UNDERTAKERS INC.

JC COMPTON

Undertakers Inc.

© 2021, JC Compton.

Paperback ISBN: 978-1-09836-7-497
eBook ISBN: 978-0-57824-6-239

1.

Tim followed Mister Gallagher into his office. The man invited him to sit in a chair and he sat opposite of him, behind a huge desk. The room was small, rather cold, and poorly lit. It was sparingly furnished with wooden cabinets and small tables neatly placed against a faded green wall, so neatly placed in fact each piece looked like it had not been moved for over a decade, and the wall behind was darker in color, perhaps its original dark green. A few solitary chairs, neglectedly scattered around the room as to seat phantom guests, were covered with old velvet of the same faded green color, and the old carpet, the closed thick curtains, all were invariably green. Mister Gallagher's eyes were also green. He grinned vaguely. In fact, his thin lips seemed unable to decide whether he should smile or not, nevertheless he did not seem unfriendly.

The tall and thin man brought his elbows to the dusty tabletop and wrung his hands as he examined the young man facing him. But more than the man, Tim's attention remained focused on the dust. It covered everything in this room, including Mister Gallagher. It was on the shoulders of his black overcoat, in the folds of his black tie, and it even seemed to have found its way onto his pale skin and the long greasy curls of his unkempt black hair.

He seemed more of a revenant than a man of flesh and bone. And yet he had those lively and piercing emerald green eyes, cat's eyes, that were the only living part of him. Tim felt as though he might like him. Men and women who lived in a whirlwind of colors, following the trends and seasons, talking and laughing loudly in the streets about the big and small concerns of a mundane life, all belonged to a world he neither knew nor wanted to know. His world was one that existed only behind closed curtains, a world in which the disturbing sunlight could not enter, in which the passing of time was forgotten. A world like this room and like Mister Gallagher. He felt relaxed as the protective atmosphere of the dark green room closed upon him. But he was there for business, and business only.

"Mister Gallagher..." he started.

"Call me Humphrey." the tall man said in his deep voice.

"As you please."

"Would you introduce yourself to me?"

"Tim Thompson, twenty-five." Tim said.

"What brought you here?"

"I read your advertisement in the London Times. I need work."

"Very well." Humphrey said. "Let me then ask you a few questions. First of all, are you familiar with death?"

"I should think so. I have lost all my family." Tim said, unemotional.

"Lost to what? Disease?"

"Yes, disease."

"Tuberculosis?"

"No. An unknown illness. I will most likely also die from it." said Tim. "No one will give me a job because of it, they think my lineage is cursed."

"So, are you afraid of dying?" Humphrey asked him with sudden interest.

"If death wants me, it can come for me. I have nothing left to lose." Tim replied simply.

"It might not come for you." Humphrey retorted with a faint smile.

Tim shrugged.

"Why do you want to work for us?" the tall man continued, leaning forward on his elbows. As he saw the puzzled look on the young man's face, he suggested an answer: "Is it for the pay?"

"I... don't really know." Tim finally said. He was a reserved man and usually had little to say, and it was all the more true since his younger sister, the very last of his relatives, had perished from the mysterious disease that cursed his family. If there were reasons to his actions before, now those reasons as well as any thought or opinion all just seemed to dance their way out of his mind playfully, and he watched them flee from him with as little emotion as he felt for the rest.

"Well it doesn't matter that much." Humphrey told him. His voice seemed suddenly warmer, as though the young man's answers fully satisfied him. He rose and held out his pale hand to the young man and said: "Welcome to Undertakers Incorporated."

London, 1888. On his first day of work, Tim found himself standing in front of the undertakers' hearse under the pouring autumn rain. Undertakers Inc. was apparently a small business and their black carriage was not so very ornate as others and had no windows – but the dead didn't need windows to gaze at the street anyway. He did not know exactly how long he had been there, but he knew he had arrived early. He had nothing else to do. The rain had soaked his long raincoat and his vest underneath. He was beginning to feel cold when Humphrey appeared behind him and sheltered him under an umbrella. Today he was wearing a long black cloak and a top hat of the same color. Two other people emerged quietly from the haze of the downpour, a man and a woman. She was holding up an umbrella for him. The man was arranging his hat and cloak when he saw Tim. He was a healthy-looking young lad, with blond hair tied into a ponytail and bright green eyes. He was, like Humphrey, a full head taller than Tim, and the short woman beside him seemed to struggle to keep the umbrella above his head. Unlike him, she was pale and listless, with curly black hair that fell softly onto her frail shoulders. She wore only a faded crimson dress, no coat, as though she could not feel the cold or the rain. She turned her lifeless eyes to Tim. They seemed perfectly black in the dim light of the late afternoon.

"Tim, this is Hanson and Miss Fiona Whittaker." Humphrey said, gesturing to his companions. And then turning to them he said: "This is Tim, our new hire."

Hanson immediately stretched out his arm and shook Tim's hand vigorously, a broad grin on his lips. Miss Whittaker tucked her umbrella under her arm to hold it still and pulled her leather gloves tighter around her hands as though the thought of touching the stranger offended her, then took Tim's hand and shook it cautiously.

"Let us go now, our *client* is waiting." Humphrey told Tim and Hanson.

Tim followed Hanson and climbed with him on the back of the carriage while Humphrey seated himself in front as the coachman. The space inside was, of course, reserved for the *client*. Miss Whittaker watched the hearse leave and then closed her umbrella, as though it did not matter anymore whether it was open or closed. As the carriage turned on the street corner, Tim caught a glimpse of the short woman standing still in the rain. She was not gazing at the carriage anymore but at the shadows from which she had emerged with Hanson, but it did not raise further questions in Tim's mind. He had come only to work.

They dashed through the city's nearly flooded streets, avoiding the markets and larger avenues, and finally arrived in front of a luxurious house. It could not be very much past six o'clock, but the sun seemed to have set already, or perhaps it was the rain that darkened the sky so much. A lonely man in a glistening raincoat walked slowly from one lamp post to another, struggling to light their little gas flames with a long pole. The wick was extinguished immediately by the rain four or five times before it finally made it all the way to the top of the lamp post and ignited the gas. It was a strenuous task.

As they finally reached the mansion, Humphrey stopped the carriage and pulled the brakes, and Tim and Hanson descended and went to the large wooden door. The house's curtains were closed and there seemed to be little or no light inside.

"What are we to say?" Tim whispered to Hanson. It was a practical question, he wanted to do his job correctly.

"Nothing." Hanson answered him with a smile. "They prefer when we say nothing."

His face then abruptly lost all friendliness and turned sober as the circumstances required. He rang the doorbell and a middle-aged woman in mourning clothes opened the door.

"Oh, you're early." she told them in a voice that meant *"You are late"*. She held a handkerchief in her hand and twisted her fingers inside it.

Hanson bowed his head slightly but did not raise his hat as would have been proper. Tim did the same as him, following him discreetly with his gaze. On the front of the carriage, Humphrey sat motionless under the rain, gazing only at the two black mares before him. Tim and Hanson followed the woman inside, through richly decorated corridors, to a room that had been especially reserved for the viewing of the decedent. He lay there in his most elegant suit, in a coffin filled with white lilies. Like all the deceased, his face had a marble-like stillness, without which he would only have seemed peacefully asleep.

"Mister Johnson." Hanson said in a respectful voice.

The women seated in chairs around the coffin turned their moist eyes to him. Two of them were young, the daughters of the client probably, and another was a very old woman who could have been his mother. The woman who had led them inside sighed.

"We will take care of him." Hanson said. "The funeral will take place tomorrow morning, when the sky is clear."

"Yes, tomorrow morning..." the woman replied, somewhat hesitant. She then turned to the mourning assembly and said: "It's time."

"If you are ready, we shall take him now." Hanson said. "You may want to leave the room, my ladies."

The woman nodded and all the others rose. They walked slowly to the coffin to bid farewell to the deceased, then exited the room one by one. The youngest was not crying, Tim noticed, but only holding a handkerchief to her eyes as though it was what was expected of her. Once all had gone, Hanson gestured Tim to help him place the lid on the coffin.

"Isn't the coffin going to be too heavy for the two of us?" Tim asked Hanson in a whisper. Mister Johnson was indeed more than just a few pounds overweight.

"Oh, I can do it alone, but it frightens people." Hanson whispered. "Don't worry, just pretend it's heavy and no one will notice."

And indeed, Hanson lifted the entire coffin with the dead man inside and held it up on his shoulder. He let the other side of the coffin fall lightly upon Tim's shoulder. There was a noticeable difference in height between them, but Hanson was carrying all the weight, and Tim barely felt it at all. They walked slowly and solemnly back to the carriage, where Humphrey was waiting under the rain. He helped them place the coffin inside and they rode away into the night. The women did not assemble on the doorstep as Tim had expected.

After a good ten minutes, Hanson, who was standing with Tim on the back of the hearse, began to knock loudly on the side of the vehicle.

"Humphrey!" he shouted. "Can we get inside now?"

Humphrey stopped the hearse and leaned out from his seat in front.

"You're a spoiled brat." he told him with a mocking grin.

Hanson laughed and opened the back door of the carriage.

"You're not going to get inside with the coffin?" Tim asked him, shocked.

"Of course I am. It's raining cats and dogs out here!" Hanson replied. "Come on in Tim!"

Tim leaned to the side to ask Humphrey if he too could shelter from the rain, but the tall man answered the question before it was asked.

"You'll catch a cold. Get inside." he told him.

"What about you? I can replace you." Tim offered.

Humphrey smiled in a way that clearly meant "no" and returned to his position.

The rain was very cold indeed, and the temperature had dropped in the last hour. Tim opened the door and let himself in beside Hanson. There was little space around the coffin and the tall young man occupied most of it. He laughed as he saw the new recruit struggling for space and pushed him onto the coffin in a playful manner. Tim frowned and slipped off it and seated himself in a corner. Hanson smirked.

"What's funny?" Tim asked him, serious.

"You make such a big deal of a simple coffin!" Hanson said.

"Isn't it strange to play around a coffin?" Tim asked.

"The fellow doesn't care." Hanson replied.

He pushed Tim aside and climbed atop the coffin. "See, nothing's happening." he said.

"I don't laugh at death." Tim replied, turning his head away.

"Tim," Hanson told him, turning serious, "you'll be seeing dead people every day with us. You'll carry their coffins, and bury them, and touch the dead, and talk to the dead. There's nothing to be somber about. If you become depressed over it, you have no business with us."

"I am not depressed or somber." Tim told him.

"Certainly!" Hanson said with irony.

He turned his gaze to the head of the coffin and sighed.

"Johnson, the banking lord. Now he's with *our Lord…*" he joked.

Tim didn't really believe in life after death or God. He didn't believe in anything.

"His daughter was not crying." he said absently.

"Of course she wasn't." Hanson immediately replied. "She was to be married, against her will and her mother's, to an old aristocrat chosen by her father. I'm sure she's happy now: she won't have to marry that old pig! And his wife – she's a wonderful actress – she will inherit his entire fortune. The old man was sick, but not dying yet. I'm sure she gave him a little something."

"You like gossip." Tim remarked.

"People talk a lot in front of us." he said.

"Why?" Tim asked.

"They think we don't listen. And that's a good thing. It means we're doing our job correctly. We're nothing, just the shadows who come and take away the dead. We must be nothing more than shadows."

The hearse came to a halt and the two young men knew they had arrived. The rain was still pouring and there was not a soul in the street, except for the distant silhouette of Miss Whittaker who, again, was holding up an umbrella. Humphrey detached the mares from the carriage and took them on to the stables. With the exact same ease he had displayed before, Hanson lifted the coffin and placed it on his shoulder. He then turned to Tim and told him: "We'll take care of the *client* from here on. You can go home now. Come back tomorrow to assist with the burial."

"I can help." Tim said.

"Go home and rest." Hanson told him. He then spun around and walked over with the coffin to Miss Whittaker, who put the umbrella over his head and followed him into the wide stone entrance of the building. It was a very ordinary building in this part of the city, with modern architecture, and there was nothing to indicate what business was conducted there but a very small wooden sign with the words "Undertakers Inc." roughly carved on it. Tim stood there under the rain, unable to think of anything. Work had ended for the day, there was nothing left to fill his mind but the silence of the empty street, interrupted only by the gentle sound of water flowing everywhere. He longed for this great silence and yet it frightened him, though he could not exactly name what frightened him in it. A hand suddenly fell upon his shoulder. He turned around and saw Humphrey.

"You may go back to your home now. Come back at eight tomorrow morning." he told him.

"May I take shelter in the entrance of the building for the night?" Tim asked him.

"Why? Do you not have a home?" Humphrey asked him, concerned.

"Yes, I have a home of course." he replied.

He turned and left, and walked quickly down the street and then, when he was absolutely sure that he was out of Humphrey's sight, he slowed down his pace. He was not heading anywhere in particular, just walking because he felt that it was what Humphrey expected of him.

The funeral home was located at the end of a small street off Whitechapel Road in the East End of London. The other buildings on that street were mostly vacant. The Whitechapel neighborhood consisted mainly of Irish immigrants, as well as a large Jewish community. It was a busy but impoverished place in the daytime and could be treacherous at night. That year, a series of murders had made the headlines in the newspapers. Some called the Whitechapel murderer "Jack the Ripper", others accused the local freak show, while some even spoke of vampires and revenants. Tim didn't care. Jack the Ripper might as well take his life too. He enjoyed the soothing darkness of the night, and, with the variety of people here, many speaking different languages, the locals socialized within their communities and paid little attention to the others. Tim was just another anonymous face among other faces, and people left him alone here, which was what he wanted the most.

He walked past a small restaurant, then another, and then he decided to enter one and eat something at least: he couldn't work on an empty stomach. He sat there at a table and removed his wet raincoat. His clothes were completely drenched underneath, something he had not noticed until then. The owner of the place, a middle-aged man with dark hair and beard, came and stood before him with a disapproving look.

"I would like a meal please." Tim said.

"No Sir." the man said.

"Why? I have money."

"I don't care if you have money, we don't want any of your kind around." the man told him roughly.

"I'm not a beggar. I just want a meal, and I can pay for it!" Tim said, irritated.

"We don't serve *what you eat.*" the man replied.

"You don't serve food?" Tim retorted.

"Please leave now. My customers are worried." the man said in a polite but firm manner, indicating that he would not change his mind.

Tim gazed across the room and saw a dozen eyes glaring at him. There was nothing strange about him and he did not look like a beggar either, he was sure of it. He wondered what kind of place this was, but it didn't matter that much in fact. If they didn't want him there, he could go somewhere else. He rose and took his raincoat and left.

In the street, the rain had stopped, and a few people had come out from their shelters: men walking alone or with friends, prostitutes waiting for lonely souls on the corner of streets, and a few drunken sailors who had drifted from the nearby docks to the taverns to drink their way through the cold London nights. A smiling young woman wearing a pale blue dress walked up to Tim and caught his arm and pressed herself against him. She was skinny but very beautiful, with alabaster skin, lovely auburn curls, cheeks like two fresh pink rosebuds and lips like cherries.

"Where are you going? I can keep you company." she offered him.

"I didn't come here for that." he told her, disengaging himself from her arms.

"I really meant it. I like you." she told him.

"Find someone else." he told her and walked away.

After being politely asked to leave a few other restaurants for no apparent reason, Tim was advised to go to the "Hell's Pit", and that he would be served there. So he went there and indeed found the owner to be somewhat friendlier. It was completely empty apart from him. A short, rounded, blond man approached him and gazed at him for a moment, then said:

"It's a little early, Sir."

"Oh, I didn't realize you were closed... the lights were on and the door was open." Tim said.

"That's perfectly alright Sir, and what shall I serve you tonight?" the man said with a forced smile.

"Honestly I'm ready to eat whatever you have at this point. I've just been booted out of every restaurant on the street. What's wrong with the people here?" Tim told him.

"You mean, you're not..." the man said, puzzled.

"I'm not a beggar. Do I look like one?" Tim asked, even more puzzled than him.

"Oh..." the man said, "No Sir, you don't look like a beggar. You just happen to look a little like the *you-know-who*."

"No, I don't know who you're talking about." Tim said, frowning. "Anyhow, can I eat here?"

"Yes, of course. Would you like the daily special?" the man said now in a jovial tone.

"That would be perfect." Tim said.

The man soon came back with a copious dish of mutton stew. Tim ate slowly, relieved to have finally found a not-so-strange place on this street, and a good meal. He noticed a shadow leaning against the window. It was that of the young woman who had approached him in the street. She was gazing at him, shivering in her thin dress. He turned his head away. There was nothing he could do for her: he was not into that, nor did he have that kind of money.

"Will you be leaving now, Sir?" the owner finally asked him just as he was finishing the last bite of his meal.

"Closing already? I thought you just opened." Tim said, surprised.

It was almost nine o'clock. It was late, but other establishments would stay open later, at least Tim thought so. The man seemed embarrassed.

"Sir," he said, "we close at nine for ordinary customers."

"I see." Tim said, thinking that the place was probably reserved for a private party that night.

He gathered his belongings, paid the man, and headed out on the streets again. The young woman was still there, waiting for him. He walked straight ahead, ignoring her, but she followed him.

"Sir," she insisted, "don't you want company tonight?" Her voice was pleading now. It was obvious that she was cold and could find no customers that night, however beautiful she was. Tim stopped and turned to her.

"I don't want your services." he told her again.

"I'm cold." she told him, losing her gay smile. "I'm very cold and I'm hungry."

"And I've no money to give you." he told her. He was not trying to be rough, it was the truth. And the other truth was that he no longer cared about any other human being. Compassion no longer existed in his heart.

The young woman wrapped her arms around herself and was about to walk away when a group of men came to her. They were all young and handsome, and dressed in fine black suits. They wore elegant hats and long black cloaks. They were all different in age, height and build, but all had unusually pale complexions, which contrasted vividly with the black of their clothes. That detail caught Tim's attention. But the prostitute was happy, she had finally found customers, and with plenty of money too. One was already wrapping his arm around her shoulders. They invited her inside the Hell's Pit, and she seemed delighted. Tim left them there and crossed the street.

He walked for a long time through the cold and unfriendly London night, unable to decide when to return home. He did not even know where his home might be, or how far he was from it. He didn't want to return there.

Hours passed and he found himself still walking, because there was nothing to do but walk. The silence and the chilling drizzle were nothing to him. He vaguely remembered a few words read in a medical journal, that fresh air ought to kill germs in the body, and he felt like laughing. If anything, London's cold dampness brought death upon people, not good health. How long had it been since he had read these words? How many years? Confused images of himself as a scholar flashed before his eyes and then disappeared. Yes, in the days past he had studied something – he couldn't remember what, but he had read a lot of books.

He had enjoyed reading, comfortably seated in the soft velvet armchair by the fireplace, while the fragile shadow of Holly danced before him on the Persian rug. She loved to sit on the Persian rug, so close to the flames they just might burn her. As a child, Holly had been turbulent, undisciplined and drawn to mischief, but she tried hard to be a good girl and, as she grew older, succeeded. She sat there in his memories, disappearing in the abundant folds of her silk dress, her black curly hair falling loosely over her shoulders, and her gloved hands turned the pages of a book of sonnets by Shakespeare. She would later come to sit beside him and recite them to him, and he would wrap a warm shawl around her shoulders and talk with her. He was proud of how good and obedient she had become, keeping herself out of trouble, and he always praised her remarkable memory and encouraged her taste for books – a very safe pastime for a girl like her. Their conversations could go on for hours, or even all night, and they never got tired of each other's company. But now, there was nothing left but silence, in his mind, in his home, in the streets. Holly had returned to the earth like their mother, their father, their older sister, their uncle and cousin... His family was a pile of bones, and their home was a stone grave. But it would not be long, he thought, until he went to lay in the earth with them. Such was the destiny of the Thompsons.

He stopped in the middle of an empty street. It made absolutely no difference whether he turned left or right on the next corner, or whether he decided to remain exactly where he was all night long. He carefully observed the shape of his worn-out leather boots on the slick paved road. Even the beggars had taken shelter somewhere. He was alone and it seemed like his presence offended even the emptiness of the night. He moved forward and turned left on the street corner; left because it seemed more inviting than right, that's all. He became aware of a presence behind him in the shadows. It could have been a thief or a cutthroat. It didn't matter. Night sheltered both the cutthroat and the outcast from the cruelty of daylight.

As he wandered down the empty docks, he heard his follower's footsteps closing in on him. Jack the Ripper? Funny thing, he thought: he owned nothing worth stealing and his life also was not worth anything. He was as free as the rats on the docks he often stumbled upon, running up the heavy ropes that tied the ships to the pier, living only from day to day. Rats, bringers of the plague, the Black Death. As he walked peacefully through this rats' nest, filled with the unpleasant stench of fish and seaweed rotting on the tangled ropes and nets, his pursuer gave up the silent chase and left him alone. He felt somewhat disappointed that the man had given up so quickly. After all, apart from the stench and the rats, there was nothing in the port.

After some time he began to feel tired, and so he headed back in the direction of Whitechapel Road, and before he knew it he was standing before the tall building again, his eyes locked on its small wooden sign: "Undertakers Inc.". A strange name for such a business, which usually went by the name of the family that owned it. But then its employees were a little strange too and neither of them seemed related by blood. There was a candle lit beside one window even though it was late in the night now, and he thought he saw Miss Whittaker's pale figure behind that window, but it disappeared almost immediately. He sat down under the arched entrance, near the large wooden doors, and pulled his long raincoat tightly around him, and he soon fell asleep there.

He was awakened only a few hours later by Hanson. The tall young man was standing before Tim, draped in his long black cloak with a matching black hat. He pushed Tim gently with his foot and handed him a black cloak and a matching silk top hat.

"You're an early bird." he said. "Wear this from now on. The mistress wants us to look good at least."

Tim rose slowly. His body was sore from sleeping against the wall. He gazed at his old raincoat: it was indeed in poor condition and had faded from its original black color to a variety of colors ranging from gray to brown. He looked more like a beggar than he had thought. He removed the old raincoat and put on the cloak he was given.

"What time is it?" he asked Hanson.

"Eight o'clock." the young one replied. He did not ask whether Tim had spent the night there or not.

"The sky is clear this morning, the weather will be fine." a deep voice said from a distance. It was Humphrey. He was gazing at them quietly, as motionless as a statue.

"Tough luck, for *them*." Hanson replied with a grin.

Tim did not understand what the two of them were talking about, but he also did not care to know. He did not like the sun, nor did he like people or conversation. Unfortunately Hanson liked to talk.

"Do you live in Whitechapel?" he asked him as they were preparing the hearse.

"No." Tim said.

"Where's your home then?"

"Does it matter?"

"No, I guess not. I hope you don't live too far away, that's all."

"I like walking." Tim said. "By the way, who do they call 'you-know-who' in this neighborhood?"

Hanson seemed to reflect for a moment.

"I don't know." he said honestly. "Maybe that serial killer?"

"Oh." Tim said.

He had never thought he could be mistaken for a serial killer.

"Do I look dangerous?" he asked Hanson, who laughed.

"Black hair, black suit, black cloak, brooding face... you look like the Grim Reaper himself!" he joked.

Well then, that probably explained the people's attitude toward him. He had looked like a wet, jobless, homeless, Grim Reaper that last night. At least now, the Grim Reaper had a job and a new cloak and hat, he thought.

There was a lot to keep them busy that day. It began with a funeral in the morning, and then three *clients* to pick up in the afternoon. Again, Hanson demonstrated his strength by carrying all the coffins mostly alone, and that suited Tim. And, as the witty blond had foretold, the sun came out that day and the dirt in the cemetery dried up, and so Tim was asked to fill in for a young man they had previously hired and who stopped showing up and dig some graves.

The City of London and Tower Hamlets Cemetery, referred to by the locals as Bow Cemetery, had opened in 1841 due to lack of space in local churchyards to bury the dead. It was larger, cleaner, and quieter too. Digging graves was not an easy task, but it kept Tim busy and kept his mind from drifting away to other matters, so he was contented with it. When he had completed the task, it was almost five o'clock, and Tim returned to the Undertakers Inc. building to ask Humphrey what he was to do next. There, he found the building locked, and all the curtains closed. The hearse was gone also; perhaps Humphrey and Hanson had gone to pick up another *client*. And so Tim sat down in the arched entrance, in the very place he had slept the previous night, and waited. He waited there for over an hour, gazing at the stone wall and the sun rays gently falling upon it.

The sun was setting and colored the bricks a very bright and disturbing orange instead of their usual light red. This orange color was truly sickening. It was absurd and out of place, as though the old funeral parlor had suddenly turned into a castle from children's fairytales. Tim closed his eyes to escape the awful sight, but still the image of the orange bricks came back to him, dancing before his eyes, mocking him, insulting him with its vividness when he felt so listless inside. Then, suddenly, the outrageous orange wall was replaced with a faded brownish crimson. Not only was this new color soothing, but it was also beautiful, adorned with a lovely pattern of roses and thorns intertwined. It was a woman's dress. It moved and disappeared from his eyes as abruptly as it had come, leaving behind it a scent of roses in full bloom. And then there was only darkness, at last, the darkness he longed for.

When he opened his eyes again, he found that the sun had set already. He had slept for a long time. Humphrey was bending over him. His face was mostly hidden in the shadows of dusk, but his eyes were as bright and sparkling as two jewels. He smiled in a compassionate manner.

"Enjoying a nap?" he asked.

"I'm sorry, Sir. I had completed my work and came back here, and..." Tim said, rising to his feet.

"Don't worry, I won't withhold it from your paycheck. You worked hard today." he told him.

"Is the day over?" Tim asked him.

"It is, you may go home now." Humphrey said. "Here, this is an advance, you will get the rest of your pay at the end of the week. Get yourself a good meal and new clothes if you need." And, saying so, he slipped a few coins in Tim's hand.

"I am not in need, Sir." Tim vaguely protested, but Humphrey closed his fingers upon the money and patted his shoulder as to tell him to go now. And so he did.

Since he was actually very hungry that night, Tim headed straight to the Hell's Pit. This time, he ordered a full plate of lamb chops and vegetables, along with bread and butter, and the owner offered him a complimentary drink – on the house. Probably because he was the only client ever there before nine o'clock, judging by how empty it was today also.

"How is the food?" the man asked him with a smile.

"It's delicious. What do you put in the sauce?" Tim asked him. He had not enjoyed food so much in a long time, especially the thick rich sauce that accompanied the meat. He could definitely taste wine it in, but also something else.

"Well..." the man said, visibly embarrassed. "I just make it the way my regulars like it..."

"Oh... secret recipe? I see." Tim said. "Can I have seconds tonight? It's not your closing time yet."

"Sure, no problem." the man said.

By the time Tim was finished eating, it was exactly nine o'clock and the owner again asked him to leave. Like the previous night, he then spent a few hours roaming the darkened streets and then found shelter under a bridge to sleep. It was not exactly the most quiet place to spend the night, as there were people crossing the bridge and talking throughout the night, but still Tim was able to sleep for a few hours, away from the rain that had come again.

The month of October passed quickly, and Tim got used to his daily work. Every day he went with Hanson to various houses, some rich, some poor, to pick up the clients and bring them back to the funeral parlor. Hanson then took the *clients* inside and Humphrey tended to the mares, and Tim was either appointed smaller tasks or sent back home, upon which he went to the Hell's Pit for his supper and then found himself a quiet place to sleep, sometimes under a bridge, sometimes in one of the filthy inns near the docks. He learned from Hanson most of what he needed to know: what to do and what to say – and especially what not to say in front of the families of the *clients*. There were unspoken rules to follow with families in mourning. Undertakers were expected to be like shadows: everything in their appearance, their face, and their words had to be discreet and respectful. They were also not allowed to take initiatives: they were to wait for the families to call upon them, and to wait for their orders to take away the clients. And they were of course forbidden from showing any emotion – ever – in front of the families. But those rules perfectly suited Tim's quiet character and Humphrey was very pleased with him.

After some time, Tim understood a little more about the position of each person at Undertakers Incorporated: Humphrey was not, as Tim had first thought, the manager of the company, but simply the "coachman" as he called himself. He spoke little but never harshly, and carefully oversaw Tim and Hanson's work. Hanson turned out to be the more mysterious of the two. For one thing, he had incredible strength, which he justified with years of labor on a farm – the explanation did not convince Tim, but then he was not really interested in learning more either. He had, in fact only ever asked two questions. The first was what Hanson did with the bodies once inside the building because the coffins seemed lighter to him the next day for the funerals. To that question, Hanson only answered that Tim would know later – maybe. The second question he had asked was who was Miss Fiona Whittaker. The woman appeared on occasion, usually in the evening or on rainy days, and sometimes accompanied Hanson in and out of the funeral home. At other times, she disappeared for several days, and then reappeared again on a dark or rainy day to offer Hanson her umbrella. When Tim asked about her, Hanson's usually cheerful face had turned somber, and he had refused to answer. Nevertheless Tim was a little intrigued by the mysterious woman. One day he dared to ask Humphrey about her, and the man simply answered: "She is the owner of the company."

The month of November passed quickly enough and then came December, and the beginning of the dreadful cold. Winters were always cold and damp in London, but the winter that year was particularly so, and Tim found it more and more difficult to spend his nights outside, as he usually did. So he wandered later and later in the streets at night, walking to keep warm, and then usually settled in some inn. Once or twice he returned to his home as well, when he had no money left, but he generally avoided it. One night, as he lingered at the Hell's Pit after a copious meal, the owner came and politely asked him to leave. It was nine o'clock and a crowd of gentlemen in black cloaks was gathering outside.

"May I stay a little later tonight?" Tim asked him. "I won't cause any trouble."

The man pursed his lips and turned his anxious gaze to the window, where the men were already peeking inside the frost-covered glass.

"I don't know." he said. "It may not be a very good idea, Sir."

"What difference does it make that they are rich and I'm not?" Tim asked him, irritated. "For God's sake, it's cold outside. I don't think my presence can be so repulsive to your regulars, I'm not a beggar."

"Alright then." the man agreed in a low voice. "But please do not mingle with them. I tell you this not because of what you are, but because of what *they* are. They are not good for us."

"And what are they?" Tim asked him.

"I don't know for sure, but you should be wary of them." the man answered.

He walked slowly to the door as though it pained him, and opened it to the gentlemen, who greeted him with pleasant words. They walked in all at once, a good dozen of them, and seated themselves around several tables. Tim gazed at them briefly: they were all young and diverse in origin and wore expensive suits: probably sons of lords and other important people, all gathering at the Hell's Pit for a cheap meal among the poor. A new fad? A thrilling social experience perhaps? All of them looked rather pale and like they could use some fresh air and sunshine. One of the men noticed him and locked his gaze upon him. He had beautiful ash blond hair tied in a ponytail like Hanson, but had very much finer features and, more noticeably, bright red eyes. Tim shook his head, surprised, but as he looked again, he saw that indeed the man's eyes were red. They were not brown or black, or any other similar color, they were ruby red. The beautiful young man smiled in a strange way as he saw Tim, enough to make him feel uneasy. He picked up his belongings, left a few coins on the table for his meal and left the restaurant.

He crossed the street quickly, as to put as much distance as possible between him and the young man. He was not really afraid of him, he had just reacted out of instinct, a gut feeling. But as he walked, he heard footsteps behind him. They were following his pace, and purposely made loud enough for him to hear. When he slowed down, they slowed down, and when he accelerated, they accelerated. There was no doubt someone was following him, and he knew that it was this young man, the very one he had been trying to escape. He wondered what he wanted. Surely the young lad had plenty of money and didn't need more. Or perhaps it was a game for him to turn into a thief at night, or worse. Could he be the Whitechapel murderer?

Tim came to a sudden halt, forcing the other to stop as well. He turned around and, as he had expected, he found himself facing the young man with the ruby eyes. They were alone in the street and tiny flakes of snow had begun to fall from the dark sky.

"I spent the last of my money on my meal, I have nothing left." Tim warned him.

"I'm not after your money." the young man politely replied.

He walked up to Tim and stood before him. He was just a little shorter than Tim, and probably a little younger. His face was even more beautiful than it had seemed from a distance: he seemed to belong in a classical paint-ing rather than in the dark streets of London. His perfect skin was as pale as a marble sculpture, and it made his eyes look even more flamboyant among all this whiteness.

"Where are you going?" he asked Tim.

"That's none of your business." Tim replied, suspicious.

The blond one moved closer to him, until he stood only a few inches away from his face and Tim could smell the sweetness of his scent, of his breath, and all of it was enchanting in a way, as though the young man had appeared from a fairytale and was not made of the same flesh and blood as him. He was captivating but at the same time a little eerie. Tim took a step back, and the boy caught his wrist. He held it firmly for a second and then his touch became gentle, like a master demonstrating his power over a dis-obedient servant. His hand was cold, even through his gloves. He kept his ruby eyes locked upon Tim's and smiled.

"I don't have *that* sort of taste. Go away." Tim told him. He had heard of those men who preyed on younger men, but he had never heard of younger men preying on older men, though if there was one kind there certainly was the other.

"Your *taste*... that does sound very interesting." the blond whispered.

"What exactly do you want from me?" Tim asked him, frowning.

"I have seen you sleeping under a bridge sometimes. Have you no home?" the young man continued in his soothing voice.

"I'm not a beggar, I'm not in need of charity." Tim retorted, freeing himself from his hand at once.

"I didn't mean to offend you." the young man said, losing his smile.

Another dark figure appeared at the other end of the street. It was that of a woman, and she was dressed elegantly. She was not a prostitute. She called out in a firm voice: "Cyril!"

The young man turned his ruby eyes to her and stood still, and she too stood still, gazing at him from a distance like a pale statue. She took a step forward, and another, and her moves were very much like those of a cat, cautious and measured, elegant and restrained. As she came closer, Tim recognized her features: it was Miss Whittaker, paler and lovelier than ever in her crimson dress. She wore her dark curls loose on her shoulders and carried a lace-trimmed umbrella, as to shield her delicate face from the snow. And still no coat. Her expression was as cold and listless as usual, but her eyes were alive – more so than Tim had ever seen them. She kept her dark eyes fixed upon the mysterious young man, Cyril, who took a step back. The silent confrontation was over, and her gaze lost all passion at once, she was again the perfect statue Tim had always known.

"He's my employee, leave him alone." she told the blond one.

He raised his hat as to greet her and then walked away in the opposite direction, as though they had concluded some kind of secret agreement without even exchanging a word.

"Miss Whittaker..." Tim started. He wanted to offer to escort her back home, as the streets were most unsafe for women alone at night, but she turned her empty gaze to him, and he forgot whatever it was he wanted to say. She was quiet, like the street, like the soft snow that fell from the sky, like the night, and it seemed that all these perfectly quiet things should not be disturbed.

"What is your name?" she asked him.

"Tim." he replied.

"Your full name." she said.

"Timothy James Thompson."

"I see. You are a Thompson." she said, and then she began to walk away.

Tim followed her. She walked quietly, a few paces ahead of him, but she was not trying to distance him.

"You know my family?" he asked her. The question had been on his lips ever since her last words.

"I *know of* them." she said.

"What do you know about them?" he insisted.

She came to a sudden halt and turned her listless gaze to him.

"Mister Thompson, if you intend to follow me back to the funeral home, I shall have to invite you in for some tea." she said, in a voice that was not quite friendly. It was in fact almost like a threat. But she had caught his interest, she had stirred something inside him.

"Yes, let's go back there." he said.

She turned around as though his answer made no difference to her and kept on walking. Within a few minutes they reached the cold and quiet building and she put away her umbrella. She pulled out a rusted key and unlocked the large wooden doors and pushed them open with an ease that surprised Tim.

"Please come inside." she told him.

He followed her into the dark corridor. It was the first time he actually ever set foot inside the funeral home, he had never been allowed in yet. As they walked quietly through the hall, Miss Whittaker pulled out a handkerchief and covered her nose and mouth with it. Indeed, there was a smell in the air that Tim had grown used to. He realized they were passing by the mortuary, where the bodies were stored.

"This way." Miss Whittaker said, as she led him up a wooden stairway.

She took him to the second floor. They entered a small bedroom furnished only with a bed, a dresser, a sofa and a table with two chairs. The room appeared to be her entire apartment and he did not know whether Humphrey and Hanson occupied the other rooms on the floor.

"I will make some tea." she said.

He gazed at her with questioning eyes. He knew nothing of her situation, but he had imagined that she lived in a little more comfort than this: there was not a candle lit, no fire in the fireplace and it did not seem like it had been used in a long time. Perhaps business had not been so good lately.

"Oh, I forget. You may want some light." she said absently.

She brought a dusty candle, lit it, and placed it on the table before him. She then disappeared into the hallway. As the candle lit up the room, Tim noticed that everything in the room, from the carpet to the velvet that covered the chairs, was a faded crimson color. It was obvious nothing new had been added to the room in a long time. Tim unwillingly continued to make up stories in his mind as to how such an obviously fine-bred young woman had fallen into such hard times, not even being able to light a fire in the winter. He didn't know why it should trouble him. He could tell she was a responsible woman, and Undertakers Inc. was still in business. She knew how to handle things, she would be alright.

She soon returned with a teapot and just one cup. The room filled with the scent of roses.

"I have made rose tea. I hope you will enjoy it." she said, and Tim thought he almost saw her smile.

She sat on a chair opposite of him and gathered her hands on her knees. If not for her impenetrable cold face, one could have thought she was nervous.

"Only one cup?" Tim asked, a little puzzled.

"The tea is for you. My tea will be served later." she said.

"Later?"

"I have my tea at four-thirty in the morning every day. It is only a quarter past ten now." she said.

"Oh." he said, still not quite understanding.

She poured him a cup of hot tea then sat like a statue, her black eyes fixed on him. For a moment he wondered whether the tea was poisoned, or if there was some other morbid explanation as to why he was the only one drinking it, but then again he would probably die young like everyone else in his family. He took a sip of the tea. It was good.

"You like the tea." she remarked.

"Yes, I do." he said.

He took another sip. The taste and smell of the tea suddenly made him feel very relaxed and at ease, despite the strange surroundings.

"Miss Whittaker, I don't mean to pry, but may I ask you a few questions?" he said.

"Yes, you may." she said, to his surprise.

"Is this your family's business?" he asked. "It just seems so... unfit for a young woman."

"Yes, you could say it is a family business." she said. "Although my family may be quite different from yours."

"My family are all in a grave." he said coldly, before realizing it was improper. "Sorry, I didn't mean to sound so... grim."

"There is nothing to feel bad about, Mister Thompson. Most of us end up in a grave. You are merely stating the truth." she said, unemotional. He wondered what she meant by "most of us", but he did not venture to ask.

"Do you enjoy running a funeral home?" he asked her. He then realized again how awkward a question it was. Of course she was either in this business because, like she said, it belonged to her family, or because she needed the money, or both.

"I do not think it is something one *enjoys*." she said. "It is something one *does*, that's all."

"That's true." he agreed.

"Have you been treated well by my employees?" she inquired.

"I have been treated very well." he said.

"Good."

He took another sip of tea.

"Miss Whittaker, may I ask what you have heard about my family?"

It was the only thing he truly wanted to hear about.

"What would you like to know?" she asked him in return.

"I'm not sure." he admitted. "I just was curious to know what you had heard about them."

"Mister Thompson, do you believe in life after death?" she asked him.

"No, I don't. Neither do I believe in God."

"What if there was no God, but there was a life after death?" she said.

"You mean as a revenant?" he said, cynical. "No. Dead bodies rot and disappear, therefore there is nothing after death."

"You seem very sure of yourself." she said.

"You haven't answered my question." he reminded her.

He suddenly found himself very sleepy and could no longer keep his eyes open. He struggled to stay awake as long as he could, but the soft candlelight, the scent of roses, and the atmosphere of the room made him feel intensely relaxed. He unwillingly leaned his head against the wall beside the table. The last thing he remembered before drifting away was Miss Whittaker leaning over him and placing a cold hand on his cheek. And in the short instant she towered over him, he realized how beautiful and perfect her features were, just like the boy who had followed him out of the inn. And her scent was equally sweet.

He was awakened by her voice again and some time had elapsed.

"Mister Thompson, are you awake now?" she inquired.

"I... I must have fallen asleep." he said, sitting up in his chair. It was still dark outside, and the candle had been replaced with another.

"You were tired. I thought I should let you sleep. But now you must go." she said.

"What time is it?"

"Four twenty-seven."

"Oh, I'm sorry, it's time for your morning tea. I will not disturb you any longer."

He rose and arranged his clothes, and took his hat, but before he could leave there was a knock on the door.

"You may come in." she said.

To Tim's surprise, Hanson opened the door. He stood there, holding a tray with a teapot and cup, looking befuddled.

"Tim? What are you doing here?" he asked, visibly unhappy to find him there.

"I invited him over for some tea last night. He was leaving." Miss Whittaker said.

"Tea?" Hanson said with a frown.

"Rose tea." she said, as though it needed to be mentioned.

"I shall leave now." Tim said, bowing to them.

He walked quickly past Hanson's dangerous glare and closed the door behind him. As he walked by though, he couldn't help but notice the strange color of the tea in the teapot, and the thickness of its texture. Perhaps some kind of exotic brew, or perhaps this morning she would be having coffee instead of tea. Yes, it was probably coffee. As he made his way down the corridor he heard Hanson's angry voice arguing with her. He paused for a moment. The argument was escalating. He returned to the door and took a peek through the keyhole, only to make sure Hanson was not becoming violent. He did not want to be the cause of any problems for Miss Whittaker.

"I asked you a question! What were you two doing all night?" Hanson said to a detached looking Miss Whittaker.

"Drinking tea." she simply said.

He grabbed her arms, but she did not appear to be afraid of him in any way.

"Fiona! He's a man, and he was alone with you!" Hanson insisted, looking more worried than angry now.

Her lips parted into a wise grin.

"Shouldn't you be more worried about him then?" she asked.

Was she provoking him or what?

"I'm worried... I'm jealous... I'm..." Hanson said, pulling her into his arms.

She wrapped her arms around him and caressed his hair softly.

"You're such a child..." she said.

"Fiona..." he said in a weak voice.

He pinned her against the wall and began to kiss her neck hungrily.

"Hanson...!" she said in a soft protest.

He fell to his knees and took her hand and kissed it. He kissed every finger, then removed her glove and proceeded to lick them. She leaned back against the wall as his tongue slowly worshipped her skin. A hand was apparently all he was allowed, and he treated it like he would her body, and she closed her eyes. Tim had not intended to watch this much, but he still couldn't tell whether Hanson was forcing himself on her or whether this was just what they liked to do behind closed doors.

"Hanson... please..." she said.

Was she was begging him to stop or on the contrary to give her more?

"Fiona... drink me!" he suddenly said in a passionate voice.

"Hanson!" she said, sounding embarrassed.

"I know you want it, and I want it too." he said. "I want to feel your teeth on me!"

"You know if we did it, it would change everything between us." she said in a whisper.

Tim couldn't believe the scene he was watching: Hanson was making an indecent proposal to his employer, or, more likely, his sweetheart. But... teeth? That sounded painful. But then again there were all sorts of people with all sorts of tastes in this world. He felt terribly embarrassed now and decided she was safe enough and he should not be spying on their intimacy. He rose as quietly as he could and left them to whatever they were doing – or not doing.

The following days came and passed quietly. The usually lively Hanson would not speak a word during working hours, and after the work was done he disappeared. Tim eventually tried to approach him one morning, before Humphrey joined them near the hearse.

"Hanson, I don't want to be the source of any misunderstandings." he told him.

"You were alone with her all night in her apartment." Hanson replied bitterly.

"I can assure you I have no romantic interest in Miss Whittaker. She said she knew about my family, and I wanted to hear what she had to say. That's all." Tim said.

"Yes, that's what she said too." Hanson said.

"Then should you not believe the woman you love?"

Hanson's face relaxed a little.

"So, did you learn anything about your family?" he asked Tim.

"No, she didn't really answer my questions."

"What were your questions?"

"I'm not sure myself." Tim said.

Holly's beautiful smile suddenly flashed before his eyes. Miss Whittaker somehow reminded him of her. And then he remembered the steamy conversation he had overheard that night, and Hanson asking Miss Whittaker to bite him. He preferred not to know *where* he wanted to be bitten. To each their own, he thought.

Work that day was done early enough, and Tim was once again sent home by Humphrey. He wandered the streets, in the dim light, until he found that his footsteps had brought him back to the place where it all begun: his family's old house, the Thompson mansion. He rarely came there, and it looked abandoned. He walked up to the door and was about to turn the doorknob, but at the last moment he stopped. He couldn't. He spun around and ran away as fast as he could. He knew if he opened that door he would be faced with the terrible truth: that all that he had cherished was gone, and there was not a trace left of it anywhere in this world. The house would only be as empty as his life.

He ran and ran and ended up in the small graveyard where his family rested. Their tombstone was just a little more ornate than the others – but a family with so many dead ought to have a special place in the grounds, as regular *clients*, he thought. He did not remember the faces of the undertakers that serviced his family members. It had all been so sudden, so fast. But Holly was there, he thought, under the stone. All that was left of her were bones and perhaps pieces of rotting flesh. And her hair, her beautiful black curls. The only place where he could still find her was here, under this heavy stone.

He fell to his knees and lay his head on the tombstone, whispering her name: "Holly…"

After a few moments, he felt a warm hand on his shoulder. It was Hanson.

"Sorry, I followed you." he said, kneeling beside him.

He gazed at the tombstone.

"So this is where she rests?" he asked.

"Yes, this is Holly's resting place." Tim said, gathering himself to his knees.

"Was she your wife or fiancée?" Hanson asked.

"She was my sister. But none of this matters anymore. She's gone." Tim said coldly.

"I'm sorry for your loss." Hanson simply said.

Tim stood up.

"I don't need anyone's pity." he said.

"I didn't come here to bother you. I just wanted to know about you, like you wanted to know about us. Fair enough?" Hanson said, rising as well.

"I still don't know anything about you." Tim said.

"The less you know, the better." Hanson said. "You've stepped into a world that is much darker and sinister than you think."

"Nothing is too dark for me." Tim said.

"Tim, the darkness never fails to find those who seek it." Hanson warned him. And with this, he disappeared in the growing fog. Tim shrugged. Hanson's words meant nothing special to him. He entered the graveyard's small chapel by dusk and walked slowly down the aisle, gazing at the frozen statue of Jesus on the cross. He looked lonely and miserable too, with his crown of thorns and his hands nailed to the wood. Maybe Jesus was just another symbol used by simple-minded people to give meaning to human suffering. For if there was no meaning to be found for the suffering in this life, what proof did they have that a meaning would be found in the afterlife? Tim was one of those who believed only in what he could see, feel and touch. Jesus was not a man of flesh and blood standing before him, the Holy Bible was just a book written by anonymous hands from the past. There was nothing there his mind could logically accept as a tangible truth. It probably took a great deal of imagination to *believe*, given such vague tools, and imagination he no longer had.

"Sorry God, but I only believe in what I see." he said.

He then noticed a young woman standing at the end of the aisle. She wore a light blue dress, and her disheveled auburn hair was covered with dust. He recognized her: she was the prostitute who had approached him once. She looked poorer and more sickly than ever. He turned and walked back to the chapel's entrance, having no interest in her. He had no sooner passed the doors than a cold hand closed upon his arm.

"Sir, have you forgotten me?" the woman's voice whispered in his ear.

"I told you I have nothing for you." he said, pushing her away.

But as he gazed at her in the twilight, he noticed with horror how pale she had become and how red her eyes were.

"I haven't forgotten *you*, the selfish man who turned me down when I was cold and hungry." she said, and as she spoke her nails began to grow into long black claws. Her lips curled upward, revealing two glistening fangs, and her brow twisted into the most horrible frown.

31

Before Tim could even react, she had him on the ground and she was trying to get to his neck while he fought back vigorously. Two unknown hands suddenly picked her up and threw her up in the air, and as she was falling back down a silver stake pierced her chest. Her body turned into ashes and fell upon Tim. A pair of gloved hands caught the stake in mid-air and tucked it under a long black coat. The young man with familiar features turned around and smiled.

"Cyril!" Tim gasped.

"How embarrassing for one to have to carry around the weapon of their own demise." Cyril said with irony. He helped Tim up.

"What... was that?" Tim asked, still stunned.

"A ghoul." Cyril said.

"What is a *ghoul*? She was a prostitute on the streets the last time I saw her!"

"Yes... that night apparently didn't end well for her." Cyril said, unconcerned.

"What in the world are you?" Tim shouted, grabbing his arm firmly.

Cyril turned a surprised gaze to him.

"I'm a vampire. Didn't she tell you?" he wondered.

"Who?"

"Fiona of course, who else?"

"Miss Whittaker? No, she never told me anything about you." Tim said, in shock.

"Oh... well, now you know." Cyril said.

Tim released him and took a step back.

"This is not real... it must be a dream!" he repeated.

"I thought you only believed what you could see." Cyril said, arranging his gloves. "You can see me, you can touch me, therefore I am real."

"Are you also after me for my blood... or whatever it is you do with people?" Tim asked him.

"Not tonight. But what if I was?" Cyril said in a friendly voice. "The other night on the port, you looked like someone who had given up on life. So what would be so wrong with me drinking your blood?"

"It was you that night also!" Tim said. "But if your intent was to kill me, why didn't you go through with it?"

"You see things in such black and white terms." Cyril said with regret. "We're not constantly hunting and not all humans are our preys. Can we not just live as we are, feed when we need, and sire a human when we feel like it?"

"Sire someone? Is that what happened to that girl?"

"You have so many questions." Cyril said. "Come, let's settle down somewhere else to talk. I also become prey at night, near graveyards..."

2.

Like the foolish hero in horror stories, Tim had agreed to follow a vampire who said he might actually kill him, just not now. What was he doing? Something different and exciting. For the first time in ages, his heart was racing with excitement as he walked briskly behind Cyril, trying to keep up the pace. The vampire's grip on his wrist was firm yet gentle. He seemed in a hurry, for reasons only he knew, but Tim felt *good* with him. Cyril took him to the darkest corner of a small tavern, where the crowd of drunken sailors and prostitutes paid no attention to them. He ordered them some drinks and food for Tim.

"You're so thin... you really pay no attention to your health. You should eat now." he told him.

"Thank you..." Tim said.

"So what's your name, curious human?"

"Tim."

"Do you have a last name, Tim?"

"Thompson."

"I'm Cyril Stewart." Cyril said.

He offered Tim his gloved hand to shake, and Tim took it cautiously. But after they shook hands, his hand lingered in the vampire's, as though he did not want to let go. Cyril politely removed his hand, looking somewhat troubled. He took a sip of his drink.

"You drink beer?" Tim asked him, surprised.

"Shouldn't I?" Cyril laughed.

"I don't know anything about your kind." Tim admitted.

"And yet you followed me, a monster, here."

"Shouldn't I?" Tim said.

Cyril laughed again. He noticed that Tim had already finished his plate.

"Done already? Shall I order more?"

"Why? One plate of food is enough."

"Why settle for *enough* when you can have more?" Cyril said, and with this he ordered more food for him.

"Now, let us get started with the questions. I know you have many." he said with a smile.

"What is a ghoul and how did that girl become one?" Tim immediately asked, his mouth full of food. He had been hungrier than he thought.

"One of my friends bit her in the heat of action... you know." Cyril explained. "But he didn't go all the way. This results in the human being partly affected by our essence, you could say, and the outcome is unpredictable. At best, the human is just a little stronger, at worst, it can create a ghoul. Ghouls are unstable by nature. They long for the completion of their metamorphosis, but they don't know how to reach it. All they know is that they thirst for blood, and they will attack any creature for it. We really try to clean up after ourselves but this one escaped."

"By 'cleaning up' you mean you kill them?"

"Yes."

"So, why didn't your friend *go all the way*?"

"To go all the way means to either kill the human or sire them." Cyril said. "He had not intended to eat her nor sire her, but when we get a little too excited, well, we want to bite."

"You mean, *in the heat of action?*"

"Yes."

"And what does it mean to *sire* a human?"

"It means to make them a vampire." Cyril said.

"Were you also sired?" Tim asked.

"Yes, a very long time ago."

"So where is the vampire who sired you?"

Cyril raised his shoulders as though he didn't know or simply didn't want to talk about it.

"What makes a vampire want to sire someone? What is the difference between that human and regular prey?" Tim then asked.

"Feelings." Cyril said. "We talk, think, and feel, just like you, and sometimes we also fall in love."

"That makes sense." Tim said, practical. "I have more questions for you."

"I'm not going anywhere." Cyril said with a grin.

Tim finished his beer and Cyril immediately ordered another for him as though he purely savored watching the human feed and drink.

"How do you sire someone?" Tim continued.

"That is a very complex question." Cyril said. "To make a perfect newborn vampire first requires a very strong bond between the master vampire and the human. They must then drink each other's blood, not too much, not too little. The first one who bites will forever be the master, and the other will be his servant. Therefore it is not wise for the youngest to bite first, unless the older vampire wants to be led around by a newborn for all eternity. Well, we can technically be killed, but if nothing too bad happens, we can also be together with them forever. That is why we think carefully before siring anyone. It's a little bit like marriage."

"I never imagined it that way." Tim said, genuinely surprised. "So there are also rules in your world?"

"Do you think we still live in the Dark Ages?" Cyril laughed. "Of course there are rules and we also have our own Dark Lord, whom we must obey."

"A vampire lord?"

"Yes, something like that."

"Tell me about him."

"Unfortunately, this is not something I can share with a mortal." Cyril said. But his eyes shone with the promise that he would tell Tim if he were an immortal like himself.

"So, if I was not a mortal..." Tim started.

"But you are." Cyril cut him.

"You followed me that night on the docks, and then again when we met at the Hell's Pit. Why? Did you want to feed on me?"

"You are very appetizing... but that was not the only reason."

"Did you want to sire me?"

"I can't sire someone who doesn't even want to live, can I?" Cyril said with irony.

"I see." Tim said. He felt somewhat disappointed, not because he wanted to be sired or become immortal, but because this ultimately dangerous creature was already giving up on him.

"You seem disappointed. Are you interested in becoming immortal?" Cyril asked.

"And never find peace in the grave with my family? No thanks." Tim said.

"I thought so too." Cyril said with a kind smile. "Well it has truly been a pleasure talking to you, but I must go now."

He rose and arranged his coat, his hat and his gloves.

"Why now? I'm not finished." Tim said.

Cyril gazed at him with somewhat sad eyes.

"Please stay a little longer." Tim said.

"You're too attractive to me. If I stay any longer I shall *have* to bite you, whether you want it or not." he said very seriously.

Tim understood and let him go, and the vampire disappeared, leaving him alone in the tavern with only two empty glasses and the memory of their fascinating conversation.

From that night on though, Tim's mind was filled with Cyril and the dangerous world he belonged to. How many other vampires were there, and how many more ghouls and creatures of the night? Of course he had heard many a folktale about such monsters, but he had never paid much attention to them; they had never been something that could fit in his reality. But now, he was finding out for the first time that death was not an end for all; for some it was a new beginning, a rebirth into something else. How good it would have been for him to acquire this knowledge before Holly passed! He would have gladly joined the world of eternal darkness with her, if it meant that she could live! He wondered for what reasons Cyril had become immortal. Who did he form this bond with as a mortal? Who had sired him and why? He longed for the next time they would meet – for there would definitely be a next time.

Work days and nights passed without him realizing it, so absorbed was he in the new and only excitement of his life. One day, Hanson dared to question him about it.

"How is everything going Tim?"

They were sitting inside the hearse, sharing the little space with a *client*.

"What do you mean?" he asked Hanson, who had taken him by surprise.

"You seem so absorbed in... something." Hanson said.

Tim shrugged and turned his gaze to the darkness.

"I bet with Humphrey that it was a woman, but he thinks not!" Hanson said with a hint of mischief.

"You shouldn't make bets on what you know nothing of." Tim told him coldly.

"Hey, Tim, we're your friends, right? If something good happened, we're happy for you."

"Something happened, yes, but I can't say whether it's good or bad." Tim admitted.

"Aren't you going to tell us?" Hanson asked.

"I will tell you when you tell me the truth about everything that's going on here." Tim told him. He gazed at him with piercing eyes now. Hanson lost his smile at once.

"Tim..."

"I have no intention of prying into Miss Whittaker's business. I fully respect her." Tim said. "However I see things that don't make sense, and no one here is willing to explain them."

"It's only to protect you." Hanson said, serious.

"How involved are you with the underworld?" Tim asked him directly.

"Too much." Hanson said. "There, are you satisfied?"

"Not one bit."

"You're not yourself today, where's the silent young man we were used to?"

"I may be silent, but I too think and wonder about things." Tim said.

Hanson pursed his lips. He didn't want to continue this conversation.

As they reached the funeral home, Tim noticed that Miss Whittaker had come out to wait for them. The sky was dark and small snowflakes blew in the wind. She gazed at them absently and then her eyes focused on Tim and became intense. She knew he was gazing at her and she knew why: he also wanted answers from her. She dealt with corpses every day: surely she knew about the undead, and, more importantly, she knew Cyril personally. But he would not ask her, not here, not now.

Hanson took the coffin inside after exchanging a quick glance with her, and she walked slowly to Tim. Humphrey went to tend to the mares, as always.

"Tim, how have you been?" she asked him. It was the first time she called him by his first name.

She stood only a few paces away from him, and in the light of a lamp post he could see the pallor of her skin and the reddish undertones in her black eyes. He remembered her conversation with Hanson about him wanting her teeth on him, and unwillingly pictured her as a vampire vixen now, giving Hanson a love bite somewhere private. He took a step back, trying to shake that thought away. She was his employer after all.

"You look frightened." she remarked.

"I'm sorry, Miss Whittaker. That was not my intention and you do not frighten me." he said, apologetic.

"Would you like to join me later for some tea?"

He hesitated. Her words were never quite inviting, and he sensed more of a trap than an open and friendly invitation. Could she be a vampire too? And what if her "tea" was not tea at all but... blood?

"Tim?" she asked again, puzzled

"Perhaps another day." he said politely.

"I forget, it is Christmas Eve after all. You must have plans." she said.

"Christmas Eve..." he repeated, turning his gaze away sadly. There were no such things as holidays or celebrations for him.

"I shall leave now. I will be here tomorrow, as always." he said. The business was always open on holidays and he was not offered to take the day off, neither did he want to.

He walked away and felt her piercing eyes upon him. But he was not sure exactly what she was, or what any of them were. The only thing he knew without a doubt was that he wanted to be with Cyril again. It was more than curiosity, more than the thrill of danger; since he had gazed into his ruby eyes and breathed in his sweet scent, he had only wanted more and more. Of course this was probably how vampires enticed their prey. But had Cyril not expressed the same attraction for him, and not quite as a prey? He needed to know. He needed him tonight and he knew where to find him.

He went straight to the Hell's Pit and ordered some wine as he waited. He didn't want food, he didn't want anything but Cyril. And indeed, at nine o'clock, the young vampire and his band of undead brothers came in with several prostitutes and seated themselves. He was somewhat relieved not to see a woman on the blond vampire's arm. As the group entertained their company, Cyril's gaze remained locked on Tim's. It was a very long and strange few minutes that went by, as though time itself was frozen. Nothing mattered, nothing else existed but the burning eyes of the vampire upon him. They were more of a brown color tonight, and he wondered why. He wanted him to come closer. His heart was racing again with excitement and perhaps a hint of fear, and that was even better. With a quick gesture of his head, he invited the vampire to follow him outside. Cyril smiled.

It took no more than a few instants for the vampire to join him on the snow-covered pavement. Everything was white and pure. Gentle snowflakes fell from the sky onto Tim's burning skin as he gazed into Cyril's shining eyes again.

"I came back for more." he said.

"Of course you did." Cyril whispered.

He took a quick glance in the direction of his peers inside. Some of them gazed at him with questioning or disapproving eyes, others had not even noticed his departure.

"Is it alright to leave your friends?" Tim asked.

"Who cares about them?" Cyril said.

He locked arms with Tim and pulled him away from the crowded restaurant. They walked fast, again. It was Cyril's normal pace, a vampire pace.

"You're not asking where I'm taking you." Cyril remarked.

"You know that I will follow you tonight, no matter what." Tim said.

"It's Christmas Eve, there will be a lot of mortals in the streets tonight. Let us go to my place." Cyril said.

"Will there be others there?" Tim asked.

"No." Cyril said. "I want to keep you to myself."

He took him to a tall house among a row of identical houses on a clean street. No thieves, no prostitutes, and no broken windows on any building. It was about as upscale as the impoverished Whitechapel could get. All shutters were closed. As they entered, Tim didn't fail to notice the warmth and the light inside. Someone had lit candles and a fire in the fireplace. It looked like an ordinary, cozy middle-class home.

"Looks like old Augustus finally showed up to clean..." Cyril said.

"Is your manservant a vampire too?" Tim asked.

"No, he's human. But he's afraid of me, especially when my eyes get too red. He comes only when he knows I'm out."

"Your eyes are brown tonight... why?" Tim asked.

"They are only red where a vampire is hungry, excited, or has just fed." the vampire said.

He removed his coat and hat, and Tim's cloak and hat, and led him to the parlor. It was well-lit and tastefully furnished. There were surprisingly ordinary paintings on the walls as in any middle-class home, and a library filled with books in the back. There were more books on side tables. The two apparently shared a common interest. Tim sat on a red velvet-covered sofa and Cyril sat opposite of him and offered him some wine.

"So you are a vampire who drinks wine, reads books and lives in an ordinary home." Tim remarked, amused.

"Have you ever read the 'Knight of the Undead' series by John Silverstake?" Cyril asked, gazing at a pile of books in a corner.

"You mean those sultry romance novels where the vampire seduces a new virgin in every volume? Please..." Tim said, rolling his eyes, and his companion laughed.

"Well," Cyril said, "those are complete nonsense. Vampires don't live in crypts and graveyards, we don't sleep in coffins or dissolve when we touch water."

"What about seducing virgins?"

"Sometimes we do. Are you interested?"

Tim took several sips from his glass while Cyril gazed at him with hungry eyes.

"You haven't answered me." the vampire said.

"Are you interested in seducing me?" Tim asked him in return.

"Do I need to?" Cyril replied, leaning forward.

"I'm here already. So, am I about to become your next meal?" Tim asked with a grin.

"Be patient, my dear human."

Tim removed his jacket and vest and unbuttoned his shirt as the wine began to warm him up, and his companion did the same.

"So, you came here because they wouldn't tell you anything over at the funeral home, didn't you?" Cyril then asked.

"You read minds too?"

"No, I just guessed."

"So are they really protecting me by not telling me anything?"

"No. It will come to you sooner or later."

"What will?"

"Our world. The world of shadows."

"Because I seek it?"

"None of us ever really sought immortal life." Cyril said, serious. "But all of us have in common that we were banished from the world of light, and at some point the shadows became our refuge."

"That's exactly how I feel." Tim said.

"I know you probably want to hear my story." Cyril said.

"Yes."

"It's a very long one, though I am still young in immortal years, so I shall try to keep it short." the vampire said. "I think I was about fifteen or sixteen when it all started, and that was about two hundred years ago. I was born to a wealthy family in Wales, and raised to be my father's successor in business, and that was truly all I dreamt about. I was a good boy, until I discovered my penchant for forbidden things."

"Forbidden things?"

"Yes, and there were many more back in those days than there are now. Nothing surprises anyone nowadays... But back then, religion was very important. King Henry VIII had cut all ties with the papacy, and this brought forth a century of terrible political unrest. Protestants killed Catholics, Catholics killed Protestants and Catholic dissidents alike, it was chaos. My family were secret followers of the Pope and had secured my engagement to the daughter of a like-minded family whom I had never met – but that was perfectly normal back then. Like most young men of my age who could afford it, I liked to frequent the city's brothels. My father just thought of this as normal practice before marriage, but I had a favorite of whom I was a regular client, a beautiful young man with dark skin, and hair as black as a moonless night! He wore a Protestant cross around his neck at all times, and if anything it made me even more thrilled to be with him. I have forgotten his name but not the passion he inspired me! I was in love, and with a Protestant too! For him, I decided to run away and convert, upon which I was disowned by my family. Within less than a year, I had fallen out of love for him and found myself on the streets.

One night, a very charming woman by the name of Sofia approached me. She was a beauty like I had never seen before, with marble skin and ash blond hair, and captivating ruby eyes. She offered to help me. I was homeless, so I accepted. She took me in and doted on me. At times she was a lover, at times a mother to me. She was the one who sired me. It was truly an act of love, at least on her part. I tried my best to love her, but in the depths of my heart, I was dissatisfied. I knew I was missing something, but I couldn't tell what. I was a selfish and troublesome newborn, and more than once the elder vampires had to intervene, but Sofia protected me. Eventually, we traveled to Europe to get away from them, and we ended up in Riga. We thought we would live there in peace, but then Sofia met and fell in love with Sergei. Sergei was an older vampire who had been around the world more than once. He was exquisitely beautiful, tall, with long auburn hair and an androgynous figure. Needless to say, I immediately fell in love with him. We lived as a sort of family for some time. I had fallen from the position of companion to that of child, while Sofia and Sergei behaved like parents around me, and I accepted it because I loved Sergei and would have done anything for him. I cursed fate for having Sofia as my mistress, and thus being bound to obey her. I wanted to be Sergei's servant! You see, it's not even like a moral obligation we have toward our masters, it's a physical obligation. The master orders and you obey, you cannot do otherwise, it just tears you apart..."

He paused to pour more wine for his guest, who listened eagerly.

"Well, obviously, that story did not end very well for either of us." he continued. "I seduced Sergei. I 'broke' my engagement to Sofia by exchanging blood vows with him, and she found out and came after us. She killed Sergei. The pain was... unbearable. I wanted to kill her but because I was her servant first, I couldn't. So I fled and came back to England. Sergei was close to the Dark Lord of England at the time, and they knew that Sofia had murdered him. Perhaps that was worse than my betrayal in their eyes, I don't know, but no one ever asked me why I came back alone. There is a bounty on her head, to this day, if she was to ever come back to England."

"The Dark Lord..." Tim said, intrigued.

"Yes, our king." Cyril said, emptying another glass of wine. His face had lost its liveliness as he recalled the memories from his past. And Tim felt compelled to go to him. He moved to the sofa the vampire was now half-lying on and lay his head on his cold chest.

"Tim, are you drunk?" Cyril whispered.

"Tell me more about the Dark Lord." Tim said.

"You will be in real danger if I tell you..."

"So what?"

He felt the vampire's cold hand fall upon his shoulder and stroke it firmly yet gently. He was controlling his strength as to not hurt him. Tim was, in fact, completely at his mercy now but he knew he was not in any sort of danger. He felt strangely safe, in fact.

"I can't refuse you anything..." Cyril sighed. "Fine then, I will share this with you. The Dark Lord is the most powerful vampire among us. The title is held until another, younger and stronger vampire challenges him and wins. Nearly all the vampires in this country obey him. His rules are not many, and the punishment for disobeying them is death."

"What are those rules?" Tim asked.

"We are allowed to interact with mortals, but they must never know what we are. We are not to befriend them or take them as our lovers, unless we seriously intend to sire them. Once a mortal knows about us, there are only two options: to kill them or sire them."

"Why is he so afraid of mortals discovering your existence, when folktales and literature are filled with vampires and revenants?"

"It's supposed to be to protect us, but I think ultimately it's just about controlling us."

"Why do you obey him then?"

"I am breaking the rules right now." Cyril reminded him.

Had he not just revealed to a mortal both the existence and the role of their Dark Lord?

"Am I going to get you in trouble?" Tim asked.

"I already am... in trouble." Cyril whispered.

He moved over the human now and let his mouth wander down his neck, enticed by the smell of his flesh and the sound of the blood pulsing through his veins. Tim knew how badly the vampire wanted him now and he didn't mind at all. In fact, the return of danger between them was particularly exciting, and now he was in the mood to play.

He moved over the vampire again, forcing him into a submissive posture underneath him.

"Tim..." Cyril said. His eyes were a mixture of surprise and admiration.

This was new and interesting, for the both of them. A human trying to dominate a vampire?

"Bite me." Tim said in a dark voice. "I want your bite. Now."

He did not know why he had said those words, but he knew everything inside him now cried for the carnal expression of his attraction to this monster. Cyril's body quivered under his, visibly struggling to restrain. He turned his head away as to block out the thought, breathing heavily.

"No, Tim." he finally said, and Tim let himself fall softly onto his chest again. He certainly was drunker than he had thought. He had never meant to be so aggressive.

"You're a fiend, Tim…" Cyril whispered, wrapping his arms around him. They were not so cold anymore.

Why did one choose to become a vampire? Why did one choose to forsake life, to defy death? These and so many questions spiraled in Tim's dreams that night.

Undertakers Incorporated. Ever since he had started working for this bizarre funeral home, strange things had happened to him. He who took pride in believing only in what he could see and touch now found himself forced to accept the existence of life after death – since he could see and touch it in the form of vampires. If only he had known sooner, before he lost Holly! Everything could have been different. Now it was too late for her though, and for him. Knowing of the undead was no use to him who wanted to be *dead*.

He rolled over on the bed and pulled the soft warm blanket up to his neck. A bed? How had he made it to the bed? He did not remember. He touched his chest: his clothes were still on. He opened his eyes and sat and gazed around him. Cyril was sitting in an armchair by the now cold fireplace in the bedroom, reading a book by candlelight. He wore spectacles and now looked more like a scholar than an undead creature. Tim's head was still heavy from the wine, but the vampire seemed absolutely fine and calm. For a bloodsucker, he sure could hold his liquor, Tim thought.

"What are you reading?" he asked him.

"So are you to my thoughts as food to life," Cyril read in a calm voice, *"Or as sweet-season'd showers are to the ground..."*

"And for the peace of you I hold such strife, As 'twixt a miser and his wealth is found." Tim continued. He knew the sonnet by heart, like many others.

Cyril moved his intense gaze to the young man in his bed and continued:

"Now counting best to be with you alone, Then better'd that the world may see my pleasure; Sometime all full with feasting on your sight, And by and by clean starved for a look..."

"Sonnet seventy-five... by William Shakespeare." Tim said softly.

"I don't only read sultry vampire novels." Cyril said, putting down the book. "Shakespeare's words are music to the soul."

"I didn't know you were a reader of poetry." Tim said.

"Reading quiets my mind and my heart." Cyril said.

Tim couldn't agree more, and now he was convinced that Cyril could read his mind. The blond youth rose and picked up a tray with a small loaf of fresh bread and brought it to Tim.

"It strikes me that you never seem to eat enough, so I slipped out before sunrise to get you some human food." he told him.

Tim took the food that was offered to him. He would have preferred it with some tea, but he doubted the vampire had any such thing around.

"How did I make it into your bed?" he then asked him, gazing around the room.

Cyril laughed.

"You fell asleep on the sofa, so I brought you up to my room. Don't worry, I didn't bite you, I only watched you sleep."

So the vampire was a gentleman after all. Tim was a little disappointed.

"I followed a vampire, expecting to be eaten... and instead he feeds me and reads me poetry." he said with a smile.

"I could still devour you."

"I'm too thin, you need to fatten me first." Tim said, eating a piece of bread and eyeing him with mischief.

Cyril broke into a wild laughter.

"My dear Tim, I think I shall die if I cannot have you for all eternity!" he said.

"I probably should be going now." Tim then said, getting up. "Hanson told me a lot of people have the awkward habit of dying on Christmas Eve and we are always on call on Christmas day. The earlier I get to work the better."

He buttoned up his shirt and slipped on his boots.

"Oh, how cruel of you to leave me now..." Cyril said with a deep sigh.

"You know it's not for long." Tim said with shining eyes.

Cyril followed Tim downstairs and watched him put on his cloak and hat while hastily swallowing the remainder of the fresh warm bread.

He left the mansion and walked in haste down the snow-covered streets. He knew he was late – later than usual that is. The streets were practically empty, as one could expect on Christmas morning. Tim knew just how many people would be celebrating, laughing, singing carols and exchanging presents with their family. But he was more interested in those who would not, those who would be in mourning, those who had nothing to celebrate and no one to celebrate with. Those banished by the world of light.

When he arrived at the funeral home, Hanson all but jumped at his throat.

"Where on earth were you? We had two calls last night, and more early this morning!" he shouted.

"Enough, Hanson." Humphrey said.

"This guy is always sleeping in the entrance of the building when it doesn't matter but when we need him he's nowhere to be found!" Hanson protested.

"Enough!" Humphrey stormed back at him, and the fiery young man grew quiet.

Tim jumped onto the back of the hearse with Hanson and they immediately left.

They answered five calls that day and brought back a total of six coffins to the funeral home. But as they arrived with the last *client*, around seven o'clock, they heard loud noises inside the Undertakers Inc. building.

"Fiona!" Hanson immediately cried, and with a speed unknown to Tim's eyes, he dashed into the building, followed by Humphrey.

Tim steadied the mares and went after them. He dashed through the dark corridor as fast as he could, but still he couldn't catch up with them. Then he heard noise coming from the mortuary and rushed there. And what he saw again defied all his beliefs: three of the *clients* had risen from their coffins as ghouls and were attacking Miss Whittaker.

Hanson and Humphrey had taken on two of them, while Miss Whittaker struggled to fight off the third. She fought back with more fierceness than Tim had ever seen in her. She picked up the heavy lid of a coffin with incredible ease and hurled it at the shrieking demon that was coming at her, sending it flying to the other side of the room. With an unearthly shriek of her own, she then flew in the air across the room and landed on its chest.

"Don't just stand there, you might as well help us!" Hanson shouted at Tim.

"What should I do?" Tim said in a panic.

"Put a stake through their hearts!" Hanson said.

Tim noticed a pile of wooden and silver stakes on a table in a corner. He jumped over a coffin, dodging the attack of one of the ghouls, and randomly grabbed a wooden one. But as he turned around he saw another one coming at him. Before he could even move, Humphrey was standing between them, growling like a beast. His stance was not human by any means, neither were the ghastly long black claws coming out of his hands. With a feline snarl, he jumped at the creature's neck. Tim immediately slipped behind the demon and planted the stake where he thought the heart might be. It was not enough. The creature hurled him against the wall and rolled on the ground with Humphrey.

Hanson, who had finished off his ghoul, crossed the room in no time to rescue Miss Whittaker, whom the undead creature had thrown to the ground, clawing at her relentlessly. Hanson quite literally picked up the ghoul and hurled it against the other, sending them both rolling on the ground. One of them landed on its back near Tim, who immediately put a stake through its heart. As he had observed before, the ghoul's body dissolved into a pile of ashes on the ground. Hanson and Humphrey finished off the others.

"See, that's what I meant when I said you needed to stay away from our world!" Hanson told Tim while trying to catch his breath.

Tim quietly stood up and shook the ghoul's dust off his clothes. Humphrey did the same. Miss Whittaker though was still huddled up in a corner, covering her face with her gloved hands. She kicked away a silver stake that had fallen beside her on the ground. Hanson immediately went to her and wrapped his arms around her. Somehow in the course of the battle the stake had cut through her gloves and wounded her hands, leaving not only scratches but burn marks around them. She appeared to be in a lot of pain.

"Are you badly hurt, my love?" he asked her.

He moved her arms to check for any other wounds.

"I hate silver..." she said in a low voice.

"I know." Hanson said. "I'm sorry, I should have been there for you. I should never have left you alone with that many corpses."

His eyes upon her were filled with pain and guilt. He kissed the wounds and brought her precious hands to his face.

"It's our job." she simply said, calmer now.

He then scooped her up in his arms and took her away to treat her wounds. He took her to her bedroom and sat her on the bed. He left her briefly and returned with bandages, which he wrapped carefully around her delicate hands. They would remain scarred. She gazed at him with sad eyes.

"You should leave me... if you stay, something will happen to you. Ghouls are dangerous creatures." she said.

"All the more reason to stay, so I can protect you." he told her gently.

"You shouldn't have to be in danger because of me."

"I chose that path and I have no regrets." he reminded her.

"We have to tell him the truth now... he is a Thompson after all." she said, lowering her gaze.

"And?"

"Then he too will be in danger."

"Tim won't reveal anything to anyone. I don't even think he has anyone in his life. The guy sleeps on the streets, even though he says he has a home." Hanson said.

"I can't fire him... not if he is already homeless." she sighed.

"Don't worry, I will talk to him." he assured her.

He was about to return to his friends, but her wounded hands grabbed his shirt.

"Hanson..." she whispered.

Fiona was so strong but so fragile sometimes, and now he knew she needed him to be strong for the both of them, to be her protector. He lay her on the bed and kissed her hands ever so softly. But, taking him by surprise, she pulled him into her arms and held him. As a healthy young man, his body couldn't help but respond to her sweet attack, but he did not want to upset her. He moved over her, making sure to leave a safe distance between them, and she began kissing his cheek, then his neck, and pulled him closer.

"Fiona...!" he gasped.

"Shh..." she whispered.

Her hands stroked his blond hair softly, then made their way down his back, sending shivers down his spine. Fiona was usually a very chaste person, but tonight she was emotional. She had been scared and needed this physical reassurance. So Hanson let her do as she pleased.

"Fiona..." he whispered, breathing heavily against her chest.

She had pinned his head down onto her soft breasts. He was in a position of weakness and total submission under her strong grip. He did not dislike that. Her hands had found their way to his trousers and gently teased the bulge in them. Her legs tightened around him, and now he was mad with desire. But they had never gone that far before and she had warned him against it.

"Fiona, please... stop." he begged her. "If you don't, you'll end up biting me."

It was what he wanted, what he had always wanted, but she was not ready. He did not want to trick her into doing it out of lust, it had to be her decision too.

"I'm sorry..." she said, removing her hands.

⁘

Tim gazed at Humphrey. His hands had returned to normal and he again looked like a human. He picked up his hat from the ground and put it back on. He leaned over the other open coffins and checked the bodies for bite marks before closing them up. Tim handed him a hammer and nails and watched him nail the coffins shut.

"So that's why your clothes are always covered with dust." he said.

Humphrey turned his emerald eyes to him and smirked.

"Come with me." he said.

They went into his office, the same green and dusty room where Tim had met him the first time, and seated themselves.

"We didn't intend to expose you to this, but now it's done." Humphrey said. "If you decide to resign, we must ask you not to reveal anything you have seen here."

Tim let his gaze wander from the dusty bookcases to the dusty curtains, and then to Humphrey's piercing green eyes again.

"I'm not going to resign because of a few ghouls." he said.

Humphrey seemed amused by his answer.

"Are you not afraid?" he asked.

"It's not the first time I've seen a ghoul or a vampire."

"I'm impressed... I did not know you were familiar with our world."

"So, are you a ghoul as well?" Tim asked.

"I suppose you could say so. I was bitten by a ghoul on the job, a long time ago." Humphrey explained. "I never did become a bloodthirsty fiend though, perhaps because it was not actually a vampire's bite."

"I see... and Hanson, what is he?"

"I am waiting to be sired by my love, whenever she changes her mind." Hanson said, who had just walked through the door.

"You are a foolish young man." Humphrey said.

"That's also what she says." Hanson said, taking a seat.

"Miss Whittaker is a vampire..." Tim said. He'd had his suspicions since she knew Cyril, but still the truth came as somewhat of a shock.

"She's not like those bloodsuckers." Hanson said. "She won't prey on the living. I provide for her, when she needs."

"I see." Tim said.

"Now that you know so much about us, you may be in danger." Humphrey warned Tim. "Vampires are a society of their own, and they will not let humans with knowledge of their existence live. It's one of their rules."

"Whether I live a few more years or die now at the hands of a vampire, it makes no difference to me." Tim said.

"Is your life not worth anything to you?" Humphrey asked with a puzzled look on his face.

"I told you already, everyone in my family died young of an unknown disease. I am only waiting for my turn so I can go rest with them in the earth."

"I don't think we need to worry. This guy is so gloomy he would probably make even a ghoul depressed!" Hanson told Humphrey.

"It is not something to laugh about. However I agree that this young man's stoicism might turn out to be his best protection in our world." Humphrey said.

Hanson escorted Tim back to the entrance and lingered there for a few minutes while Tim gazed absently at the shadows of the street.

"Wondering what bridge to sleep under tonight?" Hanson asked him in a friendly voice.

"No, I have a place to go." Tim said. He turned around and gazed at his companion.

"It's been a long day, right?" Hanson said with a grin.

"You really love Miss Whittaker... enough to want to be immortal like her." Tim said, serious.

Hanson seemed surprised at first, then smiled.

"She is everything to me." he admitted.

"You're a lot stronger than Humphrey, who was bitten by a ghoul. Did she... bite you?" Tim wondered.

"No, she did no such thing." Hanson said. "I fell in love with Fiona almost immediately when we met. I didn't know what she was, but when I found out, it didn't change anything for me. If she were human, I would have asked her to marry me, but she's a vampire, so I asked her to sire me. She refused, of course, no matter how much I begged her, and I grew angry and impatient. She said she loved me, yet she would not do the one thing that would allow us to be together forever! So one day, out of spite, I went to another vampire and paid for his blood. Yes, there are vampire prostitutes too. I thought if I had already started the transformation, then Fiona could no longer refuse me, but she took it as a betrayal. Drinking the blood of another vampire than your own is very much like adultery. Of course I had no knowledge of the rules of her world. I didn't realize how deep a commitment one made when exchanging blood vows with a vampire. If that vampire had then drunk my blood, I could have ended up his servant forever! Fiona forgave me, but it took a long time to regain her trust. By drinking that vampire's blood, I became stronger but also more aggressive. It's an irreversible process. Fiona knows that if she doesn't complete it, eventually I will start attacking humans, and her kind will know and eliminate me."

"Then why does she still hesitate?" Tim asked.

"If she drinks my blood and I drink hers, she will become my mistress and I her servant. She doesn't want to be my vampire mistress, and I can understand why. It's complicated." Hanson explained.

"I see… and when you say you *provide* for her, does that mean you hunt for her?"

"What? You think I'm Jack the Ripper?" Hanson said. "No, I don't have to kill anyone for her. We're undertakers, remember? We have a fresh and regular supply of blood for the mistress."

"You mean you take it from the corpses?"

"Yes, and I prepare it for her with rose tea."

"Why doesn't she just… drink it herself from the corpses?"

"She doesn't like to do that."

"But she's a vampire…"

"You should have left your home many years ago and married a nice young woman. Instead, you chose to live behind closed doors with your sister and behave like a married couple, am I not right?" Hanson said.

"We never did anything immoral!" Tim protested. "And I don't see how that relates to vampires anyway."

"My point is, everyone is free to live as they want. As long as it harms no one, who are you to judge another person's lifestyle?"

"True." Tim agreed. "And I didn't mean to judge Miss Whittaker's lifestyle. I'm just trying to understand."

"Sorry." Hanson said. "I know it must be confusing, but you'll get used to it. Go home, or wherever you've found a place, get some rest and come back tomorrow. We'll dig graves and stake a few ghouls and laugh about all of this."

"Right." Tim said.

He finally had the answers he had been seeking, and he knew who and what each person was at Undertakers Incorporated. But at the same time Hanson had brought up something disturbing. It was true: he had never married because of Holly, because she was there in his life, and she was closer to him than any other woman. They never behaved like a married couple, rather he wanted to keep her a child forever and dote on her. "Home" was him and Holly and their family mansion, and he never wanted anything to change. He hated change. He had never fallen in love with a woman or slept with one, and he did not know or understand the sort of passionate feelings Hanson and Miss Whittaker had for each other, nor how they expressed them. Did they sleep together or was the act of drinking blood the vampire equivalent of intercourse? He did not want to dig too deep into what his employer did with her lover though, he preferred not to know.

Cyril would be waiting for him, Cyril who read him sonnets instead of drinking his blood. The evident connection between them troubled him very much. He had felt perfectly safe and protected with him, enough to throw himself into his arms and tease him. Of course alcohol had played a part in it. Was this simply the natural reaction of a human when they encountered a vampire? Miss Whittaker had the same sort of sweet and alluring scent as him, yet the thought of her biting him left him completely cold. He did not think he would ever want to lay in her arms, nor listen to her talk and read to him. Cyril and him were kindred souls, just like he and Holly had been. That in itself was a problem. If they became any closer, as he had warned him, the vampire would either have to kill him or sire him. He didn't mind being killed but he did not want to be sired, and Cyril had respected his wish... so far.

The night was cold and damp, and Tim walked while trying to put some order in his thoughts. There was too much on his mind, between the ghouls, the vampires, masters and servants, the undead and the not-quite-undead like Humphrey and Hanson, and then, Cyril. He stopped on the docks and gazed at the black water dancing against the wooden pillars of the pier. The night had grown on him, like the moisture had penetrated deep into the wood of the pier, and like the wood would inevitably lose the fight to the salty water someday and begin to rot, so would he inevitably lose the fight to darkness someday and be absorbed into it. The light footsteps behind him came as a reminder of it. But now they were comforting to him.

"I've been waiting for you." Cyril whispered, close enough that he could feel the vampire's cold breath upon his skin.

"I know." Tim said.

"I'm not ready to let you go."

"Neither am I."

Once again, the vampire seized his hand firmly and all but flew him across the empty streets. More than once Tim slipped on the snow and almost fell, and Cyril found it quite funny. They again locked themselves away in the warmth of Cyril's home, and this time the vampire brought out some cigarettes. He offered Tim one, but he declined. He was not in the mood. He made himself comfortable on the sofa. The vampire's place was beginning to feel like home.

"I was thinking of you all day, I could barely sleep. Why didn't you come directly to me?" Cyril asked, seating himself across from him. His eyes were shining with more than hunger, and he seemed to be smoking to calm his senses.

"A lot happened today." Tim replied.

"A lot?"

The scent of cigarette smoke filled the air. Tim leaned forward and wrung his hands together.

"Today I fought ghouls again alongside Hanson, Humphrey and Miss Whittaker. I had no idea she too was a vampire." he said.

"You would have known sooner or later." Cyril said. He put out his cigarette in an ashtray, having had enough.

"I had more or less figured it out already since what happened the other day."

"Indeed."

"You seem to know Miss Whittaker very well. Why does she not live like the other vampires?"

"Is there any reason why she should?"

"No, I guess not."

He poured them both some champagne.

"Dear Tim, you may not smoke, but it kills me to drink alone on Christmas day..." he then said, offering Tim a glass, which he accepted this time. Cyril would not talk without a drinking companion.

"I have known Fiona for a few decades only." the vampire started. "Not many know of her, she is a very discreet person, leading a quiet life. The Dark Lord knows that she doesn't exactly live by our rules, but he allows it. The humans she mingles with are her employees, and nobody knows they are aware of what she is."

"So... not hunting live prey is a crime in your world?" Tim wondered.

"No, but it's... strange. Like this new fad of eating only vegetables among humans."

So Miss Whittaker was to vampires what vegetarians were to humans.

"And of course she doesn't attend the Dark Lord's court even though she could, which is frowned upon. But she's untouchable." Cyril continued.

"Untouchable?"

"She is a high-ranking Natural, like the Dark Lord. No one is allowed to harm a Natural, let alone one of her status."

"What is a Natural?" Tim asked, more and more confused.

"There are different kinds of vampires." Cyril explained. "The highest rank of vampires are Naturals. They were never sired, they are humans who naturally transformed into vampires when they reached a certain age. They are also rare. Because of their high rank and power, many have been targeted by lesser vampires. But now the Dark Lord protects them, and no one is permitted to touch them. The vampires sired by Naturals hold the second highest rank, then come the vampires sired by other vampires. Ghouls and half-dead, and other incomplete creatures hold the lowest rank."

"So she was never sired?" Tim said.

"No."

"You're also breaking the Dark Lord's rules by telling me all of this... what could happen to you?"

"That's an interesting question." Cyril said. "I guess I'm a delinquent in the vampire society. I've already broken rules, for instance by betraying Sofia and exchanging blood vows with another master."

"But now you are a threat to the vampire society." Tim said.

"Well, maybe." Cyril admitted. He lowered his gaze sadly.

Tim wanted to go to him again, but that would only put him in an uncomfortable position, having to refrain from biting him. He was sober enough this time not to play with the beast's instincts.

"Would you read me poetry again tonight?" he asked him instead.

Cyril's eyes lit up at once.

They went up to the bedroom and lay on the bed with only the light of a candle. Vampires could of course use oil lamps like everyone else, and Tim assumed some of their houses even had electricity, but, Cyril explained, many preferred the softer light of candles. Tim lay his head on the vampire's shoulder and listened as the young man read him his favorite sonnets. The usually vivacious Cyril became so very calm when reading, and his voice so soft and melodious, Tim could not help but close his eyes. He breathed in the sweetness of his scent as he read and listened to the pounding of his vampire heart. He had unwillingly moved closer and was now pressing himself against the vampire's body, who tried to ignore him. But as Tim's embrace grew more and more demanding, he finally put down the book and sighed. Tim opened his eyes.

"Why did you stop?"

"Tim, did you want me to read or... something else?" Cyril asked, removing his spectacles.

He put away the book and rolled onto his side and gazed into Tim's eyes.

"I feel very... comfortable with you, like this." Tim said.

"So do I." Cyril said.

They remained silent for a moment, then Tim spoke again.

"I know it's probably the alcohol, or maybe it's the fact that you are so alluring as a vampire, but..."

"What?" Cyril whispered.

"I want to touch you." Tim said. "I'm sorry... I know it's a strange request."

He had really, truly, only meant that he wanted to touch his skin, feel the texture of it, analyze him with his fingers. Was it some kind of perversion to want to touch the creature that could kill you? But his demand did not shock the vampire.

"It's normal to be allured by a vampire." he said. "I don't mind, Tim. You can touch me."

"I promise you I won't get carried away like last time." Tim said.

"Are you saying that to convince yourself?" Cyril asked with a grin.

He took Tim's hand and brought it to his chest, and the human explored it, feeling its cold, hard texture under the fabric of his shirt. His hand moved on to his shoulder, and down his arm, and then, his hip. His body was no longer cold as ice, it was warming up.

"Do you want to know if I am made like all men?" Cyril laughed softly. "Well yes, I am."

Tim's fingers came back up to his waist and tightened around his shirt.

"You're warm now." he said.

"It happens, sometimes." Cyril said.

Tim's hand then moved up to his face and explored its contours, lingering near his mouth. Cyril took his hand again and let his fingers brush against his lukewarm lips.

"Do you want to bite me?" Tim asked in a soft whisper.

"No." Cyril replied in a whisper. "I want to kiss you."

Tim removed his fingers from his grip, surprised. He couldn't deny that he had thought about kissing him, but a human and a vampire? Well Fiona and Hanson did it. What was his excuse since the vampire wanted to kiss him too?

"I..." he said, unsure.

"It's alright, I understand." Cyril said with a kind but sad smile.

"It's not that." Tim said.

"Then is it because I'm a vampire?"

"No."

Cyril gazed at him quietly, waiting for him to find the answer for himself.

"Why do you want to kiss *me*?" Tim asked him. "Why would anyone?"

"Because I am attracted to you... very much so." Cyril simply said.

Tim suddenly felt anxious, not about the prospect of being kissed, bitten or even killed by a vampire, but about the prospect of someone penetrating into his heart. He was not ready to be loved, liked, or even accepted. He was darkness, nothing but darkness. He sat up, shaking, and brought his hand to his head.

"Tim..." Cyril said with concern. He sat up and cautiously wrapped his arm around the human's shoulder.

"You must be mad..." Tim said in a cynical voice. "I am a man who lives in death, I have given up this world! I don't want to feel anything, ever again!"

"Because it's painful?" Cyril asked.

"Everyone dies on me! I don't want to suffer again!" Tim said as a tear rolled down his cheek.

"Then give me your pain and your tears." Cyril said, wiping away his tear. "Let me take away your suffering. I'm already dead, Tim, I can't die on you."

It was too much for Tim's heart, he was overwhelmed now, overwhelmed by the vampire's kindness and how he so easily saw through him, over-whelmed by the beauty of his soul. He no longer felt so alone in this world, and he wanted to be closer, always closer to this man who understood him so perfectly. Answering the painful longing in his heart, he turned around and kissed the vampire. Surprised at first, Cyril welcomed him in a tight embrace, and they sunk back into the bed together.

The next day, Tim arrived at work in a bad mood, and seeing Hanson and Miss Whittaker kissing through the window of her apartment before he started his shift didn't help at all. He felt weak and vulnerable now that Cyril had a piece of his heart. More than a piece. Would he too become like Hanson, a human desperately in love with a vampire, begging the undead creature to sire him and make him immortal so he could experience life, and pain, for all eternity? He wanted Cyril, but he didn't want eternity.

When Hanson came out and began to prepare the hearse, Tim gazed in the direction of Miss Whittaker, who seemed puzzled. He then turned away, too disturbed to focus. She was a vampire too and she never told him until he found out on his own. But why would she tell him anyway? He was her employee, not her close friend.

"You look like death itself today." Hanson remarked. "What happened? Lovers' quarrel?"

"I have no lover." Tim said.

It was true: Cyril and him were not lovers. They had simply kissed once. Twice. Maybe a little more than that.

"Does it have something to do with me?" the blond asked him, curious now.

"Can I ask you something?" Tim replied.

"Sure."

"Do you and Miss Whittaker kiss?"

Hanson gazed at him with surprise, then said: "Yes, we do."

"Why?" Tim asked.

"That's a silly question, Tim. You kiss the person you love; even you should know that." Hanson said, returning to his work.

"But if they are a vampire, how do you..." Tim couldn't finish his sentence.

Hanson stopped what he was doing and turned to him.

"Are you asking me if a vampire can sleep with a human?" he asked, frowning.

"Well..."

"The answer is yes they can, and no we don't. Fiona is well-behaved."

Tim took it to mean Hanson wasn't.

"But you could also kiss as... friends, right?" Tim said.

Hanson looked puzzled again then placed his hands on his shoulders and shook his head.

"Sorry Tim, but I'm not into that. I apologize if I misled you." he said.

"N-No! No..." Tim said, taking a step back. "I'm not interested in you."

"Good." Hanson said. "No romance between us."

"Right. No romance." Tim said.

"Are you two going to start working or are you out on a date?" Humphrey suddenly asked them. He had returned with the mares and looked displeased.

The day was long and uneventful. None of the *clients* were ghouls, so none of them had to be staked. Even Hanson found such days perfectly boring. Tim left the funeral home at seven o'clock, after helping with the cleaning. He had not yet been asked to help collect the blood of the *clients* and hoped he wouldn't be.

As he walked down the street, he tried to resist the urge to return to his vampire. No, he was not going to be obsessed with him, and they were not going to get themselves in the same sort of situation as Hanson and Miss Whittaker. Surely they could be friends. Good friends. Close friends. Friends who kissed? He shook his head. Who was he trying to fool anyway? He knew he would be returning to him tonight.

He passed a bookstore that was open late and noticed a crowd gathered inside. According to the sign on the window, there was a book signing by John Silverstake. Cyril probably didn't get to go out often before the bookstores closed, Tim thought. So he went inside and purchased a copy of Silverstake's latest book, entitled "Lace and Fangs." He was one of the very few men there; almost everyone in the crowd were young females who had come not only to purchase the racy novel, but also to see its author.

The man was in his twenties, pale-skinned, with short and curly black hair, and he wore a black suit with an eccentric hat and tie. He was not strikingly handsome but had a sort of dark and brooding charm to him. He seemed friendly and talkative but avoided eye contact with the women who brought him their books to sign. They all seemed madly in love with him, or, more likely, with the fantasies he gave them. Tim felt quite embarrassed as he came up to the small table where Silverstake was signing copies of his book. He handed him the book. The man lifted his gaze for a moment, only long enough for Tim to notice the reddish tint in his black eyes. He was a vampire too. Tim took a step back.

"One of my few male readers?" the man said with a polite smile. "Don't be shy now, bring me your copy."

Tim hesitantly handed him the book.

"And whose name shall I put down?" the man asked.

"It's for a friend. Cyril." Tim said.

The man stopped, gazed at him again and smiled, then proceeded to write a short message in the book and sign it. He then handed it back to Tim.

"Thank you, Mister Silverstake." the human said.

As he exited the bookstore, he opened the book to see what the vampire had written. In beautiful cursive were the words: *"To Cyril, from a dear friend. To precious encounters. John Silverstake."*

Vampire undertakers and authors, what next? A restaurant owner? Tim preferred not to think about that last one.

He arrived a little later than usual at his friend's house and was surprised to smell food. He had forgotten to pick up something along the way.

"What's this?" Cyril asked him as he handed him the book.

"I thought you probably don't get to go to the bookstores a lot." Tim said, again embarrassed.

"Oh my goodness! Tim!" Cyril shouted as he discovered the autograph inside.

The vampire threw himself at him and kissed his cheek, adding to his embarrassment.

"The author is a vampire." Tim told him.

"Really? How interesting!" Cyril said. "Let's read this one together!"

"Does the vampire bite the girl in the end?" Tim asked, lifting an eyebrow.

"No, he spanks her." Cyril said. "And then they..."

"I think I'll pass on that." Tim said, turning instead to the food on the table, and Cyril laughed.

"I convinced my manservant to prepare a meal for you, and I also have tea." the vampire then said.

"Thank you..." Tim said, turning back to him.

The table had been set for two, and in a large dish was a whole roasted chicken with vegetables.

"Two plates?" Tim asked, curious.

"I can also enjoy human food." Cyril said, and they seated themselves together at the table.

"Do you still... hunt?" Tim asked.

"I'm a vampire." Cyril replied, somewhat uneasy.

"You don't need to deprive yourself for me." Tim said.

Cyril offered him a polite smile and said: "Let's just enjoy human food tonight."

"I could come hunting with you." Tim offered.

"Tim... no." Cyril said, shaking his head.

Tim realized what awkward demands he was making, asking the vampire to take a potential prey along with him to hunt another of the same kind. It had only seemed natural to him though, now he was used to vampires.

"There were a lot of young women at the book signing today." he said, changing the subject.

"I would assume so. John Silverstake writes mainly for women." Cyril said, smiling again.

"Why would a vampire write romance novels?" Tim wondered.

"Eternity can be quite boring. One needs to have hobbies."

"True." Tim said. "And you, do you also find eternity boring?"

"It's lonely." Cyril said. "It was, until I met you."

"I'm not very pleasant company." Tim remarked. "I just come and drink your wine, read your books and sleep in your bed."

"You are the sort of company I like." Cyril said.

Tim watched his vampire put on his spectacles and read the book while they ate. Did he even need spectacles or was it a habit thing? He would ask that question later. Cyril always became so calm and quiet when reading, and Tim liked it. His world was no longer empty. It was filled with Cyril, and Cyril's den had become his home.

3.

Tim returned to Cyril that night, and every other night. He was lost, lost in this vampire, *his vampire*. Most of the time they simply ate and drank, read and talked, then lay together on the bed until Tim fell asleep. They had not kissed again and neither of them mentioned it, and Tim knew that Cyril was simply being considerate of his feelings. And Tim was unsure of his feelings. He did not know if he was ready to become so close to someone and risk being hurt, even though he could not, technically, lose Cyril since the vampire was already dead.

That night, they had downed two bottles of champagne already, smoked, read and enacted Othello and even played cards, and now they lay talking. The vampire always lulled Tim to sleep with the gentleness of his voice, and then covered him with a warm blanket before retiring to a corner of the room to occupy himself, away from temptation. He would go to bed after Tim left in the morning, as he slept during the day.

Cyril's fingers toyed with the buttons on Tim's shirt as they lay together on the bed.

"Is it hard... to be close to a human?" Tim asked him.

"Sometimes." Cyril said. "Is it hard for you to be close to a vampire? Do you never fear me?"

Tim had not meant "Is it hard because you are afraid of biting me?", he had simply wondered whether becoming close to a human, as a vampire, was more complicated than becoming close to another vampire.

"Are you still thinking about biting me?" he asked him, surprised.

"Tim..." Cyril sighed. "I am a vampire. I always think about biting you. Just like men always think about..."

"Oh." Tim said. He had never imagined it that way. "But you wouldn't bite me without my consent." he said.

"Of course not, what kind of animal do you think I am?" Cyril laughed.

"When you picture yourself biting me, what do you imagine?" Tim asked him.

"We shouldn't talk about that..." Cyril said, suddenly uncomfortable.

"I'm sorry." Tim said.

"Why don't you tell me more about you instead?"

"What about me do you want to know?"

"I found you roaming the streets at night and sleeping under bridges when you have a home. You have no fear of our world, or even of dying at my hands." Cyril said, bringing his hand to Tim's face. "What is so much more frightening in the world you come from that you seem to fear nothing?"

"Does it even matter?" Tim said sadly.

"You matter." Cyril said softly.

His eyes upon Tim were intense, piercing, but they were so full of kindness Tim wanted only to throw himself into them.

"There is nothing in my world." he said, lowering his gaze to avoid those eyes.

"That is not a satisfying answer. Try again." Cyril said.

"Do you always need to penetrate the minds of those you like?" Tim asked.

"Only yours." Cyril said. "Tell me..."

The vampire slipped his arm under his neck and let him rest his head on his cold shoulder.

"I'm going to die soon..." Tim muttered. "That is the curse of my lineage, and my curse."

"What curse?" Cyril asked.

"My earliest memory is that of my widowed aunt crying on a chair in our dining room." Tim said, uneasy. "All her children had already died, and her husband had just passed away. It is a mysterious illness that runs in my family, on my father's side. People suddenly become sick, and within a day or two they are gone. My mother had already died giving birth to my youngest sister, Holly. Soon after the passing of my cousins and my uncle, we learned that my aunt had committed suicide. My father was devastated and terrified of losing his children as well, so he locked my two sisters and I up in our house with him and we lived a secluded life. Holly and I were too young to understand the reasons why we had to hide and what we were hiding from, but my older sister Esther told us frightening stories. She said that before he died, our uncle became pale and listless, and so weak he could barely walk, yet he felt no pain, anywhere in his body. Within a day he was dead, and no doctor could tell us why. In the note our aunt left us before she died, she said that there was a curse upon the Thompson lineage. And indeed, the next to die was Esther. My father then began to lose his mind and locked himself in his room. He would not see or speak to us and asked that meals be left at his door. We were so worried for him we dared not disobey him. Then one day, without any warning, he walked away on us, leaving us only a note asking us not to look for him. We knew only too well why he had gone: he probably had developed the symptoms as well. His body was never found.

I took my father's place as head of the family and watched over Holly diligently. After my father left us though, things seemed to return to normal for several years. I enrolled in a nearby college. I had no great ambitions, but I wanted to provide for my sister. Neither of us ever wanted to leave home or marry, we were contented together. But one day everything changed, and very suddenly.

"I remember that day... Holly wouldn't get out of bed and complained of feeling weak. She was not the kind to get sick very easily, so I called for a doctor, who said that there was nothing wrong with her and it was probably some feminine weakness. I told him about our family's curse, but he only told me not to believe in superstition. He said that all the deaths in our family were unrelated, and it just so happened that every family member up to us met an unfortunate early end. He advised me to pray to God and try not to overthink it. I was not religious, but for the first time I did pray to God. I prayed that Holly be saved, by all means. Obviously that prayer went unheard, for by the end of the next day she lay dead in her bed, cold as ice... She was so beautiful, even in death. I didn't want to have her body removed, but I knew the longer it remained in our home, the harder it would be for me. Holly... Holly died a year ago, though I have stopped counting the days. And since then, I too have died inside."

Cyril listened carefully to the entire story, gently stroking Tim's head as he spoke.

"There is something I want to tell you, Tim, though I do not know if I should tell you now." he eventually said.

"You might as well say anything you want now... I am drunk, sick and miserable." Tim said.

"I don't think anyone in your family died of a disease." Cyril said.

"Are you deaf or what? Have you not listened to anything I just told you?" Tim snapped at him.

"Tim, what you have just described to me is not a disease, it is what happens to people who are bitten by a vampire and become ghouls."

"Ghouls?" Tim said, horrified.

He pushed the vampire's hands away from him at once.

"It is possible that a vampire has been preying on your family. Maybe a personal revenge." Cyril insisted.

"I don't believe it!" Tim retorted.

"Calm down, Tim." Cyril said, trying to appease him.

But Tim rose and began to take out his anger on the furniture around them.

"Lies! Lies! You and your kind are nothing but liars!" he shouted.

"Why would I lie to you? Why would I tell you that one of my kind may be the cause of your suffering, when it means that you might run from me as well?" Cyril said sincerely.

"If it was one of your kind, then maybe it was you!" Tim suddenly said, grabbing Cyril's shoulders.

"It wasn't me." the vampire told him.

"What proof have I?"

"You have none."

Tim let himself fall to his knees, shaking.

"What am I saying?" he muttered, holding his head.

"You are only speaking your mind."

"Why am I here, why did I have to hear this?"

"Tim, I understand this comes as a shock to you, but please calm down. We will find out together what happened." Cyril said. He knelt beside Tim and began to stroke his dark hair again. But the young man was enraged, furious, and yet aroused by the beast who touched him so gently. A beast who could easily give him the end he wanted, but wouldn't, just like Miss Whittaker refused herself to Hanson. He caught his arm and pinned him to the ground. His eyes were wild.

"You're not getting away from me tonight. You're gonna give me what I want this time!" he said in a dangerous voice.

"Tim... you're not yourself right now. Stop this." Cyril warned him.

"No." Tim said.

"Release me now." Cyril insisted. His voice had lost any compassion.

"No!" Tim shouted.

"Fine, you want me to feed on you? Then let's do it!" Cyril finally retorted. Using his superior strength, he rolled over the human and pinned him to the ground instead. He was strong, incredibly strong. But Tim was fearless. He wanted death now, more than anything. It was high time the vampire finally lived up to the reputation of his kind and gave him the finale he had been waiting for. He wanted him to *kill* him, and preferably make it painful.

Cyril moved closer to his neck, but only licked the skin there slowly. It felt good, really good. But they were not going to get anywhere if he remained so gentle. Tim struggled to free himself from his grip, but it was to no avail.

"Bite me, hard! I want you to suck me dry!" he shouted in a frenzy.

"So you want it hard and painful? Perhaps I should have taken a whip to you from the start." Cyril said, tightening his grip around his wrists.

"You're the one who deserves to be whipped for not giving me what I want!"

"We'll take turns then, you bad, bad human." the vampire said. His voice was seductive again but also dangerous. Tim knew the vampire was only trying to buy time, as always. But as he said himself, eventually he would either have to sire or kill the human – a human who had already chosen to die.

"I don't care what you do, as long as you *kill me!*" he said.

Cyril pulled away and gazed into his sorrowful eyes, then said: "I can't kill you."

He let go of the eager young human.

"What kind of bloodsucker are you? You can't leave me hanging on like this, just do it!" Tim said.

"I don't want to kill you." Cyril said, shaking his head.

He rolled over and lay beside him on the floor. His eyes were moist and sad. Tim turned to him and noticed a tear rolling down his cheek. A vampire tear.

"Why Tim? Why do you so desperately want me to kill you?" he asked.

"I want to die." Tim said.

"And I want you to live, to be with me." Cyril said, turning to him. "Tim, is that all I am to you? A bloodsucker who can grant your death wish?"

"No..." Tim said. His head was cooler now, and he realized his demands were only hurting Cyril. The vampire truly cared about him. He took his hand in his and kissed it for the first time.

"I'm sorry." he said. "I should not have asked you for that."

"It's alright." Cyril said. "Just know that if you go to another vampire and ask him to bite you, I will never forgive you."

If Tim died at the hands of another vampire, then it wouldn't matter whether Cyril forgave him or not because he would be no more, he thought. But he understood the meaning of his words. Offering himself to another would be a cruel betrayal, one that would hurt the vampire, as well as deprive him of the one he so adored for all eternity.

"I won't." he said.

Cyril rose and helped him up to his feet, and Tim was so drunk and so dizzy he fell into his arms.

"Looks like we need to get you back to bed." the vampire said.

"Not yet." Tim said, clinging to his shirt.

The vampire's arms were strong and supported all of his weight, and he felt safe, so safe in his arms. He pushed himself up and went for Cyril's lips, and began to kiss them softly, and Cyril responded with much more passion than he had expected. He leaned against the wall, holding the human tightly. When Tim finally pulled away, the vampire's eyes were a bright ruby red and he was breathing heavily. He let his head fall onto Tim's neck and the human could feel fangs brushing against his skin. Then Cyril moved back. He turned his head away and covered his mouth with his hand. So that was how to get a vampire in the mood for a bite, Tim thought. But he was not going to try to take advantage of him, not anymore.

"I'm sorry, Tim. I'm terribly sorry..." Cyril whispered as though he were in agony right now.

Tim fell to his knees, removing his neck from the vampire's sight, and wrapped his arms around him.

"You don't have to apologize, for anything. I was the one who was bad to you tonight." he whispered.

"I'm alright now." Cyril said, drawing in a deep breath.

His body gave every sign of arousal, and Tim understood now why Hanson had told Miss Whittaker that if they went too far in expressing their love for each other, she would have to bite him. He felt sorry now for putting Cyril in that position and began to cry. He surely was very drunk.

"Why are you crying, silly?" Cyril said, leaning over him and running his fingers through his hair. "It's not your fault if I get aroused so quickly and want to bite."

"I don't want to take advantage of you..." Tim said.

"Knowing that you care so much about me is enough." Cyril said, helping him up again.

This time he was the one who leaned forward, and he kissed away the tears on Tim's cheeks. His lukewarm lips were soft and sweet.

"Come now, let's get you to bed, my human." he said.

<hr />

The next evening Tim didn't even have to go to Cyril, for the young vampire was waiting for him quite close to the funeral home, in the shadows of an alley. And his presence made him feel young and excited again, like a boy about to get in trouble.

"Aren't you worried about my coworkers and your friends finding out about us?" Tim asked him.

"Let them." Cyril said with shining eyes. "What we have is much greater than anything else."

Tim liked his words.

"And what do we have?" he asked with a smile.

"You know it, silly." Cyril said, kissing his cheek.

They locked arms and began to walk.

"Tonight, I want you to follow me." Tim told him.

"Yes, *Master.*" Cyril said.

"Don't call me that." Tim said. "If anything actually did happen between us, you would be the master, wouldn't you?"

"I guess so, but I like to imagine that you would be." Cyril said with a bright smile.

That night Tim knew exactly where he wanted to go. The clue Cyril had given him the night before was the missing piece that completed the puzzle of his past, and now all he had to do was find the vampire responsible for all the suffering of his family and kill him. Or maybe he wouldn't kill him, maybe he would find a way to torture him, to make it a long, slow and painful death.

"How does one kill a vampire?" he asked Cyril along the way.

"Silver, stakes, sunlight, fire... are you planning on killing me?" Cyril humored him.

Tim laughed.

"Not you, but the vampire who killed all my family. The one who killed Holly."

"I see." Cyril said. "Obviously you will have a hard time taking the vampire out in the sunlight or throwing him into a fire, so I would recommend finding him when he is asleep and using a silver stake. For reasons I do not know, we can't touch silver unless we are wearing gloves. It burns our skin just like sunlight. A wooden stake will do as well but is less effective."

"Then a silver stake it will be." Tim said. "And where do vampires usually sleep?"

"In our beds..." Cyril replied, puzzled at the question.

"Oh, right. You don't sleep in crypts and coffins."

"Personally, I like to roll around in my bed, especially with a partner." Cyril grinned.

They finally reached their destination: the Thompson mansion. Without wasting a second, Tim led his companion inside. They went straight to his father's office and he opened the door. He lit a candle and began looking around the old wooden desk, pushing books and papers out of the way.

"Is this your house? What exactly are we looking for?" Cyril wondered, nonchalantly standing in the doorway.

"If this vampire is preying on my family, there must be a reason: an age-old feud, a treason, something. There has to be a clue somewhere!" Tim said. "This is my father's office. If anything, I will find a clue here."

"What makes you think you would find it here?"

"I don't know."

"I can tell you this much: vampires don't leave clues or witnesses." Cyril said.

The vampire left his companion and walked slowly down the dark corridor. He came to a halt in front of a portrait on the wall, depicting Tim, Holly, Esther and their father. It perplexed him.

"Did you find something?" Tim asked, immediately joining him.

"I'm not sure." Cyril said.

"Tell me! Anything you know might be helpful!" Tim pressed him.

Cyril pointed his finger at Tim's father.

"I've seen this face before. Is this man your father?" he asked.

"Yes, that's my father Heath." Tim said. "Did you ever come across him when he was alive?"

"Remind me when your father disappeared?"

"About ten years ago, more or less."

Cyril turned to him with very serious eyes.

"Five years ago, I saw this man." he said.

"You mean he isn't dead?" Tim said, confused.

"Oh he was dead alright. He's a vampire. A Natural friend took me to a salon frequented by the court, I saw him there." Cyril said.

"A vampire? You mean someone sired him?" Tim asked.

He was in shock, lost between the exhilarating feeling of knowing that his father may be alive – as alive as the undead might be – and the horror that the vampire who had slain his family may have turned him into his slave.

"Anyhow, let's go find him!" Tim said. "Take me to this vampire court!"

"Hold on Tim." Cyril said. "I can't just bring a mortal to the Dark Lord's court. For one thing, I'm not even allowed there on my own as a sired vampire, and I could be killed just for sharing our secrets with you. Do you really think they're going to welcome you at court?"

"My father won't let anything happen to me." Tim said.

Cyril grabbed his arm as he was about to head out of the mansion.

"Wait, Tim!" he said. "He's no longer your father! He may recognize you from past memories, but he no longer is the man you knew. He is a bloodsucker, like me. And you want to head right into the nest of the most powerful bloodsuckers... they will only make a meal out of you!"

"Let them try!" Tim said, slipping away from his grip.

But Cyril moved in front of him, blocking the door.

"Tim, if we are to go find your father, we need a plan."

"I don't have time for plans."

"Then you will have to *make* time." Cyril said in an angry voice. "I can't let you walk into their nest unprotected."

"Just try to stop me!"

Tim pushed the vampire out of the way.

"Fine then, and just where are you going to find the Dark Lord and his court?" Cyril asked defiantly. Tim froze at once.

"I... don't know." he admitted.

"I do. So if you want me to show you, you'll have to obey me."

Tim clenched his fists.

"Let me gather some information first." Cyril continued. "Give me a week. I will go around the circles and find out what I can. My friends might know something about your family."

Tim suddenly remembered his conversation with Miss Whittaker. She *knew* about his family. He decided he would visit her later.

"Fine then, I'm counting on you." he told Cyril.

The vampire then drew a pair of gloves from his pocket and put them on. He reached into his vest pocket and pulled out a silver pin, which he clipped to Tim's collar.

"This will protect you a little if one of us attacks you." he told Tim. "Of course it will not kill a vampire or a ghoul, but it will keep it away from your neck. Find a stake at the funeral home and always carry it around with you. It's your best chance of survival against one of us."

"You seem very worried about me all of a sudden. I've never carried a stake before." Tim said.

"Tim, if there truly is someone after your family, they might be after your life as well." Cyril said, serious.

"Maybe they just want to sire me like my father." Tim said.

"That is my privilege and mine alone." Cyril said.

He cupped Tim's face with his hands and lay a delicate kiss on his lips.

"Wait for me, Tim... wait for me." he said.

"I will." Tim said.

And with this, Cyril walked away into the night.

⁓

The days that followed, Tim hoped to see Miss Whittaker and request a private interview with her, but she never showed her face. One evening, he questioned Hanson.

"Where is Miss Whittaker?"

"She's out of town, she will be back very soon." Hanson promised.

"Out of town?"

Hanson put down the coffin he was carrying on one of the tables in the mortuary. He invited Tim to come closer.

"We're looking for a new place to move the business." he whispered.

"Why?"

"A messenger brought a card for the mistress the other day." Hanson said. "It was anonymous, but it warned her that the other day's incident was reported to them and needs to be dealt with. Now."

"The other day? What happened?"

"Shortly after you left to go home, Humphrey and I accidentally let a ghoul escape into the streets and Humphrey was seen by at least two humans."

"So the vampires are asking Miss Whittaker to eliminate Humphrey? Now that you mention it, I haven't seen him today." Tim said.

"He's also out of town."

Hanson opened the coffin and checked the man's neck for bite marks. There were numerous.

"Oops! This one won't be going to the grave tonight!" he said with humor.

He pulled out his stake and put it through the corpse's heart. It immediately dissolved into dust.

Tim walked over to the crate where they kept stakes and reached to grab a silver one. But his hand stopped. For reasons unknown to him, he could not touch the silver ones. He grabbed a wooden one instead and tucked it under his coat.

"Sorry we don't have gold stakes, my Lord, but silver is the most effective against the undead." Hanson said, handing him a silver stake instead. Tim took a step back. Hanson then noticed the pin on his collar.

"Who gave you that?" he asked, suspicious.

"No one. It's an heirloom." Tim lied.

"A silver pin on the collar is an old trick to ward off vampires. But ordinary people don't know of it, because they don't know that what vampires fear more than the silver stake, is silver itself." Hanson said, frowning.

"Really?" Tim said, unconcerned.

"Don't tell me you're going with a vampire?" Hanson said in a reproachful tone.

"What if I am? You go with a vampire too." Tim retorted.

He suddenly felt Hanson's large hands fall upon his shoulders and pin him against the wall. The young man was so much stronger than him that Tim could hardly move.

"Let go of me!" he gasped.

Hanson ripped his shirt open and checked his chest and neck for bite marks. He was relieved not to find any.

"Thank goodness you were not bitten!"

"Of course not, what were you thinking?" Tim said, seizing the opportunity to push him away.

There were a cursed few moments of silence while Hanson paced around the room, a serious frown on his brow. He then stopped and sighed.

"You are free to do as you please, of course." he told Tim. "Just know that a vampire's intentions are never what they appear to be."

"Then why do you trust Miss Whittaker?"

"She's... different." Hanson said.

"Yet if she sires you, you too will become charming and deceitful like the other vampires, won't you?" Tim said.

"I hope I should be different, like her." Hanson said with a sigh.

"You're the one deceiving yourself." Tim said. "You want to enter a world you despise only for the promise of eternal love."

"What is there above eternal love in this world?" Hanson asked him very seriously. His sincerity caught Tim by surprise.

"I don't know." he admitted. "But I think in the world of the undead there are many other things than love, and that Miss Whittaker is probably trying to protect you from them before you throw away your life."

"True." Hanson said. He paused for a moment then seemed to relax. "Whoever your new vampire friend might be, he or she does seem to care about your safety." he then told Tim with a smile.

Tim did not respond. He didn't want to talk about Cyril or their plans with anyone. It was his secret alone.

A loud knock on the front door startled them both. They went out to meet the unexpected guest and found themselves face to face with the most curious young lad. He was still a boy of about ten or so, hiding his pale rounded face and unruly mass of auburn hair under the hood of an old dusty cloak. He was short like a child, yet he held himself with the grace of an aristocrat. His eyes were as black as the night around him. Tim knew at once that he was a vampire.

"Could you spare a coffin for an old friend?" he asked Hanson.

"Mickey!" Hanson said at once. They knew each other.

"Long time no see." the boy said with a grin.

"You'd better come on inside before someone sees you!" Hanson said, laughing.

The boy stepped inside the funeral home and uncovered his head. He bowed to Tim as a greeting.

"Greetings Sir, my name is Michael, but people also call me Mickey." he said.

"Pleasure to meet you. I'm Tim." Tim said, unsure what sort of greeting one was supposed to exchange with a vampire when they met for the first time.

"It's been a while... traveling again, huh?" Hanson told his friend.

He wrapped his arm around the boy's shoulders and took him inside. Tim followed them. They went to the coffin storage room, where the boy picked out a coffin fit to his size and shape.

"This will do. How much do I owe you?" he asked Hanson.

"Have you any money?" Hanson laughed.

"None. But I can pay with my labor."

"Do you really think we would charge you?" Hanson said, smiling. "You know as long as you don't cause any trouble, you're free to come here anytime. Mistress' orders."

"I hate being in debt to anyone." Mickey said very seriously. "I will work for you until my new *bed* is paid off. And if you could provide a little food for me all the while, I would very much appreciate it."

"Not hunting anymore?" Hanson asked.

He opened the company's inventory book and diligently wrote down the model and price of the coffin, and name of the buyer. Mickey sat on a stool nearby.

"I have my moods." he said. "Right now I'm at odds with the rules and all."

"Until the next time you change your mind, right?" Hanson said.

"Right."

Tim stood near the door and observed them quietly.

"I thought vampires slept in beds like everyone else." he said, mostly to himself. Mickey turned his shining dark eyes to him and smiled. Less than a second later the boy was standing right in front of him, eyeing him from head to toe, and especially the silver pin on his collar. Tim did not move.

"This mortal smells like a vampire all over." he said.

"He's one of our employees." Hanson said, unconcerned.

"So, when do you plan on joining our world?" Mickey asked Tim.

"It's not in my plans." Tim replied. The vampire boy seemed quite surprised.

"You know that if your new master doesn't sire you, he will have to kill you." Mickey said.

"I'm aware of it."

"You do not fear death?"

"No."

"What an interesting young man." Mickey said.

"Oh, don't worry about him." Hanson said. "This is about as lively as Tim gets. He would probably taste as sour to a vampire as he is gloomy."

"I must agree it is most unpleasant to feed on a prey with no life in them." Mickey said. He winked at Tim and slipped back to Hanson's side.

"Where is Fiona? I can barely smell her at all." he said.

"She is out of town for a few days."

"I see. And just when does she plan on siring you?"

"I'm still waiting on her. Can you help me convince her?" Hanson said.

"I have no power over her." Mickey replied.

Tim frowned. He was getting tired of all the vampire rules, the siring, the killing, and everything else. He was beginning to understand why Miss Whittaker stayed away from her peers. He walked out of the room and headed outside. Preparing the carriage for the next day was by far more interesting than listening to the kid's gossip about who was to be sired or not and how not-tasty he would be. He was tasty enough for Cyril at least.

As he had promised, Mickey stayed in the Undertakers Inc. building and helped out with the work to pay for his coffin. On cloudy days, he accompanied them to people's homes to pick up the *clients*, though he would not set foot in their houses. Some undertakers would have a child mute anyway, a kid with a solemn face that led the funeral convoys, and the families of the clients were not surprised in the least by his presence. They brought the *clients* back to the funeral home and after Hanson made his usual round for ghouls, he bled one or two corpses for Mickey. The vampire boy stated that he no longer wanted to "feed" on humans, even dead, so Hanson mixed the blood with tea for him and served it to him as diligently as he did for his own mistress.

Tim found himself the unwilling witness of these practices, which he neither understood nor liked to watch. Even to his heretic soul, there was something disturbing in watching Hanson work on the corpses of individuals who had been alive only a day or two prior. But more disturbing even was the scene he observed one cold night, when Mickey suddenly lost all restraint before a corpse, and threw himself at its neck, and gorged himself on the fresh blood, very much like a starved beast offered a fresh cut of raw meat. And he tore at the unfortunate body, ripping flesh with his bare hands to get more of its blood. Hanson and Tim watched him quietly, bound by the mutual understanding that giving in to temptation was more painful to Mickey than to either of his observers. With a loud snarl, the boy finally pulled himself away from the corpse, covering his bloody mouth with his hand in horror. He backed away slowly from the scene, then disappeared in the dark corridors. Hanson walked over to the coffin and looked at the unfortunate man with compassion. He drew a silver stake from his coat and took a quick glance in Tim's direction, saying: "I must do it. He has other bites."

Tim nodded. There was nothing more that could be done for the man, but at least ensure that he did not become a wandering ghoul. And yet it was too painful somehow for him to watch Hanson "finish off" the poor man already torn apart. He stepped out of the room and slowly made his way outside. He felt sick and thought the fresh air might ease his senses a little. Out in the open, he leaned against the frozen wall and breathed in the winter air. Hanson joined him and pulled out a small flask of whiskey.

"You look too young to be drinking that stuff." Tim said.

"Oh, spare me, will you? I'm older than you." Hanson said before swallowing the contents of the flask in only a few gulps.

Tim returned to his silent contemplation of the night shadows.

"Does Mickey have a master?" he asked.

"Not that I know of. Vampires don't sire children." Hanson said.

"He seems too adult to be a child, and too... ferocious." Tim said.

"What you just witnessed was an accident for Mickey, but it is what others of his kind do every night. What *your* vampire does." Hanson said in a serious voice.

"I don't understand why you look forward to such a life." Tim said.

"The feeding part doesn't bother me. We eat animals, vampires eat people, what's the problem?"

"It is a problem for Mickey and Miss Whittaker apparently."

"They should have the right to live the way they want, even if others think they are strange." Hanson said. "The Dark Lord imposes rules that are supposed to keep the vampires 'free', but it's not freedom if it means they have to do what everyone else does."

Did Hanson know that he knew about the Dark Lord, or did he just let that slip? Tim was not sure.

"Is there any vampire out there who is truly free?" he wondered.

"Is there any human, anywhere, who is truly free?" Hanson said, thoughtful.

"But is Miss Whittaker happy living this way?" Tim asked him.

"I believe she would be, if my mortal life was not at stake." Hanson said. "There are some like Mickey who know about my position and wonder when she is going to sire me. Sooner or later she will be forced to do it against her will, or they will come to finish me off. That's also why she is looking for another place for us."

"It would be much more simple if she just did it." Tim remarked.

"Try telling her that... She believes that siring me would rob me of my free will because I would become her servant, and she doesn't want any servants."

A light snow had begun to fall and the moon had come out. Tim noticed a faint silhouette moving in the shadows. By now, he had got used to the way each vampire he knew moved, and he recognized Miss Whittaker.

"She's back!" Hanson said, and he immediately rushed over to her and embraced her. She gently pushed him away and locked her arm around his, like a proper lady. They walked up to Tim.

"Good evening, Tim." she said. "I'm afraid Humphrey will not be back for yet a few more days, he is making some calls about our new place."

"So you found something?" Hanson asked her.

"Possibly, but let us go inside to talk about it."

"Tim, go get the kid." Hanson told Tim. He then turned to Miss Whittaker and said: "Mickey has come to visit us."

"Has he grown weary of the court again?" she wondered.

"Most certainly."

"I am fond of Mickey, but I hope others won't come here searching for him." she said in a low voice.

"Don't worry, I'm sure he'll be leaving in no time. Life here surely isn't as exciting as the vampire court." Hanson assured her.

"Tim," Miss Whittaker said, "do bring the boy to my apartment, but please do not tell him anything about our plans to move. He is but a child and might cause us trouble without knowing."

"I understand." Tim said.

He went inside to look for the boy and the couple followed him. As he turned a quick glance in their direction he saw Hanson pressing his mistress against the wall and kissing her fiercely as she vaguely put up a fight. She finally gave in to his passion and wrapped her arms around him. He missed Cyril now, terribly, and the thought he wouldn't see him for yet several days was almost unbearable, but at the same time the thought that he *would* return, and make him feel at home again, was wonderful.

Tim had never found himself in such an awkward position as when Miss Whittaker gathered him, Hanson and Mickey in her apartment for some tea. On the table before the guests were two teapots: one containing regular tea for the mortal and the not-quite-yet-undead, and another containing her special brew of tea and blood for the vampires. More chairs had been brought in from Humphrey's apartment across the hallway to accommodate the guests.

"Please do not feel shy among us Tim. After all, you are almost like family now." she told Tim, and her eyes flashed upon the silver pin on his collar.

"Why are we here having our tea with a mortal again?" Mickey asked aloud. Though he did not follow the rules of his kind, he did not approve of mingling with mortals. Tim noticed how the young vampire made a clear distinction between him, a mortal, and Hanson, who to him was almost a vampire already.

"I just want to relax with friends, can I not?" Miss Whittaker said. "Tim is a human with no ties, he won't talk about us to anyone."

"I see." Mickey said.

"I'm an undertaker, people think we are halfway mad anyway." Tim said, sipping at his tea.

Miss Whittaker laughed softly for the first time.

"He has become more loquacious, hasn't he?" she told Hanson.

"Right? Maybe someday we'll even get a smile out of him!" Hanson said with a grin.

Tim ignored them. His gaze was fixed on the child vampire, whom he did not like one bit, and neither did the child like him.

"So, what's new in the old countryside?" Hanson asked Miss Whittaker.

"Nothing much. Our country folk are very quiet." she said.

"And I was hoping to hear some dark tales of hungry old lords in their castles, kidnapping young maidens..." Hanson said.

"There are a few older vampires, but nobody kidnaps young women." she said, puzzled. "Blood vows are exchanged only between consenting adults."

"I know, I know." Hanson said.

Tim smirked: Miss Whittaker had as little of a sense of humor as he did. They resembled each other.

"I visited Katherine, you know Katherine, Mickey?"

"Of course I do. She's boring."

"Well, I am a little boring too." she laughed.

Mickey yawned loudly and stretched out on his chair.

"May I go to bed now? I'm sleepy." he said.

"The night has only just begun." Hanson reminded him.

"I unfortunately am not all grown up like you. I need naps." Mickey said, frowning.

"Aren't you older than Fiona?" Hanson asked, sarcastic.

"I'm sorry dear Mickey, our conversation must be boring for you. Why don't you go rest in your coffin downstairs, where it is quiet?" Miss Whittaker said in a gentle voice.

"I think I will do just that." he said. He got up and she hugged him like a mother, then sent him to bed. After the door was shut, she opened a dusty old chest and pulled out a violin, which she handed to Hanson. He took it and went to seat himself near the door, and began to play a piece.

"Little pitchers have big ears." she told Tim with a smile as she came back to him.

"That kid certainly has ears, and eyes too." Tim remarked.

"He's a good kid, but he can be mischievous." she said. "But Tim, what about you? You seem so... changed since the last time we spoke."

"I am not changed." he said.

"That pin you wear could only have been given to you by one of our kind." she said. "Tim, what are you doing? Do you understand what it means to go with a vampire and accept presents from them?" Her voice was filled with concern now.

"What is there to understand?" he asked her, somewhat irritated. He didn't need a lecture from her.

"It's not something you can just back out of when you please." she said. "Once a vampire has their eyes on you, you won't be able to resist them. You cannot resist us because it is in our nature to be most attractive to your kind."

"I don't feel attracted to any vampire." Tim said. It was a lie. She had a point: no matter what, he always returned to Cyril. But in his case, he knew that the vampire cared about him and would never hurt him – even when begged to.

"What is it like to drink blood and... sire someone?" he then asked her.

"Why would you want to know that?" she asked, frowning.

"I have no intention of being sired if that's what you mean. I'm just curious." he said.

"Vampires are first and foremost predators. When we hunt and drink blood, we experience a sort of ecstasy." she said.

"Then why go through the trouble of siring a human?"

"Because we are also sentient beings, with feelings, just like you. We can have friends, lovers..." she explained. "We sire a human only when we have an existing bond of love with them. Love, sexual desire and the act of biting are very much connected for us. Masters and their sired vampires continue to drink each other's blood to strengthen their bond. So the process of siring, for us, could be compared to a honeymoon for humans. It is the consecration of our love... or so I was told."

In other words, because she had never sired anybody, Miss Whittaker would be considered an old spinster among vampires, or a stubborn virgin. Hanson turned his loving gaze to her.

"And for the human?" Tim asked.

"For the human, it comes with feelings of love and submission, which is why sired vampires are called servants." she said.

"Interesting."

"No, Tim. Depriving the one you love of their life and freedom is not *interesting*." she said in a firmer voice.

"Life invariably leads to death. So dying from natural death or at the hands of a vampire doesn't make much of a difference." he said. "Anyhow, this is irrelevant since I have no such bond with any vampire."

"If you say so." she said.

That night, as Tim left his companions, he returned to his habitual roaming of the East End's streets. Roaming and thinking. He didn't need Hanson's friendship or Miss Whittaker's concerns. He needed for Cyril to return to him, and preferably with answers. More than anything now, he needed to avenge Holly's death.

He had been sleeping in Cyril's house, and the vampire had left the door unlocked and the cabinets filled with food and wine for him. He was not only staying there because he needed shelter, but also because it was the place that felt like home to him, and every little thing there, from the furniture to the books scattered on every surface, reminded him of Cyril.

As he was walking down the dark street though, he realized that he was being followed. A light, quick footstep. A vampire, and not Cyril. He smirked.

"Don't even try." he warned the creature.

The vampire stopped and so did he. He turned around and was not surprised to see Mickey's short silhouette standing there in the snow. His eyes were a deep black. He had already fed, gorged himself even, so there was no way he could be looking for a snack.

"What do you want, Mickey?" Tim asked aloud.

The vampire did not answer.

"Were you getting tired of dead prey?" he asked him.

"Who's your vampire master?" Mickey asked him.

"I have none." Tim said.

"Why are you so intent on protecting him?" Mickey said. "I just want a name, nothing more."

"So you can go tell others who's siring who and who's not?" Tim said. "Go away. You won't get anything from me."

"I'm not going back to court, not yet." Mickey said.

"Good for you." Tim said. He couldn't care less what the vampire did.

But then another vampire stepped out of the shadows and walked slowly to Mickey's side. A female vampire this time. Unlike the boy, she wore a very fine purple dress with a long black coat over it. Her long black hair was kept in a neat bun. From a distance and with the darkness, Tim couldn't quite clearly see her face, but the moment she spoke his entire world crumbled.

"Mickey," she said in a perfectly emotionless voice, "is this man bothering you?"

"No, he was just asking me why I was alone." Mickey lied.

She took the boy's hand and they began to walk away. Tim took a step forward, then another, and shouted the one name that filled his mind now: "Holly!"

She stopped for a brief moment and turned her head back, just enough to confirm what he already knew without a doubt. It was Holly, his beloved sister, and she too was a vampire!

"Do you know him?" Mickey asked her.

"No." she said absently, and they left.

They were fast, and there was no way Tim could follow them. He ran and ran until his legs could carry him no more, and then he let himself fall into the snow, breathless and confused. It was her. His eyes and ears could have tricked him, but she responded to her name! It was her alright, and she was one of them now, like his father. And now all he wanted was to go and be with her, no matter what it took – even becoming a vampire himself! He ran back to Cyril's house and waited there.

⁓

The one-week mark came and still he hadn't returned. Tim was growing agitated. Would no one ever free him from this agony? No one would answer his questions, no one would let him do as he pleased, no one would help him, even the people who called themselves his friends... all of this to protect him from what? From finding out that his beloved sister was still alive, and that there was still a place where he could be with her! He was enraged now. He picked up one of the chairs in Cyril's bedroom and threw it against the wall, shattering it to pieces. He gazed at the pieces on the floor for a moment, shocked. He could be quick to anger, but this was different. It was a deep and dark desire for violence. He wanted to find and *kill* the vampire who had sired his family! He thirsted for the sight of blood, even though he was more likely to see ashes if his plan succeeded.

"Cyril!" he shouted, but only the silence answered him. And silence was not enough anymore.

He eventually lay on the bed and fell into a deep and agitated sleep. In his dreams, he saw the face of his father turn into a ghoul and fly away, he saw himself and his sister Holly, laying inside a coffin together, and then her cold body emerged as a vampire and flew away, and he was left alone inside a coffin... forever alone!

He eventually awakened to the familiar voice of Cyril and opened his eyes to the sight of the vampire leaning over him, and gazing at him with concern.

"Tim, what happened?" he asked him.

Tim shook his head and sat up in the bed, trying to gather his thoughts.

"What day is it?" he asked.

"January twenty-ninth." Cyril said.

"You're late." Tim said.

"I returned two days ago, but you were asleep and have been sleeping ever since."

"Why didn't you wake me up?"

"I tried, but nothing would make you open your eyes."

Tim took his head in his hands.

"I'm thirsty..." he said.

"Here, have some water." Cyril said, handing him a glass.

"Not water." Tim said, pushing it away.

"Tim, what happened while I was gone?" Cyril asked him again.

"I saw her... my sister Holly. She's a vampire!" Tim said, although now he was not so sure whether it had been real or a dream.

"Holly Thompson, yes I know. It was part of the news I brought back for you." Cyril said in a sad voice.

"So it's true then? You must take me to her at once!" Tim said, grabbing his arms.

"Tim, listen to me." Cyril said. "Holly and your father are both close to the Dark Lord now, there is nothing we can do. No mortal can even go near the court. You'll die."

"Then make me a vampire! Sire me now, and let us go to them! I have to be wherever Holly is! I have to!"

Cyril pulled away from him and walked across the room, and leaned against the wall. His dark eyes had lost all emotion and he was listless. Tim went over to him, grabbed his shoulders and shook him.

"Cyril, you've always wanted to sire me, and now I am willing! Let's do it!" he said.

"No." Cyril whispered.

"Why? Don't tell me you care about my freedom or my mortal life or such things! You've had your eyes on my neck from the very first time you saw me!" Tim insisted.

Cyril turned his head away.

"Please Cyril, you must do this for me!" he said.

"Why is Holly so important to you that you would sacrifice your mortal life to be with her?" the vampire asked him.

"She's my family... my only family!" Tim said as though it were obvious.

"And me, what am I? Your drinking buddy? Your *friend with benefits*? Your dirty little secret?" Cyril said, spiteful.

"Don't be stupid!" Tim said, angry now.

"No, Tim. I will not give you immortality so that you can go spend it with your beloved Holly!" Cyril suddenly snapped back at him. "I want you... I still want you as my immortal master, but I won't sire you only to lose you forever!"

"Damn you!" Tim shouted.

He balled his fists and Cyril closed his eyes, expecting a blow that never came. Tim pulled away and kicked the debris of the chair he had already broken across the room.

"Damn you!" he cried again. "Some vampire you are, afraid to bite me even when I offer myself to you! You're nothing but a coward!"

"And you, what are you?" Cyril retorted. "You have no respect for me or what I feel, you're only using me! I look upon you as a man, but you do not see me as a man, only as a monster! All this time... all these nights spent together truly meant nothing to you? Nothing at all?" he said, desperate.

"They mean nothing if you won't give me what I want." Tim said coldly.

Tears rolled down the vampire's cheeks as he retreated from him. He wrapped his arms around himself as to cover up the raw wound the human's words had inflicted upon his heart. He truly was heartbroken now and Tim regretted his harsh and stupid words, but still his resolve did not change.

"Cyril..." he said.

"Just go! Get out of here!" Cyril shouted, choking on his tears.

"I'm not using you!" Tim protested.

"But you are..." Cyril said. "You always said you didn't want to be sired and I respected your will. But now Holly is in the picture, suddenly you're willing to give yourself to me so you can be with her, just like Sofia sired me and then threw me away for Sergei!"

"I..." Tim started, and then he did not know what to say. Cyril's words were not exactly true but had some truth to them.

"Alright, I will go now." he said in a resigned tone.

"No... don't go!" Cyril suddenly said, throwing himself at him, but Tim pushed him away.

"You wanted me to go, now you want me to stay, you wanted to devour me at first and now you won't even bite me... you're the one playing games with me!" he snapped at him.

"Tim, please, don't go! Please!" Cyril cried.

But Tim ran out into the night. The air was bitterly cold, and he wore nothing but his shirt and vest, but nothing mattered anymore. All he could think of was his sister, and how he could get to her. He was so close to being reunited with her and yet so far away! He ran faster and faster. He was aware of Cyril chasing him down the streets, screaming his name, no longer concerned about other vampires or humans hearing or seeing them. He led him on a long chase and when he thought he had finally lost him he finally slowed down his pace. He wandered aimlessly for some time, unsure what exactly he could do. He needed a vampire to sire him, and the only one willing to do it was way too sensitive and dramatic about it. Surely if he walked up to any other vampire he would only become their meal and not one of them.

In a fit of rage, he headed back to his own house and started tearing it apart. He first went into his father's office and broke every object he could lay his hands on. Everything that reminded him of his past or his present situation had to go. He wanted to erase everything, including himself, from this world for good. He grabbed a handful of old newspapers and began to light them with matches, and throw them blindly into every room. And when he came upon the family portrait in the hallway, he took it down and crushed it, and set it on fire as well.

He then went into the only room he had spared so far: Holly's bedroom. A child's room, for she was a child woman when she died at twenty, an angel who would never age now. For some time he gazed at the china dolls, the books, and the paintings on the walls. Who would ever need them again? She could have come home anytime, but she hadn't. She didn't want anything of their past either. He lit more papers and threw them across the room, and then he fell to his knees and rested his head on the side of the bed. The entire house was filled with smoke now and he could hear the fire crackling in the hall. The violence with which he was destroying the house of the past was that with which life had assaulted him. It had taken away even his last bit of hope.

The air became thicker, hotter, and harder to breathe. His head was becoming heavy and clouded. He knew he would pass out before the flames ever got to him, and he regretted it a little, as though the burning feeling could help rid him of some of the pain – the pain of being alive. He closed his eyes. And then he felt cold hands shaking him back to his senses.

"Tim, wake up!" Cyril shouted in his ears.

"Leave me... alone." he muttered. But the vampire would not let go.

"Tim, we must get out of here now or we'll burn alive!" Cyril pressed him.

"Let go of me!" Tim resisted. He tried to push him away but his arms were too weak. "Fire can kill you... get out of here." he told the vampire again, in vain.

Cyril picked him up and threw his arm over his shoulder in order to lift him. Tim hated him. He only wanted him to let go and let him die here, but he was too dizzy from the smoke and too weak to move. The ceiling was going to collapse on them any moment. Cyril took him over to the window and he vaguely felt something burning fall upon the two of them. He heard the vampire scream and then they jumped out the window, breaking through the glass, and Tim lost consciousness.

⚬⚬⚬

"Fire mystery: the two arsonists escape unharmed." Heath read out the newspaper column's title aloud. *"Fire broke out last night in the Thompson mansion, an old building presumed to be vacant. Witnesses report seeing two suspects break in. They were then seen again after the fire started, jumping out a window on the second floor and running away with inhuman speed. The police is currently trying to contact the owner and last member of the Thompson family, Timothy Thompson."* he continued.

He turned to his daughter, who sat across his desk, playing with her new pearl bracelet.

"I wonder who did this." he said. Not that it mattered to him. Not the house at least – but catching the vampires obviously involved did.

"Probably a burglary gone wrong." she said, raising her shoulders. She gazed around the boring room, filled with boring paintings and boring statues, and everything about her life at court and her father bored her – even the new jewelry he had ordered for her from France.

Her father was a man of average height yet strong build, with thick black hair, now long, and a neatly trimmed mustache and beard. He wore a rich black suit with a white shirt and a crimson vest and tie, and gold rings on nearly every finger. They were in his private office, in their new mansion – one ten times bigger than the old one. It was gifted to them by a richer Natural who wanted to obtain Heath's favors.

"You could at least pretend to be happy with my gift." he said.

"I don't want any more jewelry or dresses, or shoes, or hats. I want to be an Apostle." she said, returning her gaze to him.

"You'll never be." he said.

"And just why?" she asked him defiantly.

"You don't have what it takes."

"And what does it take then?"

"It takes intelligence and power, neither of which you have." he said.

"So you think." she said.

"Alright, then show me this hidden intelligence of yours, you silly cow!" he said, slamming the newspaper on his desk. He rose and went to her. He leaned over her in a dominant pose, and brought his face up close to hers, and she did not move away. She did not think herself as powerful as him, but she would never admit it. She would never bow her head to him, and he would never scare her into submission. Ever since she had been brought to court, she had been the object of Heath's daily verbal attacks. He was no longer the stern but quiet father she remembered. Heath only respected those who were useful to him, and he did not think Holly was. He tolerated her presence, but he had made it clear that if she deserted him like Esther had, he would "do what needed to be done", and that meant he would kill her. You could only be under Heath's thumb or be his enemy, and his enemies all met an early end.

"Isn't it surprising, to say the least, that the Thompson mansion was said to be vacant and they seem unable to find Tim?" he asked her.

"Maybe he moved out." she said slyly.

"Or maybe he is a vampire."

"If he is, then why doesn't he come to court?"

Indeed, if he had become a vampire, surely the others would tell him where to find his father and sister. But he was not a vampire, Holly knew this. She had seen him the other day with Mickey. Tim was human and the longer he stayed that way the better. He had kept her a prisoner at home for years, doting on her when she was obedient and frowning upon any attempt she made to socialize or meet young men her age. He played on her desire to please and be loved to keep her under his thumb, as if he owned her. Thank goodness she had become a vampire and got away from him! She did wonder why their mansion had burned down, but, like the newspapers said, it could very well have been a burglary gone wrong. She would not miss the place where she had spent so many years in captivity.

"I'm going out tonight before the shops close." she told her father as she rose from her seat.

"Do I not dress you in fine clothes already?" he asked her with a hint of anger.

"I told you what I want and you won't help me obtain it. So all I have are dresses and jewelry, for now." she reminded him.

"You're a stupid girl. One wonders how I ever fathered you." he said.

"But you did. Live with it." she replied.

She eyed him with contempt now. She was not stupid, no. She would find out why he so stubbornly wanted to prevent her from becoming an Apostle. Meanwhile, she would rather not be in his presence, nor in one of his stupid salons.

Heath's new mansion was located on Gloucester Street, in the genteel Pimlico area of central London. Ladies there were dressed by the most fashionable dressmakers and seamstresses. Because she was a Thompson, she had to live with her father and live up to their rank, or so he said. He dressed her like a proper lady: her gowns, all in the latest court fashion, covered her skin from neck to toe, and he provided for her the finest jewelry. He said she was too old to wear ribbons and frills, yet too young to wear makeup. He kept her frozen in time between child and woman. She would always be the sober, poised shadow by his side, receiving guests in their salons and nothing more. She hated that, she hated this neighborhood, and she hated the old gossiping seamstresses there. So that night she went to shop with the common people for once.

She had wanted to see the new and fashionable department stores, but vampires did not shop in department stores, did they? Well, she would. There, she looked at a variety of pre-made pieces, as well as accessories she liked. She gazed at herself in a mirror and realized how appallingly ordinary she looked in her gray dress with black velvet cuffs, a matching coat and a discreet hat with a single black feather. Not a streak of her hair was out of place around her baby face.

"Can I interest you in our new models?" a female shopkeeper asked her.

She was a tall and unconventional young woman, wearing half-men, half-women's clothes and her androgynous style immediately interested Holly.

"Can you help me find something more... attractive?" she asked her.

"I see, so you're looking for a little change?" the woman said. "What's your favorite color?"

"I like red, bright colors, with lots of frills and ribbons." Holly immediately said.

"Oh dear... you must live in a very conservative home, what a shame!" the woman said, raising her eyebrows as she eyed her from head to toe.

"How dare you?" Holly said, feeling insulted.

"I feel for you, sister. But I think we have just what you need." the woman then said, placing a friendly hand on her shoulder.

She picked out for Holly a selection of outrageously low-cut dresses and ball gowns, in red and pink and stripes, with not only ribbons and lace, but also pearls and fake flowers to adorn them. The woman definitely had better taste than her father, Holly thought. She finally chose a bold red and white striped dress with a matching double-breasted blazer that revealed a lot more of her cleavage than she was used to, and tried them on. The shopkeeper removed the matching hat she had selected and let down her hair completely.

"How do you like it?" she then asked her with a smile.

"I look like a whore!" Holly said as she gazed at her new self in a tall mirror. A whore, yes, but a damn good-looking one! She had never imagined she could be so beautiful.

"You look like a modern woman, who needs not hide her charms or her hair." the shopkeeper assured her. "Hats and corsets belong in the past. You should come to our suffragette meetings."

Holly had no interest in these new "feminists" and "suffragettes", but she liked the idea of looking modern and unconventional.

Dressed as her new self, she took a cab to the East End to proceed with the second part of her plans that night. As her cab moved quickly down the crowded and not-so-crowded streets, she gazed at all the foreign faces, wondering which faraway countries each of them came from, and whether they were more interesting than the rainy streets of London.

She suddenly remembered their old home, and how she had died there. Yes, she had died. She had been buried too. She lay underground for several days until she awakened again, terrified, in the darkness of a closed casket. Moved by some strange survival instinct, she had found the strength to break out of it and claw her way through the dirt back to the surface. She had staggered in the graveyard, wondering what she was doing there – alive. Then she had wandered the streets and everything seemed new and strange. She had no idea what she was, only that she was stronger and better than before. And thirsty. She had quite naturally attacked a human and fed on him, and only afterwards had she realized what she had done and began to cry. Luckily, Mickey had been there. He was the one who had brought her to her father. Perhaps he should not have. She had only one option now: to be as cruel and ruthless as her father expected her to be. There was no other path.

The cab stopped for a moment in Shadwell, where one of the streets had been blocked off due to a fire. She noticed a foreign man gazing at her in the distance, an Asian vampire she had seen once or twice in the salons. He was handsome, very handsome. She gazed at him because he was pleasing to the eye and a distraction from the darkness of her memories. The cab began to move again and she lost him. She returned her gaze to the darkness inside the cab. The streets were cold and dark, the cab was cold and dark, and her life was cold and dark. She wanted to be anyone but Holly Thompson.

She finally arrived at their old home. The Thompson mansion had almost completely burned to the ground and a police constable stood guard while his peers gathered evidence. They would not let her inside, unless she killed all of them, but that would draw too much attention.

She walked slowly along the street, with little hope of finding any clues. And then she did find something. A wallet. It was partly burnt and had been tucked into a crack in the wall. It had no money in it, of course. It had probably been dropped by one of the arsonists as they escaped on foot, and someone had stolen the money. She smelled it. A vampire scent. She looked inside again and found several business cards. One of them simply said "Hell's Pit". She knew of the place – a low-class eatery for vampires, who could then pick up a prostitute in the neighborhood for a midnight snack. She tucked the card in her purse and replaced the wallet where she had found it. She did not expect that the regulars of the Hell's Pit were intimate enough with each other to recognize the scent on the card, but they might be able to tell her who had not been seen lately.

She walked assuredly now, suddenly aware of the eyes of men on her everywhere. No, she did not look enough like a prostitute that they dared approach her, but she looked bold and modern, just like the shopkeeper had told her. She would have to go there again, and perhaps hear what the suffragettes had to say.

She arrived at the Hell's Pit around ten o'clock. It was packed with vampires and a few unsuspecting women who would probably not see the sun rise again. She went inside and posted herself beside one of the tables. The vampires turned puzzled eyes to her.

"Who among you has not been coming lately?" she asked them.

"Who are you?" one of them asked in a suspicious voice.

"My name is Holly Thompson, and you will answer my question." she replied firmly.

Asserting dominance, was it not what her father did with all the others at court? She could do it too. And apparently it worked, for the vampires seated around the table almost choked on their food when they heard her name. Her father was that influent after all? Interesting.

"Cyril has not been around." one of them said. "Ever since he took off with that... man." he added, not willing to frighten the prostitute by his side.

"Describe this man." Holly ordered.

"Maybe twenty-five or so, black hair. He was dressed like an undertaker."

The description matched Tim, except for him working as an undertaker. Why on earth would he choose such a profession when he didn't even need to work and could live off the family fortune?

"What is Cyril's last name?" she asked.

"Stewart." the man said.

"Thank you." she said, and then she left.

She returned to her father later that night and found him still in his office, browsing through newspapers. He lifted his gaze and eyed her with what seemed like disgust.

"Taking up a new profession?" he asked in a sly voice.

"Maybe." she said.

She went to him and leaned over his desk.

"I have found the name of one of the arsonists." she said.

Heath put down his newspaper and gazed at her again, intrigued.

"Who is it?" he asked.

"A lesser vampire named Cyril Stewart."

"Why would a vampire randomly set fire to a house when he could lose his life?"

"Perhaps he was helping a human." she said. "He was seen with a human. An undertaker. Do any of our kind run that sort of business in the East End?"

"There's that antisocial, Fiona Whittaker." he said.

She moved away and gazed at him defiantly.

"Tell me again that I'm stupid." she said.

He laughed and smiled.

"No, you've proven to be quite helpful."

4.

Tim slept for what seemed like ages, and in his dreams he saw fire. A great inferno, fed by his doubts and his rage. His father and his sister were there. They gazed at him coldly then stepped into the flames, and he was going to go after them and die, but Cyril appeared and stopped him. The vampire was trying to help him escape the flames, but his body caught on fire too.

"Cyril, come back to me!" Tim cried out to him as the vampire slowly backed into the fire, gazing at him with reproachful eyes.

"No Tim. I'm not coming back because I mean nothing to you." he told him in a sad voice.

"That's not true!" Tim shouted. "Please, please let me save you! You'll die!"

But the vampire shook his head and let the flames consume him until nothing was left of him but ashes on the ground. Tim fell to his knees and ran his fingers through the ashes, searching for him, but he was no more. And then he found himself alone in Cyril's empty house. It was dark and cold. He would never be there again, never smile, never laugh with him, never lay beside him. Absorbed in his own darkness, he had failed to noticed the new light Cyril had brought into his life and now it was too late. The pain crushed his chest like a boulder. He let out a desperate cry. And then he began to awaken. He could still feel the ashes on his fingers, but now the scent of roses was also in the air around him.

"Come... back..." he whispered.

"Tim, are you awake? Can you hear me?"

It was Miss Whittaker's voice. He felt her cold hand upon his brow.

"Yes, I am..." he said. He was not quite sure whether he was awake or not, until he finally opened his eyes. The first face he saw was hers, as he knew he would. She was as calm and composed as ever. She wore a black shawl around her faded crimson dress. The room was lit only by one candle and it gave even more of a ghastly glow to her alabaster complexion. He then noticed Hanson, sitting in a corner of the room. His arms were crossed and his right leg jittered nervously. His face was angry and he stared straight ahead. In fact, he was not exactly staring ahead, he was staring at the third person in the room, who was sitting at the end of the bed: Cyril. Tim turned his gaze to him. The vampire sat there, leaning forward, his once beautiful face now marked by a large burn scar on the right side. His right hand was also covered in scars. Still, he gazed at Tim with kindness and concern.

"Cyril... you're alive?" Tim whispered. He suddenly felt a sharp burning pain around his left eye. He raised his hand and felt around it. The area was bandaged, and so were his neck and left shoulder. Hanson's angry eyes suddenly flashed toward him and he rose from his seat.

"You set your own house on fire, you damn fool, and almost killed the both of you!" he shouted, and before Tim could answer he stormed out of the room.

"It's alright. He's been very worried for you. We all have been." Miss Whittaker told Tim.

"I... can't remember much... only flames." Tim said.

"Take your time. All that matters is that you are safe now." she said.

He turned his gaze back to Cyril.

"I'm sorry... for your wounds." he said.

"For my wounds?" Cyril said in disbelief. "How much worse it would have been if you had died in the fire? Do you even realize how close we both came to burning alive?'

"You didn't have to come and save me. You shouldn't have." Tim said.

Cyril turned his head away, pained.

"Miss Whittaker, I'm sorry you had to be involved." Tim told his employer. "This is between Cyril and I only."

"Please do call me Fiona from now on." she said. "And you're wrong, it is between all of us. You think you live alone, Tim, but we all care about you."

"It's no use telling him that..." Cyril said, bitter.

As images of the scene began to come back to Tim, he recalled how the vampire had risked his very life for him. Fire was one of the few things that could kill a vampire, and yet Cyril had rushed inside the burning house to save him from the flames.

"Cyril told me everything," Miss Whittaker – Fiona said, "and I realize now that by keeping secrets from you we were only inviting you to do the same with us. I knew you had bonded with Cyril the moment you started behaving differently."

"How did you know?" Tim asked her.

"I saw how attracted he was to you that night, and... well, you seem to complement each other."

Tim turned to Cyril again but the vampire still avoided his gaze.

"Do we have anything he could eat?" Cyril asked Fiona. "I think he hadn't eaten for days before this happened. He needs human food to recover."

"Unfortunately not, but it is still dark enough outside that I can go get him something." she said.

"Please do. Oh, and will you get some more wine for me as well? No, make that whiskey. My nerves are still shaken." he told her.

"Of course." she said.

She got up and left the room.

"Cyril..." Tim said.

"What?" the other replied coldly.

"Why did you risk your life for me if you didn't want me anymore?"

"It was an act of love." he said.

"Do you... love me?" Tim asked, unsure.

"I'm just a predator, am I not? How could I feel love?" Cyril said, spiteful.

"You're not... You're a man, with feelings. And I'm an idiot." Tim said.

Cyril turned to him again and they gazed at each other.

"In my dreams, you had died in the fire and I... I..." Tim said, unable to find the words to describe his feelings.

"You were sad..." Cyril said, softening a little.

"Cyril... you're the one I never want to lose." Tim whispered.

Warm tears now rolled down his cheeks. They only intensified the burning of his wound. How long had it been since any emotion had moved his heart? He did not know. But now all sorts of feelings flowed through him and he did not know how to make sense of them. All he knew was that Cyril was alive and safe, and it was all he wanted.

"I'm not dead, I'm here." Cyril said. "I understand that you want to be with your family, but you can't just use people to get there."

"I didn't start seeing you because I wanted to use you." Tim said again. "I went to you because I like you, because we have a connection. I realized it the first time you read poetry to me."

Cyril moved closer to him and lay his head on the human's chest. Tim closed his arms around him. This was what he wanted the most after all: to be with his vampire again, holding him, feeling him, breathing in his scent.

"I didn't mean the things I said when I was angry." he told him. "Yes, I was hoping you would bite me, and kill me. But you were the least likely of all vampires to ever do it."

"You're a stupid man who doesn't know what he wants." Cyril whispered, wrapping his arms around him now. "Never do that to me again, I don't think my heart could take it."

"I won't." Tim promised.

Cyril turned his gaze to the door briefly. He then pulled a razor from his pocket and slashed his left wrist.

"What are you doing?" Tim asked him, panicked.

"Something crazy." Cyril said.

"I thought you didn't want to sire me."

"I'm not siring you, but my blood will help you become stronger, and your wounds will heal."

He presented him his bloody wrist. Though he felt like a criminal for accepting the offer from the one who had nearly thrown away his immortal life for him, Tim knew he needed that strength, and he needed to heal for what lay ahead. And he *wanted* Cyril's blood. He wanted to keep him closer to him, always closer. Though Cyril was the only one who could sire him, he wanted to *sire* Cyril.

"Hurry! Fiona will be back soon and you know what she will say." the vampire urged him.

Tim brought the vampire's wrist to his lips and licked and sucked the blood. It was good, sweet, like Cyril's skin. He was hungry for it, for all of it. He had never imagined himself drinking blood, nor how much he would like it. Cyril lay his head on his chest in a submissive manner, and Tim felt powerful as he drank. He learned much later that this was what vampires experienced when they fed on a live prey: the cruel excitement of having power of life or death over your prey, of being the only one who would decide their fate. And, in the context of blood vows, after the feeling of power came the desire to protect the one they drank from, to bond with them in body, heart and soul. And what Cyril experienced was the thrill of being *taken*, of no longer being one's master, but submitting oneself entirely to the will of the master.

"Drink me, Master." he whispered. "Drink all you want."

Tim, in fact, enjoyed the act so much he found it quite difficult to pull away from the vampire, even as they heard the loud noise of doors slamming downstairs and footsteps coming up the stairs. But Cyril swiftly pulled away from him and from their silent rapture. Within seconds, the wound on his wrist had stopped bleeding and was beginning to heal. Tim wiped away the blood around his lips, and his heart suddenly jumped in his chest. He turned to Cyril with fearful eyes, but the warm glow in Cyril's eyes let him know that what he was feeling now was absolutely normal. The vampire's blood was working its way into him, healing those wounds that could be healed, and making him into a stronger human.

The door swung open and Fiona and Hanson came in, looking agitated. Fiona took just one glance at Tim, then Cyril, before throwing a small bag onto the bed. She knew what they had been doing.

"It smells like blood. Vampire blood." she said with anger in her eyes.

Cyril held her gaze defiantly and said nothing.

"Eat, Tim – if you still feed on human food." she then told the other roughly. There was fear in her voice now, along with the anger.

"What happened?" Tim asked.

He didn't waste any time pulling out the warm, fresh baked bread from the bag and devouring it, for indeed he was very hungry. Fiona seemed relieved to see him eating human food. She pulled out a small piece of paper from her pocket and threw it on the bed near Cyril. He picked it up and read it aloud:

"It has come to the attention of the Apostles of London that the vampire Cyril Stewart has been causing trouble in our community. He has been seen repeatedly with a mortal, and made a spectacle of our kind in front of other mortals, endangering us and compromising our hunting grounds. As a criminal, he is no longer under the protection of the Dark Lord, and must be eliminated. He is believed to be in the company of an undertaker. Anyone with information regarding his whereabouts is asked to report to a Natural immediately. His mortal companion has not been identified yet but is to be killed at will. The Dark Lord likes those of his children who serve him well and generous rewards will be granted."

"They put a bounty on our heads for just being seen together?" Tim said, startled.

Cyril took just one more cold glance at the piece of paper, then walked over to the candle and set fire to it.

"Cyril, this is very serious!" Hanson said, furious.

"They know that you are here." Fiona said. "There are currently three spies on the roof of the building across the street. They will be watching who comes and goes. We must leave now, before others come."

"But how can we leave if they are watching us?" Tim said.

"I say we just hand over the criminal and let him deal with the consequences of his own actions." Hanson said.

Fiona turned around, furious.

"It is *not* for you to decide!" she hissed at him. It was the first time Tim had ever seen her so angry. Hanson turned his gaze away.

"You are all under my protection now." she went on. "And you shall come with me to a safe place, near Portsmouth."

"Hanson's right." Cyril said. "A bounty is a very serious thing. I was careless, I deserve it. Maybe I should just turn myself in."

"Don't you dare!" Tim found himself shouting at him. The vampire seemed quite surprised.

"Is my master ordering me not to?" he asked with a sad smile.

"I'm not done with you yet." Tim told him. He turned to Fiona and said: "I fear no vampires, no Dark Lord and no bounties, but we still need a plan."

"We have one." she said. "If you are well enough now to stand – and I believe you are – you and Hanson will load a coffin with a *client* into the hearse, like we usually do, except Cyril will be hiding inside with the *client*. He will slip out of the coffin during the ride to Bow Cemetery. Hanson will make sure to stop the hearse above or near the sewers. As you two carry the coffin into the cemetery, vampires will most likely attack you. You will have to fight them off as best you can. Meanwhile, Cyril will slip into the sewers and join me on another street, where I will be waiting with my personal carriage. My carriage will be stopped and searched the moment I come out of the funeral home, but when they see it is empty they will let me go. So by the time Cyril gets to me no one will be following me. We will meet up at the Dragon Gate pub, on the docks."

"No, I'm not leaving you alone against them!" Hanson told her.

"I am still under the protection of the Dark Lord, no bounty has been placed on my head despite my obvious involvement in all of this. They will not harm a vampire of higher rank than themselves." she said.

"Hold on... you're telling me I have to ride in a coffin with a corpse?" Cyril said, mortified.

"You're a vampire, you're supposed to *sleep in* coffins." Tim remarked.

"I'm a gentleman." Cyril said. "The thought of laying down in a coffin with a dead body and then going down into the sewers..."

"You didn't think twice before throwing yourself into the flames to save Tim." Hanson reminded him.

"That was different."

"Enough." Fiona said in a calm but firm voice. "We must all do things we hate at times. You will do as you are told."

Tim realized for the first time there truly was a hierarchy in the vampire world, and that Fiona had some unspoken authority over Cyril, that he would not contest. Cyril frowned.

"We must hurry." she said. "It is already past seven, the sun will be rising very soon. We have at most an hour and a half before its light can hurt me and Cyril, but it also means the vampires will retreat at that time and we can get out of the city."

"And just how will we travel outside the city in broad daylight?" Cyril wondered.

"We shouldn't use the hearse, it's way too noticeable." Hanson said.

"I know a man who will give us a ride to our destination in a closed carriage. He won't ask questions."

"Are we going to ride in coffins again?"

"Of course not, that would be too obvious. We will travel in crates." she said. "Hanson and Tim, when the way is clear, you will go to the port and talk to the old Chinese man on the docks."

"Does he have a name? How will we find him?" Hanson asked.

"He's a smuggler, he's not going to give out his name to anyone." Tim remarked.

"That's right, and he will find you. He knows of our kind." Fiona said.

Cyril raised his shoulders and sighed, astounded at the methods they had to resort to. Coffins, sewers, smugglers, what next? Within minutes though, Tim and Hanson had everything ready. There was no time to waste, every second was crucial. Fiona's carriage left first. A few minutes later, Tim and Hanson brought out the black hearse and loaded the coffin inside, as they usually would on a normal work day. Tim's wounds had healed already into scars and he needed no bandages. As they headed to Bow Cemetery they noticed that they were being followed by two shadows, leaping from one rooftop to another. Hanson pressed the horses. When they finally arrived, he made sure to park the carriage close to the sewers, where a manhole would allow Cyril to escape. The ground was still covered with snow. Tim and Hanson brought out the coffin and carried it into the cemetery. They were immediately approached by their stalkers: a vampire and his unfinished ghoul. Hanson swung around and threw the coffin on the ground before them and said: "It's not your usual hour to pick a fight."

"Beware Paul, they are not human." the elegant vampire master warned his ghoul, a barely grown man from the streets.

"That's right, we're not human and we've got something for you." Hanson said in a provocative tone. And with this, he drew a silver stake from under his black cloak. Tim also drew a wooden stake.

"Wait, there is no need to take things that far." the vampire master said, to their surprise. "We don't mind a couple of undertakers knowing about the undead, you people are always quiet anyway. All we want is to verify the contents of this coffin."

"There's nothing but a corpse in there." Hanson said. "But help yourselves if that's what you want."

With great ease, the vampire master lifted the coffin's lid, which was not nailed shut, only to discover in it an ordinary corpse.

"What did you do with the traitor?" he then asked Hanson in a voice that was like a low snarl.

"Never heard of any traitors. We're just undertakers doing our job. Can we put our *client* in the ground now? The mistress will cut our pay if we slack off." Hanson replied, unconcerned.

"Well, of course you may." the vampire said. His voice had returned to normal. "My apologies if we made a mistake."

All this time, the ghoul had its eyes set on Tim. It knew, or at least sensed something.

Hanson and Tim carried the coffin over to the grave awaiting it and put it in the ground. But when they turned around they again found the vampire and his ghoul standing right before them.

"What now?" Hanson told them. "You'd better get back to your coffins soon, the sun is starting to pierce through the clouds."

"One of you has not been honest with us." the vampire said with a wicked grin. Between his gloved fingers, he held the silver pin Cyril had given Tim. It had fallen on the ground. Tim took a step back, surprised.

"So, which one of you is flirting with a vampire?" the vampire master asked.

Both of them, quite literally.

"This one!" the ghoul said, pointing a crooked finger in Tim's direction.

The two lunged at him, and Tim and Hanson prepared to fight. Their assailants were strong, but with his newly acquired strength Tim found that he could easily stand up to the ghoul, while Hanson took on the vampire. Tim was used to fighting ghouls by now, and he immediately took his stake and aimed for the creature's heart. But something unexpected happened. With a swift move, the creature returned the stake against Tim and it pierced his shoulder with it. Tim rolled on the ground and then the stake came at him again, in his back this time. He heard Hanson shouting something and then a pile of dust fell upon him. The ghoul had been killed. The vampire was coming at them now, but the sun came out from behind a cloud and his body caught on fire before them. With a loud and terrible shriek, he rolled into the snow, but it was too late for him. He already was no more.

Tim was in a sort of daze. He felt Hanson shaking his body vigorously. He pulled his hand away from the wound on his chest: the stake had gone through his back all the way and he was bleeding profusely. Hanson was screaming, but he could no longer hear him. He was losing consciousness, fast. He felt Hanson lifting up his body in his arms and then everything went black.

And black it was, not like he was asleep, comfortably cradled by the darkness until he woke up to another day. It was pitch black and cold everywhere. There was no light, no warmth, nothing. Now even the burning flames that had nearly engulfed him seemed sweeter than this cold and quiet darkness. Was he dying? Most certainly. But if so, where was the light? Where was God? There was no God in all this darkness, there was nothing at all. The only thing that surprised him was that he still felt somewhat conscious and aware of his surroundings, even if there were none to speak of.

He wondered what had been the meaning of all of this. He would never find out who murdered his family after all. He would never see Holly again. Neither would he ever see Fiona, Humphrey, Hanson. And Cyril. The poor vampire had saved him from the flames, only to become hunted by his kind and see the object of his affections die in the end. What a pitiful and meaningless ending! He wanted to laugh but no sound could escape from his lips.

And then suddenly he felt something pounding in his chest, faster and faster. It was his heart. It had been at a complete stop until then, and now it was beating again. How could it? Had Cyril's blood saved him in the end? He knew very well that the transformation into an immortal was not complete until the vampire also drank the blood of the mortal, and surely Cyril hadn't.

Why was his heart pounding again? He had no logical explanation. But he *saw* himself, as though he was floating above his body. He saw himself laying in this darkness, and his body was changing. His already pale skin went from the color of death to that of marble, and his brown eyes became a bright crimson like those of a vampire that had just fed. The wounds on his chest and shoulder stopped bleeding and healed on their own. He couldn't believe it. He was watching himself change into a vampire, though he had never been fully sired. What happened? Had Cyril returned and bit him while he was unconscious? Or was it Fiona?

Someone was calling his name now. It was Hanson.

"Yes, I'm alive." he wanted to tell him, but *alive* was not quite the word.

He breathed in and air filled his lungs again with a burning sensation. He heard himself saying the words aloud: "Vampires breathe?"

"You sure scared the hell out of me, you bloody fiend!" Hanson screamed in his ears. But it was a cry of relief. He felt strong arms squeezing him and then he opened his eyes. He was laying on the cold stone floor of a crypt, and Hanson was towering over him.

"Where are we?" he asked.

"In a crypt at Bow Cemetery. Thank goodness you're alive! It's a miracle!" Hanson said.

"I'm not quite sure I am." Tim said. He sat up and gazed at his marble hands. He touched his chest and shoulder: the wounds were completely gone.

"Am I really what I think I am?" he then asked his friend.

"I don't know what you are, but you sure look like a vampire to me." Hanson said. He seemed more relieved than surprised.

"Was I bitten by a vampire after I passed out?"

"No."

"Did Cyril bite me any time before that?"

"No, you were never bitten by a vampire."

"Then how?"

Hanson crossed his arms and frowned slightly.

"Honestly, I have no clue. We'll have to ask Fiona, she might know." he said. "But for now, we have to wait until night-time to move. The sun is bright outside and I don't want to see you turn into a pile of ashes."

"What about Fiona?"

"We'll meet her at the Dragon Gate pub, near the docks, as planned – just a little later."

They waited until the sun set and headed out to the place where Hanson had moved the hearse out of plain sight. They rode in it to the East End's docks, where they met a hooded man in the shadows of an alley. He was fully human, an old Chinese man, but he was not surprised to see them.

"Looking for something?" he asked them.

"We have goods to transport to Portsmouth." Hanson said.

The man eyed them carefully.

"Boat, train or carriage?" he asked with shining eyes.

"Carriage. Our friend told us you would be waiting." Hanson said.

"The carriage has been prepared and paid for. You travel at your own risk." the man said.

"Deal." Hanson said.

"This way." he then said, bidding them to follow.

They went inside the Dragon Gate pub, a place filled with Indian and Chinese sailors. Their ships traveled around the world, bringing back to England the common and less common things the people of London now wanted: from tea to spices, even opium for some. Smuggling a few outlaws was not a problem for them – besides, Tim, Hanson, Cyril and Fiona were only outlaws in the vampire world anyway. They found Fiona hidden in a small storage room in the basement. She immediately threw her arms around Hanson and he held her tightly, while Cyril gazed at Tim with stupor.

"Did one of us bite you?" he asked, sounding betrayed.

"No, I don't know how this happened." Tim said.

"It was crazy!" Hanson said, now all excited. "The ghoul put a stake through his chest, and one minute he was bleeding to death in my arms, and the next he started healing and woke up like this!"

"Tim!" Cyril said, horrified at the thought he might have lost him.

"I know what he is." Fiona said, stepping closer to him. "Tim, you're a Natural, like me."

"A Natural?" Tim repeated.

"I will explain it all in detail to you later." she said. "Let us get ready to head out now. Mister Yang, the owner of this place, has kindly agreed to create a distraction while we get into our carriage."

"What kind of distraction?" Tim wondered. But it was not long until his question was answered. Indeed, as two shadows peeked into the windows of the lively pub filled with drinking and cussing sailors and mahjong players, a young waiter stepped on the foot of a client, making him lose his tile. The man immediately rose and shouted something in his language, to which the waiter answered in his own. Since they couldn't understand each other but were quite sure they were being insulted, they started pushing each other around. The sailors from each of their countries respectively then rose and surrounded them, each cheering for their champion as the two men resorted to fists. No one seemed worried about the outcome, clearly this happened all the time and the sailors found it very entertaining. Money even exchanged hands as bets were being placed. If not for the circumstances, Tim would probably have watched the bar fight, out of curiosity. He would have bet on the young slender waiter, who seemed a little more athletic than the other.

During the commotion, the vampire and not-quite-yet-undead party escaped through the back door and slipped inside a closed carriage of which the doors had been left open. The interior smelled strongly of opium. There, they got into four crates large enough to each hold a person, if they crouched. A young man who had been smoking a cigarette on the corner of the building then nonchalantly walked back to the carriage and closed and locked its heavy wooden doors. They were locked inside now, for better or for worse.

⌒∽

They traveled to Portsmouth like this, and it seemed like a much longer and more uncomfortable journey than they had imagined. There, the crates were taken to the port and placed in a hangar along with other crates destined to be shipped to the Americas and Australia, and abandoned there overnight. Tim and Hanson waited until nightfall and the port grew quiet, then carefully opened the crates and slipped out, followed by Fiona and Cyril. But they were not the only ones. Another, larger crate opened and a man came out, followed by his wife and two children. Tim was startled but Hanson gestured him to pay no attention to them. "Just stowaways getting some fresh air before the journey across the Atlantic." he said. The family watched with curious eyes as this strange party of four escaped into the night.

The streets of Portsmouth were fairly busy at night around the port, so they had no problem mingling with the already diverse crowd there. They walked for some time, then Tim suddenly stopped and said: "I'm hungry."

All of them came to a halt and turned curious eyes to him. He looked puzzled himself. He had been fine until moments ago, but now he was desperately hungry, thirsty for blood. Human blood. So this was what it felt like, being thirsty and so close to humans. Clearly it was not the time and place, but the urge was so strong it was almost irresistible. All he could see now among the crowd were walking meals, walking necks he wanted to suck dry.

"Oh great, just what we needed." Hanson said in a low voice.

"He has never fed yet." Fiona told him in a voice that begged for indulgence.

"I'll handle it. Come with me." Cyril said, taking the newborn's hand and leading him into a dark alley.

"This is terrible, is it always like this?" Tim asked him when they were alone.

"You'll get used to it and it won't feel so bad." Cyril assured him. "Well, I guess we'll have to hunt."

"Will Fiona hate me for it?" Tim wondered.

"No, she will not hate you. You must feed."

"I'd rather not do it in front of you or anyone though." Tim said.

"I can't let you go out alone and risk missing your kill. You would draw our enemies' attention right back to us." Cyril said. "Wait here for just a split second, and I'll be right back with food."

And indeed, he soon returned, seemingly helping a drunken sailor to walk – except the man was already dead. He dropped the young man's fresh body in front of Tim, who threw himself onto it and sunk his teeth into the man's neck. Cyril turned his gaze away, letting him feed without having to feel guilty about any mess he might make. When he was done, Tim felt an awkward mixture of contentment and disgust. He did not like the taste of human blood at all, Cyril's was the only blood he had enjoyed, and yet he knew he needed to feed. He now understood some vampires' distaste for the whole process though. Cyril knelt beside him and wiped off a smear of blood from his face, like a mother cleaning her child's face after he ate.

"How was it?" he asked him with interest.

"I can feed on humans, but I only like *your* blood." Tim said.

Cyril laughed softly.

"Am I that tasty?" he asked.

"You're delicious and I want to drink more of you." Tim said, gazing at him with predator eyes now.

"Later, darling." Cyril told him with a wink.

But Tim had meant it: his body needed blood, but he had an insatiable thirst for Cyril's in particular. And not only that, he was hungry for him in his entirety. Cyril was his love prey. He breathed in deeply, trying to calm his wild young fangs.

"Sorry." he then said.

"You've just become a vampire, it's normal to experience wild feelings at first." Cyril told him. "But soon you will learn how to differentiate hunger for prey and hunger for a mate."

"Hunger for a mate..." Tim repeated.

Cyril gave him a seductive grin.

"We should go back now, or they will wonder what we're doing." he then said.

"R-Right!" said Tim, whose thoughts had unwillingly drifted back to the subject of Cyril's neck.

They found Hanson and Fiona enjoying some quiet private time around the street corner. In a neighborhood filled with sailors and prostitutes, a young man and woman embracing was not unusual at all, and no one paid any attention to them.

"Excuse us for interrupting..." Cyril said.

The two immediately parted, blushing slightly.

"We're done feeding." Tim said, back to his composed self.

"Good, let's go." Fiona said.

They purchased a simple covered carriage and horses from a merchant, and traveled out into the quiet countryside. They were not followed, their enemies had probably lost track of them now or thought they were trying to escape by boat.

Just before the break of dawn, they reached an old castle on the heights of a lonely hill. It was not in ruins but did not look inhabited either: the heavy iron fence around the property and the gates were old and rusted, and the gardens seemed overgrown and abandoned. Whoever lived there either did not care about maintaining the property, or received so few visitors it didn't matter. The gates were open, but closed immediately on their own after the carriage had entered the property, as though under some magic spell. Fiona didn't waste any time: the sun was rising on the horizon. She jumped off the carriage and threw open the door, and bid them to follow her inside. Hanson ushered them forward: as the only still-somewhat-human, he would take the horses to the stable.

They entered through a small door to the side of the courtyard, and went up several flights of stairs before they came to a great hall dimly lit with a row of candles on either side of the wall. The floor was covered with an old red carpet, and the walls with equally old tapestries depicting medieval wars, Vikings, French and Saxons. There were no windows.

Their host was waiting there for them, seated in a modest wooden throne at the end of the hall. He was a handsome vampire with the features of a middle-aged man, long, very long straight black hair, and piercing black eyes. He wore a golden ring and luxurious clothing from the last century. By his side, Humphrey stood quietly and smiled at them.

"Fiona..." the vampire said in his deep voice.

She walked assuredly toward him and knelt before him, not like a lady but more like a knight would in front of his lord. He extended his hand and she kissed the ring on it. He was clearly higher in rank than herself in the vampire world.

Hanson joined Cyril and Tim, who stood there observing the scene, not quite sure if they were also expected to kneel in front of the man.

Fiona rose and gestured them to come forth.

"What have you brought me?" the man asked, intrigued.

"This is Cyril, he is in danger." she said, stepping beside the blond vampire. "And these two are our friends Hanson and Tim. Tim Thompson."

"Interesting." the man said, finally rising from his seat. He was very tall, even compared to Humphrey who had been the tallest among them. He was in fact a giant by human standards.

"My name is Yvan Thompson, and you may all stay here as long as you wish." he said.

"Thompson?" Tim repeated, startled.

"I think it is time for all of us to sit down and talk." Fiona said.

They all gathered in a smaller dining room around a table covered with food. Not vampire food, human food. There were roasted meats and poultry with vegetables, venison pies and soups. It lacked nothing of a tasteful banquet. No servants were to be seen but the food was fresh, so Tim and Hanson assumed there had to be at least a cook in this castle. *What* he cooked most of the time, that was a different story. Like Cyril, Yvan appreciated the finer things in life. Humphrey, Hanson, Cyril, who enjoyed delicacies, and Tim, who had retained a lot of his human taste in food, helped themselves to the banquet. Yvan then poured a glass of blood from a bottle and offered it to Tim, who refused it. He then offered it to Fiona, who hesitated.

"It's goat's blood." he told her.

She took the glass reluctantly, eyeing it with disgust.

"Humans are rare around here, and I am too much of a misanthrope to go to the city very often. So I hunt and raise animals here instead." he explained. "It's not a moral choice, but a choice based on my own comfort." he added, turning his gaze to Tim.

"Have you any tea or wine for the lady?" Hanson asked him politely. "She has very delicate taste."

"But of course." Yvan said. "Please forgive this old man who likes his drinks coarse."

He snapped his fingers and an old man soon came in.

"Wine for the lady." he said in a dominating but respectful voice.

The old man disappeared into the corridor and soon returned with the requested wine. Hanson poured some into her glass which contained the blood.

"You have to feed, my love." he reminded her and she nodded.

"Can I try that too?" Tim asked.

He was poured a glass of goat's blood mixed with wine and drank it. It was not bad at all and complemented the piece of venison pie he had been eating. He offered the remains of his drink to Cyril, who politely refused.

"I had enough with that sailor. I don't need to feed for some time."

"You're stuffing yourself with pie." Tim remarked.

"That is a completely different thing." Cyril said, taking another bite of the delicious pie and savoring it thoroughly. Fiona and Yvan laughed.

"Now, if you will allow me, I am curious about this young man who appears to be of our lineage." Yvan said, gazing at Tim.

"We hired him as an employee for our funeral company, but he turned out to be a Natural." Fiona said.

"Can someone explain to me again what a Natural is?" Tim asked.

"Naturals are humans born to become vampires. They never need to be sired by anyone." Yvan explained. "When the time comes, they wither away and die – or appear dead to the human eye. Then their vampire side awakens and they come back to life, or undead life, however you prefer to call it."

"I was stabbed in the back by a ghoul and thought I was going to die. My heart stopped for a long time. Then I came back like this." Tim told him. "But what about the rest of my family? They all died of a mysterious illness. Did they become vampires too?"

"Naturals are rare but it often runs in a family. It is possible that some of your relatives were Naturals and bit others." Yvan said.

"Tim is the son of Heath Thompson." Fiona said, and Yvan frowned.

"He is?" he said with interest.

"Is my father some important figure I should know of in the vampire world?" Tim asked.

"He serves the Dark Lord..." Yvan simply said.

Indeed, Tim was already aware of it. He understood now that his father would be hunting him and Cyril down, because he was an observer and an enforcer of the rules.

"Is he... an Apostle?" Tim questioned him, remembering the words on the piece of paper. He had no idea what an Apostle might be in their world.

"I'm not sure about that." Yvan replied. "But he is the most feared vampire at court."

Tim grew somber and quiet again. Cyril placed a comforting hand on his, but the young man stood and left the table.

"Please excuse him, this must have come as a shock to him. I will find him." Fiona said. She rose and went after him. She found him in the corridor, standing still and gazing at the wall before him, trying to process all he had just heard.

"Tim..." she said.

"You knew everything. From the beginning. You knew everything about who I was, and who my father was, and you didn't tell me!" he told her coldly.

"I knew that, as a Thompson, you might be a Natural. But there was also a chance that you wouldn't be." she said. "If you were only human, there would have been no point in me filling your mind with hopes of becoming a vampire."

She had a point.

"I thought we were... friends." he said.

"When we had that conversation, I was your employer. Your vampire employer, trying to protect you, a human, from the dangers of our world." she corrected him.

Another point.

"What am I supposed to do now?" he said, cynical. "Just when I find out my father and sister are still alive as vampires, they put a bounty on my head and Cyril's!"

"That will be your decision." she said.

"What decision? There is only one decision to make."

"Is there?"

She was right, there was – technically – no bounty on Tim the vampire, only on Tim the human. If he was a vampire now, then he was not violating any of their laws by being around vampires. There was nothing to prevent him from joining his father and Holly at court if he wanted. Nothing, except Cyril.

"You're encouraging me to join those who oppress vampires like you and have been hunting us?" he asked her.

"No, I am only telling you the truth." she said. "I do hope you will stay with us, as my friend. But that choice is not mine to make, neither is it Cyril's. He is not your master."

Indeed, he was not. They had not completed the siring ritual yet. What would happen if they did? Cyril had suffered at the hands of his former mistress and his attempt to find a new master had only led to more suffering.

"What is it like, truly, to be someone's master?" he asked her.

"It means controlling but also protecting your servant. People with dominant personality traits usually enjoy it." she said.

"What about you?"

"Me..." she sighed. "I am afraid of hurting Hanson. The fact that he is human and I a vampire provides just enough distance between us that we don't lose ourselves in each other, and remain equals. If we become one as master and servant, we will no longer be equals."

"I don't think he would mind yielding to your will." Tim smiled.

He went to the room he had been assigned in the castle: a sparsely furnished but very comfortable bedroom with its own small library. A servant – perhaps the only servant – had lit a fire in the fireplace and laid out two fresh, clean suits on a chair. He assumed one of them would be for Cyril, who would no doubt join him later. He sat heavily on the side of the bed and let his head hang low. So much had happened in just a few weeks: his entire life, reality as he knew it had been flipped around. He was no longer a dark brooding young man with a death wish, mourning the loss of his family and his sister. They were very much alive, at least his father and sister Holly, and they were all vampires like him and Fiona, Naturals without any other master than perhaps the Dark Lord. He had a guaranteed place now at court among them, if he wanted it. The only thing holding him back was Cyril, the vampire who had risked his immortal life and become a renegade for him. It would not be fair to turn his back on him after what he did, and at the same time Tim had not asked him to do it.

He soon heard footsteps behind the door and Cyril slipped quietly inside the room. Rather than go to Tim, he leaned his back against the wall near the door and gazed at him, hesitating.

"Have I become a stranger to you all of a sudden?" Tim said, stretching out his arms to him.

Cyril immediately crossed the room and threw himself into his arms.

"I should never have left you alone." he whispered. "What if you were only human and that ghoul had killed you?"

"Well, it didn't, so there's no reason to worry about that." Tim said, stroking his blond hair softly.

Yes, he was bound to him, but not only because of his sacrifice. He felt a new tenderness for him, he wanted to dote on him, touch him, feel him; he needed to fill himself with his affection.

Cyril turned his anxious gaze to him.

"What's wrong?" Tim asked him with a smile.

He invited him to lay on the bed beside him, as they used to do.

"You know who you are now. You have your place at court with your father, if you want it." Cyril whispered.

He too had thought about it.

"But you are here." Tim said.

"So you're not going to leave us?"

Tim couldn't truthfully answer him, not yet.

"Fiona said she didn't want to sire Hanson because she doesn't want to be his master and him to be her slave." he said. "Is that what would happen if we finish what we started?"

"I wouldn't see myself as your slave..." Cyril said.

"But would you have to *obey* me, even if you disagreed?"

"Maybe. But on the other hand you would feel compelled to protect me."

"I already feel that way." Tim said, cupping his face with his hand.

Cyril closed his eyes and sighed.

"If you went to court and met Holly again, would you forget me?" he asked.

Tim had all but forgotten about that part of his past. It all seemed so small, so unimportant now. He didn't even remember what had been so comforting in the memory of her. But would that change if he met her again?

A sudden fear gripped Tim's heart, the fear of losing Cyril. As a mortal, he had only been playing games with him. But they were not playing anymore. The bounty on Cyril's head was very real, and he could not escape to Europe, where Sofia might still be after him. He had nowhere to go. He was in danger.

"I will protect you." he promised.

"Why? You didn't ask for any of this." Cyril reminded him.

He was asking him to decide now what would become of the two of them. Tim closed his eyes and let his hand wander down Cyril's arm slowly.

"But I did ask for this." Tim said. "The moment I decided to follow you, I knew there would be only two options: to become immortal and stay with your forever, or to be killed by you. I was the one who made that choice, you didn't force me."

"So you mean..." Cyril said, surprised.

"You will neither kill me, nor let me die, nor sire me. That leaves us only one option." Tim said with a smile.

"You will become my master?"

"Don't use that word." Tim said. "Let's just say I want to become your protector."

"Then take me, protector." Cyril said with shining eyes, and Tim drew him into his arms.

His heart was racing again, and the sweet scent of Cyril's skin awakened his senses. He remembered what Fiona said about the siring ritual being like a honeymoon, but he was too thirsty for him, too eager, too impatient to even take the time to savor the experience. Cyril pushed him away gently, just long enough to remove his shirt, and Tim gazed at him like a hungry animal. The blond took his hand and kissed it, and Tim sat and brought his face up close to him. His body was trembling now as he tried to control himself.

"You're so hungry for it..." Cyril said.

"For you..." Tim said, slowly laying him back down on his back.

Cyril was also breathing hard. He had not yet drank his blood, not once. He too had been holding back, and for so long. It seemed unfair not to let him bite first but he had decided that it should be Tim.

Unable to hold back any longer, Tim sunk his fangs into Cyril's neck. He bit him hard and held him firmly in his arms as he did. Cyril let out a soft cry of pain and joy, and Tim drank him, and drank him. Cyril's arms fell limply on the bed as his new protector took control of him, and he enjoyed the bliss of surrendering entirely to him. With tremendous effort, Tim finally let go of him before he drank too much of his blood, and now he felt too full, full of blood, full of passion, full of love, as though he was going to burst. He gazed into Cyril's subdued eyes, begging him to help him release some of it, if he had any idea how. The blond smiled and wrapped his arms around his neck. He gave him a slow amorous bite and began sucking the blood. Tim gasped as a new feeling of ecstasy came over him. He had never imagined that what had sounded like a bizarre and gruesome ritual to his human ears could be such a beautiful and meaningful thing as a vampire. He was overwhelmed with feelings of love at first, and then they turned into a new kind of desire. The desire to eternally belong to Cyril.

Tim remembered how lost he had been as a human. Even before he had lost his family, he had never felt like he belonged anywhere, he had never felt like his existence really mattered. His was not a close-knit, loving family. It was one where each member had responsibilities, and they each knew their place and what was expected of them. He had always done what his father expected of him, nothing more, nothing less. Only after he was left alone did he begin to live the life he actually wanted. He could have become a lawyer like his father, a professor, anything he wanted. It was not out of sadness or despair that he shunned that world, the world of light and all its normal, smile-bearing people, and sought instead the darkness and solitude of the streets. It was who he truly was. And knowing that his father and sister were alive had not suddenly lifted any of the darkness in him. He was attracted to everything dark, dangerous and morbid. That was why he had wanted to work with the dead, and why he had been attracted to the world of vampires. But there was a place for him in that world, with Fiona, Hanson, Humphrey, and now, forever, in Cyril's arms. He was accepted as he was, and he was free.

He stroked Cyril's hair and kissed him as the vampire slowly drank his blood, promising himself forever to him in return. And when Cyril was done drinking, they took care of their other needs at length.

They lay together all night and the entire next day, unwilling to move. There were no more words needed, no more questions, only peaceful smiles exchanged. Tim was contented at last, and so was Cyril.

"I feel like... I have a place now." Tim told him.

"Your place is with me, it has always been." Cyril said.

Tim now understood what it meant to become a master and feel compelled to love and protect one's servant, and he knew of the feelings Cyril experienced, and what he had sought from him from the beginning. Cyril was solitary because he was fragile and had been hurt, and Tim was the man who could make him feel safe and complete for all eternity.

He eventually left his companion's side to get them some fresh blood. They needed to feed. He put on the new clothes that had been laid out and headed downstairs. He had no clue how much time had elapsed, but it was dark outside, and he found Fiona standing on a balcony. The cold air shook Tim out of his daze as he stepped outside to join her.

"Where is Hanson?" he asked.

"Preparing my rose tea." she smiled.

"I was also looking for some... for something Cyril and I could feed on." he said, unwilling to say the word she disliked.

"You are allowed to say the word 'blood' around me." she said with a smile. "So, I guess it has happened after all."

"Yes."

"How is Cyril?"

"He is resting... I may have drunk a little too much of him." Tim said, a little embarrassed.

"I disagree with your decision, but it is done now. There's no going back, ever." she said, gazing at him intensely.

"I have no regrets." he simply said. "Where are the others?"

"Yvan is out hunting – deer. And Humphrey is in the library."

"Yvan is a Thompson, isn't he? Are we relatives?" he then asked her.

"Distant relatives, yes." she said. "Like you, he is a Natural."

"What are we going to do? Are we going to remain in hiding for now?" he asked.

"We will have to, for some time. Then, I will reopen our undertaker business somewhere else." she said.

"And they will let you? With Humphrey?"

"Word has been sent to court that he has been eliminated. My word is proof enough, because of my rank." she told him.

"Then can't you just do the same for Cyril?"

"I could... if he wants to remain in hiding for all eternity." she said. "Humphrey is a human, he will age and eventually die. They're not going to verify whether or not he has been eliminated. Cyril, on the other hand, will live forever. Someday he will want to come out of hiding and other vampires will know. He has broken our laws, I can't use my rank to try to obtain his pardon or it will set a precedent for other criminals."

"Why? What crime has he committed?" Tim asked, growing angry.

"He ran out in the streets after you, screaming your name. He was seen by many humans. And what they saw was a man running with unbelievable speed, shrieking louder than their ears could bear. Then there was that fire in your house. They saw two men jump out a window on the second floor then run away on foot like it was nothing. There was a column about the incident in the Times the next day. Religious men then came forth and told stories about demons and the undead. Luckily, in this age of great stoicism, few people believed them."

Tim hadn't realized just how much attention the whole incident had drawn to them, and all by his fault.

"The Apostles are the ones who found him guilty, right? Who are they?" he asked.

If they could issue a bounty, then surely they could also pardon a criminal.

"Apostles are the Dark Lord's lieutenants." she said. "Most of them are Naturals like us, and dominant vampires. Their role is to carry out the Dark Lord's justice and maintain order in the vampire society."

"What if I went to court and asked them to pardon Cyril?" he wondered.

"What makes you think they would?"

"My father was a respectable man as a human, surely he can't have changed that much."

"He serves the Dark Lord, and that is all I need to know about him." she said, turning her gaze back to the night.

"What does that mean exactly?" Tim asked, frowning. He was not trying to defend his father for he truly did not know what kind of man he was now, but he was curious to know why she disliked him so much.

"It means he is a follower of the rules. Someone who would tell me my place is at court, ordering lesser vampires because of my rank. Someone who wouldn't tolerate my relationship with Hanson, and would try to force me to sire him."

"Much like the church controls how humans live." Tim said.

"The Dark Lord is, by nature, a dominant and power-hungry vampire." she said. "But his power lies in controlling us with all these rules, to make us an obedient society, constantly watching each other. I could never live like that."

"I see."

"As I told you before, you are free to leave anytime." she continued. "If you decide you want to live by the rules of the Dark Lord, you can. As Heath Thompson's son, you have your place at court, and you can rule over sired vampires."

"It doesn't sound like a very interesting place. Probably like the court of England for humans, I guess."

"Probably." she agreed.

"Were you happy in London?" he asked, changing the subject.

"I ran a business that provided for my needs and I had Hanson. We could live a quiet life there. That is all I ever wanted."

Hanson came out with her tea on a tray and she sat with him at a small table to enjoy it outdoors with the man who made her happy. Tim remembered the hungry vampire in the bedroom still needing to be fed.

"I must go get something for Cyril." he told them, excusing himself.

He wandered around the castle until he found what he thought were the kitchens. The old servant was there, cleaning up.

"Good evening, Sir. Can I please have some... well..." Tim said, hesitant.

"Goat or deer?" the old man said with a loud sigh. He was not disturbed in the slightest by the request, only that he had to bring out more glasses after he had just finished cleaning them.

"Deer please. And some wine. And whatever leftovers you might have." Tim said politely.

The old man sighed again. He placed a large tray on the table and on it two bottles, two glasses, and a half-empty dish of stew.

"Venison *Bourguignon*." he said proudly.

"That sounds French... and delicious." Tim said, taking the tray.

He brought it back to his sleepy companion, who drank the wine mixed with deer blood and ravaged the stew. Tim laughed as he watched him attack the meal like a famished wolf.

"Leave a little for me." he said affectionately.

"Yes... Master." Cyril said, pausing.

"Let's make a few rules: first of all, I don't want you to call me 'Master.'" Tim told him, serious now. "We don't live under the Dark Lord's rules, do we?"

"No, we don't. Not anymore." Cyril said. "What is the next rule?"

"You must always leave half of the meal for me." Tim grinned, and they laughed together.

"You're changing." Cyril remarked.

"For the better... hopefully." Tim said.

"When I met you, you wanted me to kill you. Now you are asking me to feed you. So I should say it is for the better."

"As a mortal, I was constantly thinking about my own death. Now I'm dead, or undead technically, so I don't need to think about death anymore."

"But how do you feel about being a Natural?"

"I don't know yet. It is something I will have to find out on my own."

"With me." Cyril corrected him.

"Yes, with you." Tim said.

They remained in Yvan's castle for several more weeks, enjoying a carefree life away from the city and from any more trouble. He took Tim hunting with him – not hunting prey on foot with their fangs, but hunting deer on horseback with a rifle, because they were aristocrats after all, and Tim enjoyed it as much as he enjoyed the old servant's venison dishes. As for Cyril, it wasn't long before he was fully recovered and went with them. Meanwhile, Fiona remained in the castle with *her humans* Hanson and Humphrey. But they knew this life couldn't go on forever, and Yvan was also beginning to grow weary of having company. Tim knew what he had to do. One night, he approached Yvan in his private salon, away from the others. The old vampire put down the book he had been reading by candlelight.

"How can I help you?" he asked, raising an eyebrow.

"I've decided to go to court and ask the Apostles to pardon Cyril." Tim told him in a determined voice.

"Ah... well, good luck with that." Yvan said, with what looked like a sarcastic grin.

"You don't think I will succeed." Tim said. He had expected such a reaction from him.

"That you will go to court and be accepted there, I have no doubt. For the rest, I don't know." Yvan told him.

"This whole situation is largely my fault and I am the only one who can change it." Tim said.

"Maybe." Yvan said.

"I need you to tell me where I can find this court." Tim continued.

"Find it? No, Tim. One does not *find* our secret court. It will find you."

"That's good enough. What should I do? Is there somewhere I should be, someone I should talk to?"

"Go to any place where vampires gather and tell them who you are." Yvan said, picking up his book again.

"I have a favor to ask..." Tim went on. "Until I come back, could you please let Cyril stay here? There is no other safe place for him at the moment."

"I don't mind the company of one." Yvan said.

Tim thanked him and excused himself, and returned to his room. From the look on his face, Cyril immediately knew something was going on.

"What happened?" he questioned him.

"I've decided to go find the Apostles and ask them to pardon you." Tim said, taking his hands in his. They were not lukewarm today, but cold. Just cold.

"No... no Tim, please, don't leave me!" Cyril said in a panic.

"I am responsible for the bounty on your head, I have to do something, and I have the power to!" Tim insisted.

"But if you fail, they will put a bounty on your head too and kill you! You can't just enter the court and escape it when you want!"

"My father won't let them kill me."

"Tim, there is no such thing as family ties in the vampire world. We obey dominant vampires, we submit to the authority of Naturals, those are the only relationships we respect!"

"But I am a Natural, and I think I am a dominant vampire too."

"Yes, I also think you are..." Cyril said.

He moved away and brought his hand to his forehead. His entire body was shaking with fear now.

"Tim, it's not worth it. Let them come after me if they want, who cares?" he said.

"I care!" Tim said. "I care about you..."

"You don't, you're going to leave me and endanger yourself when we could be safe here together!"

"But for how long? I want us to be able to live the life we want, just like Fiona and Hanson."

Tim stepped forward and placed his hands on his shoulders.

"Do you remember when you got that scar, for me?" he said, brushing his fingers softly on the vampire's scarred right cheek.

"It was an act of love." Cyril whispered.

"An act of love that saved me from the darkness I was trapped in." Tim said. "I lived my mortal life like a dead man, thirsting only for darkness and revenge. Now, I want to *live* my undead life with you. And free."

"You can't do this for me. I won't allow it." Cyril said, turning his gaze away.

"Cyril, I owe it to you, after the way I treated you and all the trouble I caused in your life."

"I let you into my life. It was mutual, you didn't force me." Cyril reminded him.

"And so will I come back to you." Tim promised, drawing him into his arms. "I don't want to be away from you, it will kill me. But I would do anything for you. Anything."

"I didn't choose you as my master so you could go out and die stupidly." Cyril said.

"You chose me as your protector, and I am doing what a protector does." Tim said.

It pained him to have to leave him. He wanted nothing more than to bury himself away with Cyril somewhere, and live a quiet life together. But to do so – freely – he had to distance himself from him first.

"You must let me go. For us." he insisted.

Cyril let out a soft whimper and let his head fall onto his shoulder. His body shook now with silent tears and pain, the pain of losing the one he adored again – even if there was a chance he might come back someday. Tim took him to the bed and lay beside him. He needed this closeness one last time before he left. Cyril was a strange, unique, and endearing soul. A soul kind enough to have sought him out and dragged him out of his coffin of regrets like he dragged him out of that fire. He was grateful now that the vampire had followed him in the streets, had not given up on him upon their first encounter. He never knew that all he needed was to be found in the darkness, to be met there by someone like Cyril. With his fingers, he wiped away his savior's tears, but they would not stop tonight. He wished he had enough words to tell him all that was on his mind, to reassure him, but words never quite seemed to make it to his lips. So he brought his lips to him instead, and kissed his forehead, his cheek, his neck. And Cyril pressed himself against him and wept even more.

The next evening, after dusk, with a heavy heart, Tim left the property alone on horseback, taking only Hanson's silver stake as protection... and Cyril's love. He was on his own now, just for a little while. He would come back soon. He would obtain Cyril's freedom and come back to him.

He rode to Portsmouth, where he stayed overnight, then went on to London. He knew exactly where to find vampires and he knew exactly what to do. He went straight to the Hell's Pit and posted himself by the door. As he had expected, around nine o'clock came the group of regulars. He stepped out in front of them and blocked the way, naturally adopting a dominant stance.

"Who are you?" one of them asked, recognizing another of their kind.

"My name is Tim Thompson and I want to see my father, Heath Thompson." Tim said firmly.

5.

Magdalena knelt before the small corner altar and the large statue of Mary towering above it. At the Virgin's blessed feet were dozens of candles lit by the afflicted and the humble, and her painted eyes looked down upon them with an all-encompassing mother's love. Mary was her shield, her protectress against the dark forces.

"Sister Magdalena." a man's voice said behind her. It was that of Bishop Smith.

The nineteen-year-old Magdalena had joined the orders only two years ago in Barcelona, and, while not a part of this diocese, she had been invited there on an important mission. She rose and arranged her clothes. She had abandoned her order's habit for more practical attire: she wore an all-black dress, slit on both sides for riding purposes, and same-colored breeches and boots underneath. A fresh white standing collar and cuffs, a black hairband in her auburn curls, cut short under the ear, and the silver crucifix around her neck were the only indicators that she belonged to a religious order. She wore a heavy belt around her waist with a holster containing a customized Lancaster pistol, and twelve blessed silver bullets in a cartridge belt.

"Your Grace." she told the man, kneeling before him and kissing his ring. Though still a member of her order, she was there as a secular person. Nevertheless, Catholic nuns in any country were under the authority of the male clergy, and the Holy Bible dictated that woman should submit to man like the apostles and the church submitted to Jesus Christ.

"It is a pleasure for us to have you here." the old man said, smiling. He invited her to follow him into the confessional where they could talk privately. He was a man of sixty or so, with white hair neatly combed back and a grandfatherly benevolence in his features. The All Saints Church of Poplar provided a quiet, discreet meeting place, away from the inquisitive eyes of the Archbishop – and their enemies. Because this was not exactly church business – not directly.

They seated themselves in the shadows of the confessional.

"How are you liking the East End?" he began.

"It's a filthy place filled with scoundrels and sin." she replied coldly. "But I did enjoy seeing the Tower. Criminals must be punished."

"Indeed." the bishop said. "God can only grant pardon in the other world. In our world, we must make sure that criminals are brought either to the light of the Lord or to justice if they won't repent."

"Do many criminals repent here?" she asked with a hint of sarcasm.

"No." he said.

There was a moment of silence as the man leaned forward against the wooden screen separating them.

"I received a letter from the Mother Superior of your order." he said in a lower voice. "So you have encountered *them* too..."

"Yes, Your Grace."

"Tell me what happened."

"Before I became a nun, they killed my fiancé Diego. Or rather, changed him." she said in a voice tainted with anger and grief.

"I see." he said. "So you were engaged, not married, right?"

"Yes?" she said surprised.

"Good. Keep your purity, it is a powerful weapon against demons." he advised her.

"Of course." she said.

"You have come to a dangerous part of London. But that is also their preferred hunting ground, because the people here have little value in the eyes of society. Murders and disappearances are not thoroughly investigated."

"It makes sense."

"And what is your goal?"

"To kill every bloodsucker out there."

"Good." he said.

He invited her to exit the confessional and they went to a back room which contained a chest with various books and artifacts. He picked up a book of demonology and handed it to her.

"This books contains all the information we have gathered about them over the centuries." he said. "Forget old folktales and legends, they live among us, everywhere."

"What is the best and fastest way to identify them then?" she asked.

"Of course they avoid sunlight, but also they cannot touch silver. Wear silver on you at all times."

"Where do they gather in the East End?"

"Solitary hunters haunt the docks and dark alleys at night. Groups may gather in pubs and taverns, or even theaters and high-end salons. Those will be the hardest to identify as they may look like any other gentleman or lady, except, you will find, they are unusually attractive and friendly to humans."

"I see." she said.

He then handed her a silver stake.

"In case those bullets fail." he said with a smile. "Don't worry sweet child, you are not alone. Our *sweepers* patrol the streets too, to protect the innocent."

She tucked both the book and the silver stake in a small leather bag and headed out into the night. She was aware the East End was a dangerous place for any woman alone at night, but she was not alone. She was blessed by the light of the Lord and wore Mary as her shield at all times. And that night, she *swept* the streets.

She walked through the night with an assured step, passing through the darkness as though it was nothing more than an illusion. And those who lived by night, the prostitutes and smugglers, the crooks and cutthroats, the sinners, were all part of the same picture to her judging eyes: that of Sodom and Gomorrah. Humans had not learned anything from God's wrath, she thought, they only rebuilt cities of sin elsewhere. The people here were probably not worth saving, but this is where the enemy operated, where they could be found, and that was why she was there. God would take care of the sinners, she took care of the vampires.

Hers was a dangerous job, but a rewarding one. Every time she put a bullet or a stake through a vampire's heart was another victory, and the hunt itself became a thrilling, exhilarating pastime, something to look forward to after her loss.

Diego. Her beloved, the man who was hers to marry, was a kind and pious young man. They frequented the same church in Barcelona and became acquainted. They were not the sort to go out alone without a chaperon, they only met in the presence of their families, who approved of their engagement. But one day, Diego began to act differently. He would no longer see her as often, and when he did his gaze was absent, longing for something else. She never knew what. She asked him what had happened but he only withdrew from her more. Concerned about him, she crept out of her home one night to go to him. She, the chaste young maiden in love, climbed up to his balcony like Romeo to his Juliet, and what she saw there broke her heart. Diego was not alone in his room, he was with another young man. That alone was not suspicious in that day and age, he could have been a friend or a visiting relative. She observed them talking for some time, unable to decipher their words. Then, the stranger cupped Diego's face in his hands and bit his neck. Struck with terror, Magdalena – then Carmen, saw the vampire drink Diego's blood slowly, kissing and biting his neck at the same time, and the worst part of it was that Diego showed no signs of protest: he was *enjoying* it! When the vampire was done, he slashed his wrist with a razor blade and presented it to Diego, who fell to his knees and sucked it hungrily. With trembling limbs, she climbed back down to the street and ran away. Diego sent a note to her family the next day, saying that he was breaking their engagement and leaving town.

She did not know what she had witnessed at the time so she went to the local priest and told him about the two men kissing and drinking each other's blood. He did not believe her. Thinking this was probably some sort of female sexual fantasy, he recommended her family place her in a convent for some time to keep her out of trouble until another suitable husband was found. What she thought a punishment at first had turned out for the better. The sisters were kind and not too surprised when they heard her story. They reminded her how the Holy Bible warned against witches and demons. Satan's realm was very real to these women of strong faith, and to Magdalena who had witnessed it herself. Vowing to never marry, she chose Jesus Christ instead and announced to her family that she would be joining the orders under the name of Sister Magdalena.

Protected by the light of the Lord, she thought the underworld could never harm her, and she was contented with her new life. Until a new resolve began to grow inside her. Shielding herself was not enough, she had been *chosen* by the Lord to fight! And so she went to the Mother Superior and asked for permission to temporarily leave the order to bring justice to all the innocent victims of these monsters. To her surprise, the Mother Superior agreed, and told her she was not the only one. There were other *limpiadores*, "cleaners" or "sweepers" like herself all around the world. These devoted Christians worked behind the scenes to rid the streets of demonic filth. They were called cleaners or sweepers because their work had to remain quiet and behind the scenes, and they were humble in the eyes of God; they were not soldiers, only men and women of faith doing their duty.

Despite the rampant vampire activity in Barcelona, the Mother Superior chose to send her instead to the East End of London, where she thought she could be of use. Disappointed at first, Magdalena understood however that obedience was a virtue and serving God through the Mother Superior was more important than carrying out her personal revenge locally. So she went to London, armed only with a pistol and her faith. And anger.

It was anger than moved her more than devotion, she had to admit, and she prayed Mary every day to help rid herself of sin. God frowned on murder, it was a sin, but not the murder of demons. It was legal and permitted in their world, and that was all she needed to know. It gave her a perfect outlet to express her anger and grief, and there was never any end to either. One night, though, she made a mistake.

She had been *sweeping* the streets for hours that night and not a soul – or an undead soul in sight. Winter would soon be over, and the air was growing warmer. It no longer chilled her to the bone when she walked alone on the docks. Stepping into a world of sin and living in it, she had unwillingly began to wonder about those who partook in it. What was it like to be a prostitute and make money from the lust of men? What was it like to be a thief and take what you wanted when you wanted? The East End was growing on her. She needed to go to Mass again to cleanse herself from all this filth. Her fingers brushed upon the pistol in its holster, reminding her of her mission. And then she saw a little boy all alone on the docks. He looked around him, frightened and lost. She immediately went over to him and knelt beside him.

"Are you alone? Where are your parents?" she asked him.

Like many here, he was probably orphaned. He was not as little as she had thought, he could have been between ten and twelve, it was hard to tell.

"They... they left me here." he sobbed, as sad tears poured out of his black eyes. He was very beautiful with his pale skin and perfectly rounded cheeks surrounded with auburn curls. He looked just like a little cherub from a painting. He was obviously well-fed and not poor. Perhaps his family had run into some hard times, she thought. She did not know what she should do. Find a police constable? Here, at this hour? And where would they take the child? Orphanages were full already. He could end up in a workhouse.

"Your parents left you alone here?" she asked him again.

He nodded.

"Do you know where you live? Perhaps we can try to find them." she said, trying to sound cheerful. And then what? They clearly didn't want him anymore. But she could always refer them to the local church and charities. Yes, perhaps if a charity could assist this family they could keep their son.

"I know my address but... but I don't know how to get there." the boy wept.

"That's fine, I can take you there. You're safe with me." she said, parting her cloak to show him her pistol. His shining black eyes moved with interest.

She took his hand and walked with him in the direction of the street where he lived. It was not very close, of course, they obviously didn't want him to find his way home. Shameful parents, dumping a child on the docks in the middle of the night like this! She would let the bishop deal with them though, she was not enough of a diplomat.

"What's your name?" she eventually asked the little boy.

"It's Mickey." he told her with a friendly smile. "You don't sound like us, Ma'am, why is that?" he then asked candidly.

"That's because I come from far away." she smiled. "My name is Magdalena. Sister Magdalena. And I come all the way from Spain."

"I thought sisters wore a habit?" he said, perplexed.

"I'm a different kind of sister." she said.

"It's here." he then suddenly said.

They stopped in front of a tall middle-class house in a row of exactly identical middle-class houses. Everything was dark, and there were no lights inside. She knocked on the door loudly several times but no one answered.

"Mum and dad keep a key under that stone there." Mickey said, pointing at a large flat stone near the doorstep, and indeed she found the key there.

She realized entering unsuspecting folks' houses at night could be dangerous, but after all they were this boy's parents, and she was armed if needed.

They entered the silent house and Mickey shouted "Mum! Dad!" but there was no response.

"Maybe they are asleep upstairs." he said, pulling Magdalena's hand.

She followed him up the dark stairway, her hand on the pistol, and he took her to a dark room. The door closed and locked behind them.

"Mickey?" she said.

A candle was lit, then another. There were three people facing her, three adults and none of them looked like the boy's parents. The first was a very beautiful and elegant woman in her early twenties, with black hair and heavy eyeliner around her Asian eyes. She wore a luxurious black sleeveless ball gown and a tight corset, and long black lace gloves on her arms. Her hair was gathered into a tall bun and neatly curled around her face. The man next to her was also tall and handsome, in his twenties, blond of hair and well groomed. He wore a dark blue striped suit with a yellow tie and a gold watch in the pocket of his vest. The blue and yellow of his attire seemed to have been strategically picked out to match the gold of his hair and his general pale complexion. The third and last one was a shorter man in his late teens, robust for his age, with thick and curly brown hair. He wore a black suit over a gray shirt embroidered with roses and a crimson tie matching the color of his fierce eyes. Diego.

Magdalena gasped as she saw him. It was him, there was no doubt about it, except he was one of them now – a vampire.

"What is this?" she asked, turning to Mickey.

The little boy removed his cloak and went over to the group of three, and as he stood beside them her eyes opened wide with terror. How could she have been so stupid? His angelic face and endearing tears, they were nothing more than a bait! She had been lured into a trap by a child vampire!

"Good evening." the blond man said with a French accent.

"Who are you and what do you want?" Magdalena said, frowning. What did they want? Why even ask? Her of course. She was their dinner.

"Let me introduce myself." the man said. "My name is Didier Deschamps, and this is my wife Thi." He gestured to the aristocratic Asian woman by his side, who stood absolutely still like a statue. "The boy's name is Mickey and this is..." he continued but she cut him: "Diego."

Diego gazed at her with puzzled eyes for a moment, then said: "Carmen?"

"It's Magdalena now. Sister Magdalena." she told him in a dark voice. "*Soy una limpiadora*." she added and he knew exactly what she meant.

Her hand reached for her pistol but her gun belt was gone.

"Are you looking for this?" Thi asked in a sultry voice, holding up the gun belt and the small leather bag containing the stake in her gloved hand. When had she snatched it? Magdalena had not seen her move.

"It has come to our attention that you have been causing trouble to our kind." Didier then told her in a tone that could otherwise have been interpreted as friendly.

"I am a *sweeper*, I hunt you fiends." she said coldly.

"Why?" he asked her, as though it needed to be explained.

"Because of me." Diego then said, stepping forward.

She took a step back and prepared to fight with her bare hands.

"Well then." Thi said, somewhat disappointed. "We were going to kill you but it seems like you two know each other."

There was an unspoken rule among vampires that if a human belonged to one of them – whether as food or a potential servant, the others would not intervene, so long as that vampire either ate or sired the mortal. Diego was a sired vampire, but he could sire others as his servants too, though this sort of polygamy was not very common among their kind. Vampires usually went in pairs of two and two only.

"Carmen was my fiancée before I was sired." he told the others.

So a servant she would be, not a meal.

145

Thi placed the gun belt on a side table as though it was no danger to them anymore and she, Didier and Mickey quietly exited the room, locking the door behind them.

"Aren't they going to kill me?" she asked Diego.

"We do not kill each other's humans." he simply told her, and he invited her to sit on a sofa with him.

She knew she could no longer trust him, he was a creature of the night now, but her love for him had not quite disappeared. It never would. She sat with him and waited for him to speak.

"How have you been, *mi amor*?" he asked her in a gentle voice, the voice she remembered.

"Alive. Unlike you." she said.

They spoke in their mother tongue now, as they always did, and it was comforting to her in a way.

"I am alive in a different world, that's all." he told her. "I'm still the Diego you knew, and loved."

"No, you're not. And I am no longer Carmen, I am Sister Magdalena." she told him roughly.

"Relax, love." he told her. "You're safe with me here, I'm not going to kill you."

"I will not become one of your kind." she warned him.

"I cannot sire a human against their will, it is against etiquette." he said, stretching out his arms on the back of the sofa.

"Then what do you want?"

"I was surprised to encounter you here." he said. "I've missed you, you know."

She wanted to believe his sweet words, but she knew vampires were cold, deceitful creatures.

"I came to London to hunt your kind. It's all I have left now, all I live for." she said.

"You're still beautiful, even though you cut off your hair." he said.

He moved closer to her. Her heart was pounding in her chest like a young girl again. She remembered their sweet courtship, his devotion to her, his kindness. And then she remembered him and the vampire kissing and sucking each other's blood, and how, with all the horror it inspired her, it had also awakened her senses and given her forbidden dreams thereafter. He inched closer to her and breathed in the scent of her hair. She couldn't move. Her limbs were frozen, stuck between the urge to run away and the desire to give in to him.

"For someone who claims to want to kill me, you sure smell like something else. The scent of arousal is all over you, my sweet virgin." he whispered in her ear, only fueling the problem even more.

"If you're not going to kill me or change me, then what do you want?" she asked, turning to him. Her voice had lost its combativeness, and so had her heart. She really was *that weak*...

"The same things anyone would want when reuniting with a lover." he said.

His lukewarm fingers came down upon her hand and stroked it softly. It was his touch, the same patient, respectful and yet enticing way he had always touched her hands before.

"Diego, you broke our engagement." she reminded him in what was now nothing more than a weak whisper.

"Because I didn't want you to become like us. I wanted you to live a normal life." he explained. "I was allured by a vampire. But Carmen, I still love you. Nothing has changed for me."

He lay a soft, lukewarm kiss on her neck and she shuddered.

"Diego..."

"There is no reason for us to be enemies. Not anymore." he told her.

"But you're a..." she said and was not able to finish as his lips came down on hers and kissed her softly and languidly. And she let him.

He lay her on the sofa and kissed her longly, and she lay there, her heart racing in her chest, trying to fight the burning fire he lit everywhere inside her. She had never been with a man before, but even she could sense his arousal. His fingers intertwined with hers as he kissed her for what seemed like hours, never growing tired of her taste.

"Diego..." she whispered as their lips parted briefly.

"I can still take care of your needs, my love, even as a vampire." he assured her.

And now she wanted him to. No, she couldn't. Shouldn't. But then if she did, who would know? He was her love, her fiancé, her Diego after all. He was different in body, but their love was still there, burning perhaps stronger than before.

"Let me go... Please. If you truly still love me, let me go Diego." she begged him.

He removed himself from her and invited her to sit again.

"You're not a prisoner in my house." he said, turning his gaze away. "But if I let you go, they will come after you."

"Then protect me." she said.

He turned to her with shining eyes.

"I want to protect you..." he said. "Will you at least let me escort you back home then? They won't follow us if they think you're *my human*."

She didn't like the term, but he was truly offering her his protection, at least she thought.

He returned her gun belt to her and let her out of the room. He then walked her back to the small room she rented in a respectable old lady's house not too far from there. As he had promised, no one followed them. On the doorstep, he gazed at her longly, unwilling to leave.

"Carmen..." he said.

"It's Magdalena." she corrected him.

"Magdalena, please, give up this life and return to Barcelona." he said. "You can return to a normal life there, even in the convent if that's what you want. If you stay here, you will either die or become one of us, it's inevitable."

He took her hands and she lowered her gaze.

"I... I need some time to think." she told him truthfully.

"I will not come back to your place, nor will any of my kind. You will be safe if you stay home." he said. "But if you want to find me, you know where I live."

He kissed her hands softly and bid her farewell and she stepped inside quietly.

She did not sleep that night, or the next day, she could only lay in bed thinking of Diego. Had she been wrong all along? Were his kind not just thirsty bloodsuckers who hunted her kind? The three other vampires had seemed well-mannered too. Nothing was like she had imagined it.

Needing answers, she returned to the church the next evening around eight o'clock. The church doors were locked at that hour but Bishop Smith had given her a key to let herself in if she needed to pray. She found the church empty, of course, yet she could hear vague sounds somewhere. Following them, she found a small door in the back of the building, with a staircase leading up to the belfry. She climbed the stairs quietly and loaded her pistol. And there, at the top of the stairs, right beside the bells, she saw the bishop. *Fornicating.* And not even with a woman: with a female ghoul! The demonic creature moaned along with him, and dug her fangs into the skin of his back and bit him over and over, and the man, oblivious to what he was doing or the danger, carried on, lost in the lustful rapture the creature was giving him.

With a trembling hand, Magdalena drew her pistol and fired two shots.

She stood there in a trance for a moment, observing the man's naked body lying in his own blood, and underneath him only ashes. And then, slowly, the reality that she had not only eliminated another monster, but murdered a man – granted, a sinful one – struck her. Other humans would not understand. They would not know that he was with a ghoul, that he might become one himself if left alive. She put her pistol back in its holster and quietly went down the stairs, thinking about what she should do next. Turn herself in to the police? And then what? Who would *sweep* the streets at night and protect the people of London? And now she was a murderer, there was no way she could return to the convent, let alone show her face before Christ in a church. She held her breath as she quietly crossed the main hall of the All Saints Church, careful not to turn her unrepenting gaze to any of the statues that seemed to be judging her now.

⚬⚬⚬

She walked the streets aimlessly that night, almost hoping a vampire would stalk and attack her so she could cleanse herself by shooting another fiend. But no one came after her, nor did she spot any. Perhaps that night they were all gathered somewhere else. She needed to tell someone what she had done, but of course she could not go to the police or they would arrest her. Diego... He would listen to her, wouldn't he? Would he understand? She did not know.

Her pace suddenly quickened and she darted off toward the street where he lived. There, she took the key from under the flat stone and let herself in. Not a very good hiding place for a spare key, she thought, but then again any burglars in a vampire's house would quickly turn into a meal. Or was it even a private house? It could be a whole nest of them for all she knew.

The house was dark and quiet. Having no intention of snooping around, she went straight to the upstairs room where she had been taken the last time she came. It too was dark and empty. She lay on the cool velvet sofa and began to cry. More than the guilt of murdering a man, a bishop, she cried for the loss of her immortal soul. Yes, God would never want her now; even Jesus Christ and Mary would not intercede for her, nobody would. She had murdered a holy man in cold blood, because he was a sinner.

Later, much later though, Diego came in. He took one glance at her then went to light a single candle and placed it on a side table. He then closed the door. She gazed at him quietly, her eyes red and puffy.

"Something happened." he said, sitting down beside her.

"I... I murdered the bishop. He was... with a ghoul." she muttered, still in shock.

"Well, that is not a great loss." he said softly.

"What do you mean?"

"The man had been frequenting one of our favorite pick-up spots for some time. You could say he was a regular. We let him be since he would just end up being a meal for one of us. It saves us the trouble of hunting."

"You mean, he went with ghouls... regularly?" she asked in disbelief.

"Ghouls, half-ghouls, vampires... That lecherous old man could write an entire encyclopedia about our sexual habits." Diego said. To him it was funny, but he tried to keep his tone respectful in front of her.

"Maybe he was just investigating though." she said.

"Investigating our females' anatomy?" he said, turning to her. "That man was the biggest sinner in town. Don't let his rank fool you."

"But... but..." she said, shaking her head. None of this made sense. He was a man of Christ, he could not be as Diego described him – and yet she had seen him with her own eyes.

"Magdalena, you are not a child." he said, taking her hands. "You know of the behavior of men, why does any of this surprise you?"

"I don't know... Oh Diego, what will I do now?" she told him, desperate.

"You can do whatever you want." he replied, not truly understanding her concerns.

"I can't surrender to the police, they wouldn't understand. And I can't return to the convent, God will never forgive me!"

"You could just return to a normal life." he suggested.

"I can't... I am a sinner now!"

"And you weren't before?"

"I didn't think of myself as one, though I suppose in the eyes of God we are all sinners." she admitted. She suddenly burst into tears and he took her in his arms. They were not warm like a human's anymore, only lukewarm, but they were still comforting. He bid her to follow him to the bed and lay down. He lay beside her and placed a gentle hand on her arm until she had let out all her tears.

"You are too pure for our world." he said with compassion.

"But this is the world I live in now, and so do you." she said.

"It's not as bad as it seems." he assured her.

"Diego..." she whispered.

She wanted to be in his arms now, but he was kind and respectful and remained at a safe distance from her. And that only enticed her more. She moved forward and kissed him, and he finally wrapped his tender arms around her.

They kissed, again, for a long time, and she felt better. Contented. What she had done was not so bad after all. Like he said, the man was a lecherous scoundrel. And vampires were not so bad after all. Diego was one of them, was he not? She had lost the protection of Mary and Christ now, there was no going back.

"Can we still be together?" she asked Diego softly.

"You know it is what I want." he said.

His hands found the buttons on her dress and began to unfasten them. Undressing a woman in those day was not exactly easy, nor could it be done alone. She helped him unfasten buttons, undo laces on her corset, and remove this damned straight jacket of a dress. By then, he had loosened his tie and unbuttoned his own shirt. And then he moved down to her thighs, unfastening her stockings from her garter belt, and rolling them slowly down her leg, where he placed kisses along the way.

"Diego..." she whimpered.

He then proceeded to remove her corset and adorn her neck, her chest and her belly with as many kisses. She grabbed his shirt and tore it open. He removed his tie and lay on his back, and let her explore him. She breathed in his scent. It was a musky, manly scent but had some floral component to it. It was incredibly enticing. She did not want to wait any longer and he knew it. His black eyes shone brightly as he appraised her in the poorly lit room. She removed whatever clothes she still had on, and his, and let him bring her most forbidden fantasies to life. And for a sister, she had fantasies that surprised even him the vampire. She wanted to try everything, every move, every touch, every position. Nothing was off limits for her hungry lips or her inquisitive fingers. And he fulfilled her every dream like the passionate young man he was.

As she lay naked in the bed, half-asleep in the early hours of morning though, she sensed something different in the room. Diego had got up and the candle was out. She rolled over in a panic and saw his piercing, hungry red eyes upon her in the darkness. He was no longer her sweet, respectful lover, he was a bloodsucker, and she knew exactly what those eyes meant.

"You said you loved me!" she gasped.

"I do... and we can be together forever, as immortals." he said. "I love you so much, Magdalena!"

"If you loved me, you wouldn't do this." she said, on the defensive.

"Am I so horrible that you wouldn't consider being like me?" he said, saddened.

"You're a vampire." she said.

"I'm the man you love. Just let me do this, it will only hurt for a second." he said, now growing impatient.

"Never." she stated firmly.

"You weren't so feisty about parting with your virginity."

"That was different."

"Really? I don't think you can ever confess to a priest the things we did last night."

"Do not touch me." she warned him as he moved closer, but he ignored her.

And as he lunged at her she rolled out of the bed, grabbing her gun belt along the way. She aimed coldly, mechanically at the vampire, and shot. The silver bullet pierced Diego's heart and he caught on fire, and within a few minutes he was no more. So this is what it came down to: being with Diego meant becoming a vampire. Giving herself to him came with a price tag: that of her mortal life, and he wouldn't have it any other way. A silent tear rolled down her cheek.

Without any emotion, she got dressed, took her things and left. The sun had not risen yet and a thick fog bathed the empty streets. She wandered deep into the fog, staggered, her eyes locked on the wet paved road. One step, another. *Walk*, she thought, she must *walk away* from it all... but to go where? She thought she could hear Bishop Smith and Diego's voices crying for revenge in her ears. Would they turn into ghosts and haunt her? She was no longer blessed with the light of the Lord and Mary was laughing at her misery.

One step, another. Crushing. Crushing night coming to an end and pushing her against an invisible wall she could not cross. The night ushered her away but between her and another day was a hard stone wall she could not break through. Was she just going to die like this, crushed between the shadows of the night and the impossibility of moving on to the next day?

Her body was sore and heavy. Her hands hung by her side as she staggered across the streets. Her soul was crying, loudly, and yet her lips did not make a sound. There were no words left. There was the mission. Yes, of course there was the mission. But she had lost her greatest strengths: her purity and the protection of God. God didn't reward murderers. She needed to repent but something inside her didn't want to. Another voice inside her told her that she needed to kill more, to put a bullet through yet another vampire, as though it would ease her suffering. But even if Diego had lied to her, the three others had behaved quite politely in leaving him the prey out of etiquette. Was it right to kill such well-mannered people because they ate her kind? Of course it was right. Or maybe it wasn't. She didn't know anymore, and she could not take one more step.

She stopped as she realized she was standing on the edge of the docks. *Use the pistol, kill.* Her hand longed to pull the trigger again and her soul thirsted for someone's blood at least. Well, there was one person who had lost her right to God's kingdom and that no one would miss. She drew the pistol and applied it to her temple, and...

Before she could pull the trigger something hit the back of her head it seemed, pushing her forward, and she realized that the pistol had actually been the one hit, but with such strength that her entire body had been pushed forward. Time almost came to a halt and she saw herself falling slowly into the Thames, until she received another blow in her stomach this time, that knocked the breath out of her. She fell backward into a tall person's soft arms, and she stood there, stuck in a stupor, until a woman's voice resounded right behind her ear.

"That was close, what were you thinking?" she said.

Magdalena turned around and saw a beautiful, angel-faced woman. In her mid to late twenties, she was very tall and blond of hair, and had a healthy and friendly demeanor.

"You're one of them. Well, just do what you want with me." Magdalena immediately said in a listless voice, stepping forward. She didn't even want to fight her, didn't need to. The vampire would either eat her or go away. Either way, it didn't matter.

"What's wrong with you?" the woman said loudly instead. "I just saved you from putting a bullet through that pretty head and falling into the Thames. Is that all you have to say?"

"What do you want me to say?" Magdalena asked.

"*Thank you*' would be a good start." the other said. "And then perhaps tell me what is worth throwing away your life like this?"

Magdalena clenched her fists and said: "I'm a filthy whore..."

The vampire seemed baffled.

"You don't look like one... but even if you are, what's wrong with a woman earning a living?" she asked.

"And a murderer." Magdalena added.

"So are you wanting me to turn you in to the human police?" the other asked, confused.

"They wouldn't understand..." Magdalena said sadly. "Besides, I've lost the light of God: Hell is where I'm going, so why bother? I just wanted to shoot something. Especially those two, Didier and Thi."

The tall woman frowned as she heard the names.

"I don't know about the light of God, but if you just want to shoot things, I may have work for you." she said.

Vampires never did anything for free, and now came the negotiations.

"And after the work is done, you get to eat me?" Magdalena laughed, sarcastic.

"I can if that's your deepest desire, but I'd rather not. You intrigue me."

She dropped her large arm onto the young woman's shoulder and led her down the foggy streets to her place, a modest three-story building in a slum.

"You live here?" Magdalena said, surprised.

She had assumed that vampires, who did not need to work for money and could obtain as much of it as they wanted simply by killing a rich human and stealing his wallet, lived in classy high-end homes and apartments.

"It's the safest place ever, plus dinner walks right into my den." she said, unconcerned.

In other words, she *ate* burglars and cutthroats who followed her inside.

She took the young nun – or not-so-nun-anymore – inside, and they seated themselves in a blue salon with old broken furniture. The window had been boarded shut. The woman served her a glass of strong gin, which she swallowed at once. It burned her throat, but did calm her nerves a little. She gazed at the vampire now, wondering what would happen next. The woman was dressed in a simple blue dress under her long cloak, which she removed. She wore her long hair loose on her shoulders, much like a prostitute would – and most certainly went about like this to attract unsuspecting prey.

"You're not polite... like them." Magdalena remarked as the vampire slouched on an old sofa.

"Do you think I'm rude?" the other said, laughing. "A human worried about a vampire's manners... now you have to tell me your story. Here, have some more gin!"

And she poured her another glass.

"You could start by telling me your name." Magdalena said.

"And you yours. I'm Astrid."

"I'm Sister Magdalena."

She was not ready to give up the title yet, but was she still married to Jesus Christ after losing her chastity to a vampire?

"Sister..." the vampire said, appraising her with shining eyes. "Do continue."

Magdalena told the unsuspected listener her whole story, because she needed to tell someone and preferably not the police. The tall woman was all ears and seemed captivated.

"And then, I murdered Diego." Magdalena concluded.

"What a story..." Astrid said, leaning forward. She seemed more amused than condescending, and that was a good thing. Magdalena did not expect nor want her pity.

"It's done and over now." she said, lowering her gaze.

"I'm curious about one thing though." Astrid said. "You said that you were impressed by Didier and Thi's manners, yet you told me earlier you especially wanted to kill them..."

"Well, of course..." Magdalena said, surprised she even had to explain. "My kind and your kind are mortal enemies. We kill each other. Vampires are only one thing, and that is evil! I won't let them confuse me by pretending to be polite, respectful people!"

"You have very clear cut ideas of what is good and what is evil." Astrid remarked.

"I'm a nun. I'm on the side of God and all things good... I was until last night." Magdalena stated.

"And now, what side are you on?" Astrid asked.

"I don't know anymore."

"What if I told you I also don't like those two vampires and I want to eliminate them and a few others? Would you work for me?"

"Work with you to eliminate your own kind?" the young woman said.

"I've heard about you, the new *sweeper* in town. You've taken out many more vampires and ghouls than any other mortal around here, and they say you're a damn good shot! Are you a good sniper too?" the vampire said.

"I've never missed my target." Magdalena said.

"Good. Then you are just the person I need." Astrid said, satisfied.

"Why would you ever need a human as your hitman?" Magdalena asked in utter disbelief.

"Because you're just a human, they won't be wary of you. If I introduce you to the court as my pet, it will cause quite a scandal! The people I'm seeking to identify will most likely reveal themselves. Once we've spotted the targets, we retreat and you eliminate them in the shadows."

"And after that, you kill me?" Magdalena said, suspicious.

"If you're a good pet, I won't have to." Astrid said with a grin. She poured her another glass.

"We think of your kind much like you think of animals. Some are pets, some are food." she continued. "You may eat beef or mutton, but you don't necessarily throw yourself on every living cow or sheep and devour them, do you?"

"True." Magdalena agreed.

Again. Another vampire was trying to convince her that they had their own morals and rules, but it could not be... it simply could not be that way. It was not what she was taught!

"So you want me to behave like a good and loyal puppy in front of your kind, is that it?" she asked, downing the glass.

"Would that be so difficult?"

"I guess not. In my order we are taught that obedience is the first and foremost of all feminine virtues."

"What a dreadful place you come from!" Astrid said, frowning. "But anyhow, if it helps you play your part, I'm fine with it. I will make sure we get you all the weapons you need for the job."

"I can't believe I'm selling my soul to a vampire now..." Magdalena said, sarcastic.

"I call it a business partnership." Astrid said, smiling again.

⌒∽⌒

And the court she spoke of was, much like the court of England for humans, a place of intrigue and danger, even for the undead.

Holly knew this only too well. It had not been that long since she had awakened as a Natural and had been invited to join her father Heath at court. There, she had quickly learned that there were many other kinds of vampires: sired vampires, and lesser vampires sired by sired vampires. And then, at the very bottom, were ghouls, humans who had only been partly or incorrectly transformed. Only Naturals were allowed at court, along with their sired servants. And among each of these ranks were dominant vampires and submissive vampires. Dominants naturally asserted their power over the others, and the others accepted it. It was an unspoken rule: you knew whether you were dominant or not. And she was dominant, just like her father.

The vampire court was ruled by the Dark Lord and the Apostles. No one knew their names or faces, but they made the rules, decided what direction the vampire society would go and, more importantly, who lived and who died. Vampires were always on the lookout for a new bounty, an excuse to hunt down one of their own – mostly for sport but also for a reward. She had heard about the bounty on the vampire Cyril and that alone left her completely indifferent, however she was curious about his obvious involvement in the fire that had burned down the Thompson mansion. But there were other priorities right now, and one of them was a group of unwelcome guests in her father's salon. She knew them well – too well, and she knew they coveted the throne of the Dark Lord, much like herself and her father.

Her spiteful glance first landed on Ashok and Rathika, the Indian over-seers of the whole East End. Distant and elegant in their colorful kurta and saree, adorned with more golden jewelry than many a king or queen, they returned to her a disdainful glance. Next were Allan and Casper, who controlled the smaller Tower area, always a little withdrawn and seemingly appraising the others. She was not too worried about them. Much like the always silent Japanese vampire Yojinbo and his child companion Yurei. Nobody really knew the purpose of their presence at court – and that was troublesome, but nothing in their behavior indicated the slightest ambition. Her eyes browsed quickly over the crowd of regulars in the salon, spotting there Mickey, Roland and Mary, the oldest and least dangerous at court, and finally the pair she hated the most, Didier and Thi. She hated them because they were powerful, dominant, and more importantly, they were not a master and servant pair, they were two Naturals who were already husband and wife in their human life. Two Naturals meant twice the power and twice the scheming. They had an unfair advantage over other Naturals who went with a sired servant.

"You're not enjoying yourself tonight." her father remarked. He was sitting in a chair, enjoying a drink while his guests gathered and entertained themselves.

"I see some faces I don't like." she said in a low voice.

"And why do you not like them?" he wondered, amused.

"They're dominant." she responded. "Especially that woman, she wants to become an Apostle, I just know it."

"Then challenge her and become an Apostle in her place." he suggested. "Or is this new *style* of yours just for show?"

He emphasized the word as though it were some stupid act of adolescent rebellion that would not last – and he did not think it would. Except Holly had become immortal at twenty, she was not a girl anymore.

"She is stronger than me." she said.

"A Thompson never admits defeat. If you have already accepted that you are weaker than her, then I have no use for you." he said coldly.

"So you're saying you will kill me if I don't challenge and kill her?" she replied, not surprised in the least. She was used to his constant threats now.

He continued watching his guests and did not answer.

"I will take the place that is mine, and get rid of those who stand in my way – even if that means *you*." she whispered in a dark voice.

"I'll believe that when I see it." he said, smirking.

There was a sudden clamor in the crowd followed by silence as Astrid walked in, followed by a *human*.

Tonight's salon was not an official court gathering, but Naturals only ever brought their sired servants. No one had ever brought a lowly ghoul, or worse, a human. Astrid was known to be bold and provocative behind the scenes, but she had never openly sought scandal and everyone wondered whether she had lost her mind that night.

"Who is *she*?" Holly whispered, gazing at the meal – or pet that had just walked in like any other guest.

Astrid, who had dressed up and even fixed her hair for the occasion, walked assuredly ahead of an angry-faced Magdalena in her half-nun half-sweeper attire. The pair stopped in front of Heath to greet him and he eyed them with interest. Was Astrid provoking all of them by showing a mortal their world, in plain sight? Or was she just testing their limits before eating the girl?

"Good evening, Heath Thompson." she said, bowing before him. Like most Naturals, she sensed that he was dominant over her, and yet she did not bow low enough. An undisguised insult.

"Have you brought dinner or are you keeping her for later?" he asked with a sly grin.

"Sister Magdalena is my pet." Astrid said with a friendly smile, pushing the provocation even further.

"Sister?" he said. He noticed the silver crucifix around the girl's neck.

"So have you turned to religion now? Or to women?" Holly asked her in a provocative tone.

"Aren't these clothing the latest fashion in the Whitechapel brothels?" Astrid replied with a grin, as she eyed Holly's rather bold attire. The young Natural wore a black silk dress embroidered with gold threads, with a leather corset of the same color tied with black and gold laces that beautifully pushed up her blooming young chest. Feathers adorned the loose black curls that fell over her shoulders and she wore black diamonds as her jewelry. All she was missing was a whip, Astrid thought. She did not expect Heath would intervene, and he didn't. But another vampire stepped in.

"Good evening ladies, Mister Thompson." the man said, bowing his head. "Miss Holly, if I may, you look absolutely ravishing tonight." he then said with shining eyes.

Holly gazed at him with astonishment. He was the handsome Asian she had seen in Shadwell. It was rude enough for a sired vampire like him to invite himself into a conversation between Naturals, and even more so to compliment her in front of her father, who was one of the highest-ranking Naturals. She was rather pleased that the man turned out to be so daring.

"Who are you?" she asked.

"Holly, this is Shen, servant of Xiaolian, the Chinese ruler of the Limehouse and Shadwell districts of the East End." Heath said.

The man seemed displeased to be referred to only as a servant.

"Oh." Holly simply said, somewhat disappointed that he belonged to that woman. She was a very powerful Natural.

"We haven't seen you at court in some time. Have you any business with us, or... with my daughter?" Heath asked him, slightly annoyed.

"No, Sir. I merely came to see these newcomers and thought I would greet you. And Miss Holly." Shen said, excusing himself afterwards.

Heath smiled, satisfied, but he was not pleased to see his daughter gaze at the man as he walked away.

"Astrid!" a woman suddenly called out sharply.

Didier and Thi had joined them. The female vampire came up to the human close enough to breathe in her scent, then said: "Where is Diego?"

Magdalena did not answer – as Astrid had instructed her.

"It appears that Diego had a little accident and is no longer with us." Astrid replied in her place.

"She is the vampire hunter we had captured! She killed Diego!" Thi then said, turning to Heath. Had they been outside, Didier and Thi would have challenged Astrid, slightly higher in rank than them but outnumbered. But they were in Heath's salon, surrounded by his allies and some Apostles.

"A vampire hunter?" he said with a smile.

Astrid laughed.

"Not this one!" she said. "I found this fresh young virgin on the streets and thought I should keep her... for later."

Both statements were lies, since Magdalena was indeed a vampire hunter and was no longer a virgin. As for her ending up as a meal, she did not know yet.

"When we captured her, she was carrying a silver stake, a book of demonology and a pistol with silver bullets." Didier intervened. "Helping a human hunt our kind is high treason."

"And that's all the evidence you have? A few objects?" Astrid replied. "Well then, let's take her to court. Take us both to the Apostles!"

Another open challenge.

"Why are you so eager to go to trial before the Apostles?" Heath wondered.

Astrid raised her shoulders, unconcerned. Around the corner of her eye, she noticed that Ashok, Yojinbo and Yurei, had all moved closer to them.

"I was merely pointing out the lack of evidence against my pet." she said.

"Fair enough." Heath said. "Just make sure she doesn't leave your sight until you eat her or sire her, or then you *will* face the Apostles." The warning was serious.

"I'll excuse myself now, father. It smells like fish here." Holly said, glaring at Astrid. She was referring to the tall woman's origins as the daughter of a Norse sailor. Astrid was not usually seen in London, and she spent most of her time on the northern coasts. Some said she had inspired the legends about mermaids enticing and devouring sailors.

"I'll have a bite out of you too, someday." Astrid said, eyeing the feisty Holly from head to toe.

The crowd lightened around them, now assured that at least someone among them was an Apostle and that Astrid would be dealt with if she took the slightest step out of line. And the tall woman took her pet to a sofa and sat with her.

"What exactly are we doing?" Magdalena whispered, aware of the many eyes still on them.

"Confirming who are the Apostles in this crowd. They're all here, as I thought. Perhaps even the Dark Lord himself."

"How can you tell?"

"There are five vampire Apostles, so it's safe to assume the first five vampires who came forth when I provoked Heath are the Apostles."

"So now we know, what do we do?"

"We wait." Astrid said.

⌾

Meanwhile, Holly had retreated to a secluded chair behind a curtain. She hated this stupid vampire court and she hated her father. She wanted to be powerful enough to just get rid of her enemies, not so much to please him, but first and foremost to ensure her own survival. Power was the only thing that mattered at court, and if she lowered her guard even for a second she would be eliminated, either by her father or another Natural. But she was not that powerful, she was only pretending to be, for now at least. Her weakness infuriated her.

Shen again came to her. She didn't dislike him, and his boldness amused her. He was not afraid of angering her father like the rest of them. He was a tall and handsome man sired in his late twenties to early thirties, with an oval face and piercing black eyes. He wore his long and smooth black hair loose over his shoulders, and was well-groomed and clean-shaven. He looked quite dashing tonight in his traditional blue changshan tunic embroidered with dragons. She had never really been attracted to British men – they all looked the same to her and they were boring. Shen was different, not only in looks but also in character. He was exciting, and a little excitement was very welcome in this dreadful place.

He brought another chair close to hers and sat facing her.

"May I join you, Holly?" he politely asked her.

"You already have, so why ask?" she said, trying to look like she didn't care all that much what he did.

"I unintentionally overheard your conversation with your father. Holly, is he always like that?" he said with concern.

"I'm not afraid of him." she said, avoiding his inquisitive gaze. "Is there anything you need from me?"

"Just conversation." he said.

"Why would anyone want to talk to me?" she wondered.

She was the daughter of Heath Thompson: no one talked to her, for fear they might anger her father. But Shen was not afraid apparently.

"Why would I not want to?" he asked with a smile. "I saw you the other night in Shadwell, you were in a carriage. You went to investigate the fire in your family's mansion, didn't you? And you were the one who found out that vampire's involvement."

"And?"

"And I was very impressed." he simply said.

She finally broke into a gentle smile.

"I'm sorry for my attitude." she said. "Everyone at court is my enemy, so I am used to being suspicious of people."

"It makes perfect sense." he agreed. "This court can be treacherous, and I like how you put them all back in their places. Your straightforwardness is so very refreshing."

She smiled. She had heard rumors about him at court. Shen had the reputation of being a liar and a cunning man, but he was so very attractive she was quite willing to fall into whatever trap he had laid out for her.

"You're not very fond of Astrid, Didier and Thi." he remarked.

"I hate them... especially Thi. She acts like an Apostle!" she said.

"I only know that she was an aristocrat in her country as a mortal, who married a French officer." he said, always keeping to the facts.

"Well that probably explains her attitude." she sighed. "I wish I could be an Apostle too, but my father wants me to prove myself by..."

"By challenging and killing an Apostle." he said. "And if you don't, he will kill you."

"I'd like to see him try!" she said defiantly.

"Dear Holly, you are an amazing and strong woman," he said, "but there is no reason for you to fight so hard and on your own. Let me be your friend, your ally."

"Thompsons don't have *friends*." she said, lowering her gaze sadly.

"You hate this court, yet you covet the title of Apostle. Why, Holly? Is it to please your father? Is he that important to you?" he continued.

"No." she said hesitantly. She did not want to please her father, yet it would definitely earn her his respect if she did become an Apostle.

"I know why." Shen told her gently. "You are a dominant Natural. You have strong survival instincts and you can tell that other Naturals like Thi would eliminate you at the slightest chance. You are absolutely right to suspect everyone at court and want to protect yourself from them. And what you have seen leads you to believe that being an Apostle would place you in a safe position."

He could see through her very well.

"Am I wrong about that?" she asked him.

"I do not think you are wrong, and I would like to help you, if you would let me." he said.

"And then you would have an Apostle as an ally."

"Then I would be closer to you, Holly." he said. "Do you think I like this court, where people call me a 'dog without a leash'? Where Naturals insult me for trying to hold my place without the rank that goes with it? For trying to be someone without my mistress?"

"The vampires at court are stupid." she said. "You are someone, even without your mistress."

"Holly, you are so... precious." he said in a sensuous voice.

He took her hand and kissed it, and she removed it immediately.

"Are you offended that a sired vampire likes you?" he asked.

"No..." she said, blushing. "I was just... surprised."

"Then this means I trouble you." he said with a smile.

Of course he troubled her. How could he not?

"Not at all." she said, turning away from his piercing black eyes again.

"Please do not fear me, Holly." he said. "Why don't you come to my opium den in Limehouse sometime? We could talk in a more relaxed environment, away from the dangers of court."

He did not fail to notice the spark of interest in her eyes.

"I will think about it." she said with a smile.

Holly knew how much it would displease her father to see her frequent a sired vampire when she could make servants of her own, and that alone was a good enough reason to go to Shen. And she liked him. They were both frowned upon, she for her independent character and he as the neglected pet of a distant mistress who had no more use for him. So why shouldn't they see each other after all?

Limehouse was one of London's two Chinatowns, surrounding the Limehouse basin on the northern bank of the Thames. Shen's White Lotus was a rather upscale opium den among many cheaper establishments. Locals knew of vampires and suspected he was probably one of them, but he was a good businessman and the clients never got bitten – at least not in his den. The neighborhood had a very bad reputation and was said to be full of scoundrels and cutthroats, but all a vampire like Holly could see was fresh meat. She swept quietly through the dark streets that night, eyeing a few potential snacks for later, and entered the White Lotus. It was decorated in the Chinese fashion, its walls were white and the wooden floors covered with rich gold and blue carpets and mats, where Shen's human and non-human clients lay. He greeted her again with a kiss on the hand, like the refined man he was, and took her to a private salon to talk.

"Your opium den is crowded. Did you invite me here for dinner?" she asked, leaning over the small table between them. That night, she wore a red ball gown and a tight corset, layer upon layer of lace, frills and silk, and her hair was beautifully curled and adorned with red feathers. When outside, she wore a thick black velvet cloak, like many clients of his would, and he was delighted to discover her charms underneath.

"You mean you?" he asked, his eyes shining with promises.

She smiled, and he poured her a cup of green tea.

"I want you to feel at home here." he said. "This is a place where you can be yourself without always watching your back."

"You want me to feel at home, yet you are the one who is far away from home." she said. "I noticed that you speak English without any accent. You must have been here for a long time."

"Not so long, only ten years or so. But you are right, my home, Shanghai, is far away."

"What is Shanghai like?" she asked with interest.

"It is a very large and very crowded city, and a center of trade." he said. "In Shanghai, it is said you can buy anything. Because of its wealth, you will find there beautiful palaces, temples and pagodas. And because of your people, we are now partly under the colonial influence of the French, the British and the Americans." he told her, perfectly honest.

"Because of the Opium Wars?" she asked, frowning.

She had read about the wars between the British and the Chinese that took place before she was born, but of course only from the perspective of the British. She was curious to hear his version, as someone who had actually lived through them. There was a lot he could teach her.

"At first, the British wanted to trade with us and we agreed, but the product they wanted to sell in China was the opium they produced in their Indian colonies. This caused widespread addiction and social problems in our country. When we decided to put an end to it, they simply attacked us, and won. They used other incidents to attack us again and acquire more and more of our country." he explained.

"I didn't know that part, of course they don't mention it in our history books. I do hope the Chinese strike back!" she said with passion.

"The Chinese are strong and smart. I have no doubt someday we will rise again and remove the invaders. Meanwhile, I do profit from the situation. The British went to war with us to impose the sale of their opium in China. So I went into the opium business and sell it to the British instead. The money I make from the British goes back to Chinese banks. An eye for an eye." he said with a smile.

Holly would not have done the same, she thought. She would have led a riot and removed the foreign invaders from Shanghai. But Shen was a businessman, and he fought his enemies as a businessman.

"I must sound very stupid. All my knowledge comes from books and is limited." she said, lowering her gaze.

"Holly, you are not stupid in any way, and it is my pleasure to teach you anything you want to know." he said.

"I would like to see your country, someday..." she said, vaguely turning her gaze to the window beside them that had steamed up behind its wooden screen from the cold outside.

"Chinese winters can be as cold and miserable as here." he said. "But the summers are very hot and humid. It rains a lot."

"Hot and humid..." she repeated, gazing at him with shining eyes now.

He leaned forward and smiled.

"*Very* hot and humid." he said.

Holly was definitely beginning to feel the heat. Despite Shen's calm and composed demeanor, the sexual undertones in his deep voice left her quivering underneath her clothes.

"I see business is going well tonight." she then said, changing the subject.

He turned his head to a wooden screen by his side, behind which they could peek into the other room.

"Tonight we have a few bishops and cardinals. They often come on Saturday." he said. "And that man over there, he's a vampire, a Natural."

She had noticed the vampire when she came in.

"An Apostle?"

"Not him. But he frequents the court." he said. "I also brought you here to show you the sort of place where the human court and people of influence mingle with the vampire court. Decisions are made here, behind closed doors. The rulers of England are aware of us vampires and want to work with us. We have a common goal: to keep our streets peaceful. They leave us alone, we eat their lowlifes and criminals. It has always been that way and always will be."

"Why tell me this?" she asked, leaning back in her seat.

Minor decisions were, perhaps, made here behind closed doors, but the Dark Lord and the Apostles made the rules. She wanted to become one of them, not mingle with humans to get what she wanted.

"Because you want to be an Apostle." he said. "Do you even know how one becomes an Apostle?"

"They are nominated by the other Apostles. One can also challenge an Apostle to a duel and take their place, but since nobody knows who are the Apostles, challenging them would be difficult." she said.

"Some of my human customers know who are the Apostles." he said. "If I provide them with what they want, they provide me with information."

"And what could humans possibly want from us?" she wondered.

"Drugs. Food." he said.

"Food?" she repeated, perplexed.

"Have you ever heard of the Shanghai tunnels?" he asked with a grin.

"No." she said, embarrassed at how little she knew about London.

His eyes shone like two obsidians upon her, making her once again uncomfortable, but in a good sort of way.

"Of course when you go with vampires, you end up with a few bites." he said. "People like the Archbishop of Westminster, who is close to the Apostles, are already partly undead. They often want a little *extra* in their diet. I supply the fresh meat through special tunnels. My men lure wasted sailors to the back rooms of pubs and taverns, a revolving floor trap door opens and they fall into our tunnels, where we tie them up and shackle them, and ship them to the client. This service also provides for vampires who are too busy to hunt, or those who simply prefer to pay for a meal rather than get their hands dirty."

"Interesting." she said. "So you have another line of business."

"Indeed."

"But why share this information with me? What if I reported you?" she asked.

"You won't report me because everyone at court is your enemy." he said with a smile.

"You're not my enemy." she pointed out.

"Tonight, the Apostles are meeting in a secret venue. I couldn't get the names of those present, but I know the time and place, and what will be discussed. If we wanted to wipe them all out, with the right number of sired vampires, we could. Like I said, information is power." he said.

She gazed at him now with deepened interest. He understood that she knew very little about the vampire court, and he was willing to educate her, in exchange for her friendship, or, hopefully, more.

"Is my father an Apostle?" she asked him.

"I cannot confirm it yet, however I know that he is close to the Dark Lord."

She bit her lip to hide her anger. She would find out more about that.

"Be patient. Everything takes time." he told her.

"I'm not patient." she said, and he laughed.

"Well then, shall we skip the formalities and take off our clothes?" he joked, observing her reaction.

She certainly had not come only for his conversation, she was hoping for a little action, but of course that was not what a vampire of her rank was supposed to be thinking of, or saying to one of his rank.

"You're not answering..." he remarked, appraising her with his eyes.

"I can't wait to see you take off your clothes." she replied, taking him by surprise. Her eyes were the ones shining upon him now. And his face was no longer that of the wise businessman, but that of a young man who had just been shot with the flaming arrows of love. He was the one who was troubled now. She suddenly realized the awkwardness of her response and blushed.

"I mean..." she said.

He too blushed slightly and lowered his gaze for a moment, searching for his words.

"So you like older men?" he finally said.

"I like you." she stated.

She could tell he was not used to women approaching him so boldly, but he seemed to be liking it. He smiled at her now.

"Well then, Holly," he said, taking her hand, "let us leave politics aside for tonight and get to know each other better – in private."

He invited her to follow him to a bedroom upstairs, and she went with him. There, he prepared for her a special blend of opium which they smoked together while talking. Then, they lay on the bed and gazed at each other quietly. In the darkness and intimacy of this room, there was no need for masks.

"You're so quiet all of a sudden." she whispered after some time.

"I am savoring every moment spent with you tonight." he said.

And then she grew quiet, as words failed her. Her heart was racing in her chest and did not seem intent on calming down. She wondered whether he was pretending not to see it, or whether he needed her permission, as a Natural, to touch her. So she took his hand and placed it on her waist, and he moved closer.

"Weren't you the one who wanted to skip formalities and take off my clothes?" she said.

"You are so appetizing, I am debating where to start." he replied.

"You should start with a kiss." she suggested, trying not to sound too eager.

He leaned forward and kissed her, and she kissed him in return. He drew her closer and pressed his chest against hers, and she could feel his heart racing too. He was the one who was eager in fact. They kissed longly and his hands held her firmly while caressing her body gently. He then began to unlace the back of her dress while laying kisses on her chest. He removed her corset and skirts and proceeded to her belly, where he lay another trail of kisses. She stretched out on the bed, letting him do as he pleased. He took great care in removing her stockings and garter belt, enjoying the taste of her skin. It was dangerous play that could end with an unfortunate bite – and he was already taken. But he did not bite her.

He removed his clothes and let her play with him as she wanted now, gently pushing her back when she became too hungry for him. She ran her fingers through his long black hair that fell around her like a gentle curtain, and he caught her hand and kissed and tasted each of her fingers one by one. She traced the contours of his lips, his cheeks, his neck, and then his slender but muscular body. He then moved down and played her with his tongue and fingers like an expert, making her quiver and moan with delight. Shen was a treat, one to be enjoyed slowly and patiently, and she was the queen receiving this royal gift, or so he made her feel.

But Holly was eager for more. She whispered her demands in his ear and he finally offered himself to her with the devotion of a kind god, embracing her with gentle and caring arms. He rocked her slowly, careful not to hurt her inexperienced body, he teased her, kissed her, licked her, fueling her arousal until he finally took her over the edge a first time, and many, many more times after that.

"What are you thinking?" he asked her as they lay naked together afterwards, she on her side and his now warm body pressed against her back. His fingers moved slowly up and down the contours of her body, her breasts, her waist, her hips, her thighs, as she smoked his special brew. The smoke from the opium pipe made the air thick and heavy. He lay a kiss on her neck, then licked her skin slowly.

"Why do you need to know?" she asked him.

"You had never been with a man before. I need to know if I met your expectations." he whispered in her ear.

She had not wanted him to know that, but was there anything she could hide from him? He was too wise – and clearly too experienced with women – for that. As for her expectations, he had not only met them but surpassed them. He was so good in fact, that if not for his physical exhaustion, she would have been begging him for more.

"I'm not telling you anything." she teased him.

"Really? Then I will just have to make love to you again and again until you say it." he said, laying a kiss on her cheek.

She wouldn't mind that. Not at all.

"Be careful, you might end up falling in love with me." she warned him.

"Would it be such a bad thing?" he replied

She rolled over and gazed into his eyes intensely. She was the one who was falling in love, and she had been since that night when they spoke at her father's salon, and the more she got to know him, the more she fell for him.

"I know what those eyes mean." he told her gently and she removed her gaze from his.

"Don't hide from me..." he said. "A man wants to see a woman gaze at him with those eyes."

"Why would she, if the man does not gaze at her the same way?" she replied.

"Perhaps if she turned around, she would see that he does." he said, bringing her face back to his.

He kissed her slowly, taking all his time to taste her. No one had ever kissed her like this. No one had ever kissed her at all before him. No one had ever made love to her.

"Holly..." he said again, enjoying the sound of her foreign name. She gazed into his eyes and saw there the same spark she knew he had caught a glimpse of in hers. She wanted to bite him now, or for him to bite her.

"I love you and I want to bite you!" she suddenly said.

"You know I am already claimed." he reminded her.

"What if I claimed you instead?" she asked. "I would never treat you like a servant, I would treat you like a man."

He tightened his embrace around her, burying his face in her shoulder. She was reckless enough to challenge Xiaolian for him, but that would cause scandal at court because Holly was the daughter of Heath Thompson. Nevertheless, Shen liked the idea of belonging to a woman who would look up to him and respect him, a woman he could also look up to, a woman who would never to go another man because he was her first lover and no one could ever compare to him. He liked the idea and now it would never leave his mind.

6.

Tim once again found himself sitting in a room, except this was not a faded green and dusty room, it was a bright, flamboyant, red room, with red walls and carpets, luxurious mahogany furniture and marble statues of antique heroes and nymphs. He had not known his father to have such bad taste. But he was here, now, in his father's new mansion, and in front of him was not Humphrey the undertaker, but Heath Thompson. And, by his side, Holly.

Heath sat quietly behind his desk as though in the middle of important business, except there were no books, no papers, not even a fountain pen on his desk. Tim remembered him as a quiet lawyer, who kept his clients' secrets and never drew attention to their family, not as some royalty living in all this extravaganza. As for Holly, his dear little sister, so pure and innocent, there was nothing left of the child she was in his memories. The seductive temptress before him, almost bursting out of the corset of her ball gown, her hair decorated with feathers and pearls, was not Holly. He realized what a mistake he had made coming here, and the image of his sister he had clung to so desperately, the one he had been willing to die for as a human, had been nothing more than an illusion. He wondered how his memories could be so wrong, or if he had simply wanted to embellish them.

All this grief, the roaming, the desire to die to be reunited with his family again, the desire to rebuild the home they had together, all of it had been for nothing. His family was alive indeed, but they no longer were the same. Nothing would ever be the same again.

"So you too have changed, my son." Heath said, and Tim couldn't tell whether he was satisfied with what he saw or not. "What took you so long to join us at court?"

"Where is Esther?" Tim asked, evading his question.

"She also changed, and then she ran away with some handsome Swede." Heath said.

"He was someone else's servant." Holly added.

Her eyes flashed upon Tim and he understood the disguised warning. She knew or suspected something about the reasons for his presence with them. Tim knew that Cyril was his, but technically still Sofia's servant. If he told them the truth now, that they had exchanged more than blood vows and more than once, would that not just add more charges to Cyril's criminal record? Nothing would be as easy as he had thought.

"You haven't answered my question." Heath said.

"I changed a few weeks ago." Tim said, cautious. "I was attacked and, technically, killed by a ghoul. Then I woke up like this in a crypt. I had to figure out what I was and where I belonged on my own."

"Was this before or after the vampire Cyril Stewart set fire to our mansion?" Heath questioned him.

Holly's eyes flashed upon Tim again, silently warning him not to answer.

"You were misinformed, Father." Tim said. "The fire was an accident and I was the only one present. Please have this vampire's name cleared."

Heath laughed.

"The decision is not mine." he said. "But you haven't finished telling me your story. How did you find us?"

"One night, I walked into a place called the Hell's Pit." Tim said. "There were many vampires there. I told them my name and a man by the name of Joe the Mad Hatter brought me to court."

That last part was true. A few days prior, Tim had gone to the Hell's Pit and stood in front of the door, effectively drawing the attention of the regular vampires who went there. One of the vampires had come forth and introduced himself: he said people called him Joe the Mad Hatter. Tim recognized him as the vampire author he had once met. Joe was both shy and eccentric at the same time, and had a style of his own. Like many of his peers, he wore a black suit that night, but also a bold checkered tie and his hat was decorated with a playing card. He invited him to a private table, where they dined together. Joe was not as antisocial as Tim was, but only moderately social, and was not a regular of the Hell's Pit. He showed Tim a few card tricks to make him comfortable as he listened to the parts of his story Tim decided to share with him. Tim did not know Joe's rank but the man said he could take him to court to see his family, and he had not lied.

"Joe the Mad Hatter?" Holly asked, turning to her father. "I've never heard of him."

"Joseph Stein. He is a very old and eccentric Natural." Heath said. "Well, dear Tim, now you are here, hopefully you will stay for some time. I have great plans for you."

Tim appraised him with his eyes and his father did the same. They did not trust each other.

"Might as well." he said.

To his surprise, his father trusted him enough to let him stay with them and attend his salon, where he would be introduced to the elite. And they were all curious about this newcomer. Naturals and their servants flocked to Heath's salon now, and greeted Tim with seeming respect. Having been briefed on the vampire court customs, he understood that they were assessing how dominant he was and what were his chances of becoming an Apostle, or perhaps a future Dark Lord. This assessment had nothing to do with character or ambition, only with their senses, their perception of where he stood in the Naturals' hierarchy. And he found that, contrary to his reserved nature, he was considered a strong dominant, second or third perhaps in the hierarchy. And at the top was Heath, rumored to already be an Apostle or close to becoming one. And as his rank was established, so grew his sister's distrust of him. He didn't like what she had become, he didn't like her fancy dresses and jewelry, and she made no secret of her jealousy toward him. Still, he hoped that this was all for show, and that, inside, she was still his sweet little sister, the one who would never grow up and he could dote on forever.

One evening, when they were alone in their father's mansion, he caught her as she was about to leave dressed like a whore in his eyes, with a royal blue and gold silk gown that left little to imagination, a tight corset she seemed about to burst out of and a matching cape and small feathered hat. Her eyes were heavily painted but not her naturally rosy lips. She knew of her charms and how to accentuate them.

"Where are you going dressed like that?" he asked her.

"Is it any of your business?" she asked him defiantly.

"Are you seeing a man?"

"What if I am?"

Indeed, she had the right to see another vampire, or to play with a potential future servant, though he hated the idea.

"You've changed." he said.

"So have you." she said.

There seemed to be nothing left of the strong bond that used to exist between them, and it broke his heart. He wondered if there was any way to rekindle it in the stormy youth before him.

"*Unthrifty loveliness, why dost thou spend upon thyself thy beauty's legacy?*" he said, reciting one of the first sonnets they learned together.

She knew it by heart, he was sure of it, and yet she gazed at him with anger.

"Stop it, Tim. We're not children anymore." she said coldly.

"What is it you hate in vampire Tim? You used to love your older brother." he said.

"What is it you despise in me?" she asked him in return.

"Throwing on all those laces and feathers and accessories doesn't make you any more or less beautiful, it only makes you look cheap." he said in a reproachful tone.

He did not know why he didn't want her to dress that way: after all she was a grown up woman and there were other women at court who dressed provocatively. Holly did not have a reputation yet, but she was making a bad one for herself. Whoever she was seeing, it would soon be known. Hopefully, it was not an affair that would bring scandal upon her. Like she said, it was none of his business as Tim the vampire, but he felt that it was as Holly's older brother.

"You're an arrogant bastard like Father!" she said. "You only liked me when I pretended to be what you wanted and you could control me. But now you can't anymore; I will never let anyone control me again!"

Control her? When? How? He was not aware of having ever imposed anything on her. And yet perhaps he did. Perhaps she did not want to be that quiet little girl he doted on, but simply did not have the courage to stand up for herself back then. Perhaps she would have grown up this way anyway. Changing into her Natural form had certainly brought out the fierceness in her.

"I... I'm sorry if I ever tried to control you." Tim said, lowering his gaze, and she relaxed before him.

"Why didn't you tell Father about our encounter?" she asked him.

"I don't like the look in his eyes. And you, what do you know about Cyril?" he asked.

"Tim, we can tell if a vampire has exchanged blood vows with someone. And you came to us without a servant." she said. "This means that either your servant is dead, or that you want to protect them. After our mansion burned down, I went there to investigate and found Cyril's wallet. And now you want us to believe that you were there alone. So I take it he is the one you exchanged blood vows with."

"If you know this much, then why didn't you tell Father?" he asked her, frowning.

She gave him a cynical smile. Neither of them looked upon Heath as a father, and they were no longer brother and sister, at least for her.

"We're not a family, Tim." she said. "We are three dominant vampires competing for the title of Apostle and ultimately for the Dark Throne. In our world, one needs to keep themselves informed of others' moves. However, your involvement with a sired vampire is no threat to me."

"Could it be because you too are seeing a sired vampire?" he asked her.

"You know who I'm seeing." she said.

He had indeed seen her spend most of her time with the sired vampire Shen in the salons. So it was scandal she had chosen.

"I know it's none of my business, but Father says Shen uses people. He is cold and deceitful." he said.

"And you believe everything Father says?" she retorted. "Nobody truly knows Shen at court, they look down on him because he is not seen with his mistress. Do you think that's fair?"

"No, it's not." he agreed. "This whole system of master and servant is beyond ridiculous."

They agreed on one thing at least.

"Does he love you?" he then asked.

"Yes, I believe that he does." she said in a softer voice.

"As long as he loves you and treats you well, it's all that matters." he said.

Her eyes were gentle now, almost vulnerable.

"He does." she said, before leaving him.

❧

Like his sister had said, Tim found that this court was nothing but a place of schemes and intrigues between dominant vampires, and he disliked how his father pushed him to make allies and take sides. He made it very clear that Tim would be one of those who would dominate them and as such he might be challenged – and possibly killed, by those who sought power, including his sister. But Tim did not want to play those games, nor consider his own sister an enemy, no matter how much she may have changed.

He had never attended parties as a mortal, and they bored him as a vampire. He sat alone in a corner, observing the others, until he knew all their names and faces. Roland and Mary, the old couple from Cornwall, were probably the least dangerous to him. They came to him and introduced themselves, and sometimes made polite conversation with him after that. They seemed to have long given up any ambition at court. Perhaps they too understood the frivolousness of it all. Allan and Casper, much like Ashok and Rathika, were well-known and respected figures at court. No one stepped on their feet, or contradicted them. Allan was a Scottish knight and a Natural, and Casper was his sired follower. Tim preferred to use the term "follower" rather "servant" which seemed incredibly disrespectful to him, but then it did not seem to bother any other vampire to be called so.

Ashok was also a Natural and he called Rathika his "little Radha" though, unlike the Radha portrayed in legends, she was neither sweet nor lovestruck for him. Nevertheless they had a bond of a kind, and worked as a team on all fronts. Another peculiar couple were Didier and his wife Thi. They were a married couple as mortals, and both turned out to be Naturals and embraced the dark life. They seemed eternally enamored with each other, and often slipped away from others' sight to kiss and touch, as though they could not keep their hands off each other even for a few minutes. Thank goodness Cyril and him were not that immodest, Tim thought.

And then there were solitary Naturals like Mickey, who had transformed early in life and now was stuck forever in the body of a child. He used his appeal to get attention, and many of the female vampires at court doted on him. He never saw Joe the Mad Hatter at court, but he was told he too was a solitary.

The strangest characters though were Yojinbo and Yurei. Yojinbo was a short, muscular Japanese man, who wore the traditional samurai armor minus the helmet. Like the samurai were portrayed, he shaved the top of his head, above which was gathered his topknot, giving him an air of power. Most vampires, unless caught in their sleep, could easily avoid a stake and had no need for armor. It made Tim wonder whether he was protecting himself from something else. His young companion Yurei was even more mysterious. Pale white of skin and hair, he looked like an ageless child and moved almost like a ghost in his pure white kimono with vaporous sleeves. He never spoke, and let Yojinbo speak on his behalf. Tim could sense that Yojinbo was a Natural and he was not sure what exactly Yurei was, but they behaved as though the child was dominant over him. Siring children was a crime punishable by death in the vampire society, so Yurei had to be a Natural too, like Mickey. He was just... odd. He and Yojinbo came to him one night, in the secluded corner of a salon and bowed to him.

"You are always alone." Yojinbo said. It was more of a statement of fact than a conversation starter. By his side, Yurei gazed at the newcomer with shining eyes – eyes that did not belong to a child.

"Not anymore..." Tim said, slightly irritated, and it seemed to amuse the both of them.

"What do you not like at court?" Yojinbo asked.

"This..." Tim said, gesturing toward the rich furniture, the paintings, the statues, everything that needed not be there. He had no interest in objects, and little in people.

"The court is more sober where I come from." Yojinbo said.

"So, are you an Apostle?" Tim asked him directly, since they were alone.

"Are you looking for Apostles?" Yojinbo asked in return.

"Maybe." Tim said with caution.

Yurei turned to his companion and they exchanged a silent glance.

"Yurei says you can speak to him." Yojinbo then said.

So it was, as he had thought, Yurei who made the decisions in this pair, and the child had ties with the Apostles, or perhaps was one of them.

"How? Aren't they supposed to conceal their identity?" Tim asked, frowning.

The two in front of him stood perfectly still, waiting for him to speak, until he realized *they* were Apostles. Both of them.

"I see..." he said.

"You do not trust the Apostles. Why?" Yojinbo asked.

"They put bounties on innocent vampires." Tim risked saying.

Again, the short man and the child exchanged a glance, then he said: "The Apostles are willing to reopen a case and examine new evidence brought to them."

"And if the evidence does not convince them, what next? Do they kill the vampire who brought it forth?"

"Only if he has committed crimes too."

Tim rose from his seat and stood before them, conscious that he was asserting his dominance.

"The vampire Cyril Stewart has committed no crime." he said. "I was the 'human' he was seen with. As you can see, I am a vampire. And I was the one who accidentally set fire to my own house and jumped out the window to save myself from the flames. Cyril was not even there."

Would they believe his story when there were numerous witnesses?

"Human witnesses saw two men escape." Yojinbo stated.

"Humans are easily deceived and imagine things." Tim said. "And yes, I was seen trying to save my own life, alone. Will you prosecute me for it?"

He stood there, gazing at them defiantly.

"The Apostles will examine your situation and that of the vampire Cyril Stewart." Yojinbo finally said, excusing himself with Yurei.

So now it was all on the table before them – a big fat lie destined to appease them, and if his father was an Apostle, he too would know that he and Cyril were actually involved with each other. Tim would be in danger from now on, and have to watch his back every moment. But he had come here for Cyril, and he would not leave until justice was rendered, or what he thought should be justice. He knew it would be safer for him to stay somewhere else than with his father, but then would that not be the same as admitting that he had lied to the Apostles? He was like a criminal waiting for his trial now. There was however, one venue to get out of the mansion, at least for a few hours. He had to feed.

He excused himself and left the salon, and went down to the streets of London. Tim hated this upscale and fashionable part of town, so he took a cab back to the East End, his favorite walking and hunting ground. He found prey quickly. He had learned to hunt on his own and was both quiet and deadly. He was not the sort of vampire who seduced their victim and made the feeding process like a slow climax to ecstasy for them as they met their demise. He fed savagely, covering their mouths with his hand when they tried to scream. He did not enjoy giving pain or giving death, he was only doing what was natural for his kind. And his prey knew the dangers of being out in the streets at night in this part of town, just like he had known as a mortal.

After having fed on a sailor, he wandered the streets back to the place where it all began: the now abandoned Undertakers Inc. building. A "For Sale" sign now covered the business' name. He missed working there and earning a living like an honest man. He missed Fiona, Hanson and Humphrey. Would he ever see them again now? He had been a fool to go to his father alone and expect that he could intervene to pardon Cyril. The decision was probably not even in his hands, and if it was, Heath was no longer the man to listen or care. He had found that his father was now an ambitious man, interested only is asserting his power and influence at court. What had he been thinking?

He walked slowly down the empty streets until he spotted a humble-looking pub. He still had an appetite for human food, so he went in. Dressed in the fine clothes provided by his father, Tim expected to draw attention but he didn't. This was the sort of place where people of all classes gathered. He seated himself at a secluded table and ordered a full meal. He had pockets full of money now and could eat as much human food as he wanted. He made sure to take all the money his victims carried – both for his own use and to lure the police into thinking the dead bodies were just the result of a common robbery gone wrong. As he was eating, he noticed a curious pair seated in another corner. One of them was a tall female vampire with long blond hair who looked like a tavern wench, and the other was a human. The vampire was *feeding* the human rather than *feeding on her*, and seemed to take great pleasure in fattening her, or keeping her alive – whatever this sort of game was.

"Eat, my dear Magdalena." she said, offering her another bite of food.

Magdalena ate it, gazing at her companion with cautious eyes. Seeing the tension in her, Astrid then pretended to bring the next bite to her lips. When the human moved forward to grab it, the vampire laughed and let her have it. Eventually, Magdalena too broke into a smile and began to laugh at how silly she was behaving.

"You probably need to feed too." she said.

"I will take care of that later, and alone." Astrid said with a smile.

"There's no need to be shy. I've seen it all before." Magdalena reminded her.

"Well then." Astrid said, and she leaned forward as though she was going to take a bite out of the human, and instead licked the corner of her sweet mouth with her cold tongue. Magdalena opened her eyes wide and the other began to laugh.

A man in the pub then pulled out a fiddle and began to play an Irish tune. Several people began to clap their hands and others got up to dance. Two waitresses jumped over the counter and joined them. Astrid rose and invited her human to dance too.

"What is this dance?" Magdalena said, trying to follow the fast steps of the crowd around them.

"It's a jig!" the lively Astrid said, pulling her along.

"What should I do?"

"Just move your feet!" the vampire said.

Shamelessly lifting her skirts like the waitresses around her and dancing to the tune of the fiddle, Astrid looked no more vampire than anyone else in the crowd. It was hard for her human to believe that she just might *eat* any of the dancers later that night. Magdalena followed her, and danced, and laughed.

The daughter of a Norse sailor, Astrid had grown up between the coasts of Ireland, Scotland and Norway, and spent her youth in places like this, dancing to the sound of a fiddle and listening to the old sailors' tales. A bold girl, she had dressed like a boy and worked on her father's ship from a young age. She liked to drink, cuss and fight with men – and sleep with them afterwards. She had not lost any of the life in her as she transitioned to her Natural form. She knew she lacked the modesty and restraint to earn respect at court, and she didn't care. She saw in Magdalena a kindred spirit, but one bound by the shackles of society's impossible expectations of purity and goodness for women, and she was on a mission to break those shackles for her. And the vampire's constant efforts to wear out the human's solemn, grief-stricken demeanor were finally paying off, and she rather liked it after all. Magdalena realized that before she came to London, she had never enjoyed herself. She was a proper young lady, and then a proper sister, and then a proper vampire hunter. She had never experienced passion, danced a jig with a vampire, or truly been able to express her talents as a marksman. In London, she had known pain also, and grief. But it was not so bad now, with Astrid. Happiness was permitted with her, it was not a sin, nor shameful. Astrid did what she wanted and encouraged her to do the same. She was good to her, as a *friend*, she dared to think.

Tim was now one of the few customers remaining seated, and he observed them. They reminded him a little of himself and Cyril, when he would bring food to a reluctant and brooding human Tim, and entertain him with card games and books.

Soon, the female vampire noticed him but continued to dance. He turned his gaze away, embarrassed. He had not meant to spy on what now seemed like a pleasant evening between friends. He finished his meal and left the pub. Unsurprisingly, they followed him.

He led them to a dark alley where they could talk privately.

"What do you want from me?" he asked them, turning around.

They stood quietly before him, and the human, who had seemed so happy earlier, now was pointing a pistol at him. He could smell silver along with the scent of gunpowder. She was one of those *sweepers*, humans who thought they could rid the streets of vampires.

"Sorry but I can't leave any witnesses." the tall woman said.

"Why would I care what you do?" he asked.

"You're the son of Heath Thompson. I cannot trust you." she said in a dangerous voice.

"I did not come to court to be around that man, nor do I share his ambitions." Tim told her. "I don't care what you do or with whom. Leave me alone and I will leave you alone. But if you want to pick a fight, just know that I also fought vampires and ghouls as a human before I changed." His eyes moved to the young woman by her side.

The vampire's face relaxed and she gestured to her companion to lower the pistol.

"Well then. You're not the sort of man I assumed you were." she said.

"Why do you all act like it's a crime to interact with a human?" he said, irritated now. "I was simply watching you because you reminded me of me and..." He stopped before revealing Cyril's name.

"It sounds like we have a few things in common. My name is Astrid, and this is Sister Magdalena." the woman said.

"I'm Tim Thompson." Tim said.

Astrid suddenly broke into a loud laughter and now she reminded him of Hanson.

"Don't worry, I don't bite. Well, not that hard." she said. "I'm just a tall woman who likes the sea, taverns, and dancing a good jig."

"Can I go now?" Tim asked. He had nothing against her but he had not come here to make friends, nor did he have any interest.

"Oh, a solitary, huh?" Astrid said. "Of course you can go."

She moved aside and let him walk away.

"Target?" Magdalena then asked her.

"Not him. Not now." Astrid said. "Come, sweet one, we have work to do."

The two of them slipped out of the alley and moved quietly among the night crowd. They walked until they found what they were looking for: an old church with a high tower where Magdalena could hide as a sniper.

"Not fantastic, but it will do." she said.

"Will vampires come this close to a church?" Magdalena asked her.

"If we lure them, they will."

"And how do we lure them?"

"Provocation. Lust. It's not that hard. We'll start with a practice target, someone whose disappearance will not be investigated too thoroughly."

"Who... Mistress?" Magdalena said for the first time. She had learned the word while spending time among them at court. Shocked at first by their use of "master" and "servant" to define their place, it had grown on to her, much like their lifestyle, and she had secretly longed to call Astrid so, because Astrid was good to her. Even if it was only to eat her eventually.

Astrid gazed at her with puzzled eyes.

"You don't need to call me that. I have no intention of siring you." she said.

"Neither do I want to be sired."

"Then... why?" Astrid wondered.

"You make me feel... comfortable." Magdalena admitted.

"Well..." Astrid said, a little confused. "Don't get too comfortable with me. I am a vampire after all."

"I know that." Magdalena said. "So have you picked a practice target?"

"Yes." Astrid said, her face shifting into an evil grin. "Holly Thompson."

Tim returned to his father in the early hours of morning and found him alone in his office, reading a newspaper and smoking a cigar.

"A bishop was brutally murdered in the East End and ashes were found under him... interesting." Heath said, paying little attention to him.

"Father." Tim said, seating himself across from him.

"Is your sister out with that Chinese vampire again?" Heath asked, raising an eyebrow.

"Is it any of our concern?" Tim replied.

"It isn't, so long as they don't exchange blood vows." Heath said. "Holly is a high-ranking Natural like us, she has no business stealing another's pet."

"Shen is a *pet*?"

"He is the servant of a Natural, so yes, he is a *pet*."

Tim would not reply to such a stupid statement.

"And where were you?" Heath asked, putting down his newspaper.

"Hunting."

"All night?"

"I hunt in the East End. The prey tastes better there."

Heath laughed, satisfied with his son.

"I am pleased to see how well you have turned out... as a vampire." he said.

"Father... what happened? How and when did you change? I want to know." Tim said.

He at least wanted answers before the Apostles heard him, judged him, and, most likely, killed him. His had been a sudden transformation, but all his family members had become sick and appeared to die before some of them returned as vampires.

"It was a slow process." Heath said. "It was like a long sickness. Every day I grew angrier, weaker, more wary of daylight, and I thirsted for blood."

"Our blood?" Tim asked. He remembered how his father had shut himself away from them.

"Yes, your blood." Heath said.

"And then? What happened after you disappeared?"

"I wandered into a cemetery and lay in a crypt. I don't know why. I just knew I *had* to be there, it was the safest place for me. And then I died, and awakened again, and I knew what I was – and my place."

"Your place?"

"We Thompsons are destined to rule over all the other vampires. We are the supreme dominant clan." Heath explained. His eyes were filled with ambition and ambition only.

"So are you an Apostle?" Tim asked him, frowning.

"And so will you be." Heath grinned.

"What if I don't want to be?"

"You can't resist it. It is in your nature to dominate others."

Tim knew what he meant. From the beginning, he had wanted to dominate Cyril, to possess him, and the same feelings rushed through him when he killed. He did not want to subordinate others, but he *enjoyed* it.

"What about Holly? What are your plans for her?" he asked.

"Holly is immature and stupid." Heath said. "She fails to understand that the court rejecting her is proof of her dominance over them, and rather than face them, she accepts their judgement, and acts like a whore. But this rebellion won't last. She wants the title of Apostle and she will fight for it. I'm waiting to see how she will fight back."

"Holly is anything but stupid." Tim contradicted him.

In fact, he now believed that she had a lot more common sense than their father. She was choosing what made her happy rather than what made her powerful and respected, and her happiness was with Shen, no matter what others said.

"If you say so." Heath said.

"Surely you don't intend for all three of us to be Apostles though?" Tim said.

"That is right. I am dominant over you and Holly. I plan on becoming the next Dark Lord, and you will be my first lieutenant. Holly will be second lieutenant once she proves herself."

Tim was surprised at how easily his father shared his ambitions with him, and how he naturally expected his son's instincts to propel him to the highest rank next to him. He did not even know his son anymore yet he had already decided that he was fit for the role of Apostle, while his daughter had to prove herself before he would even trust her.

"We, the Thompsons, will bring forth a new era." Heath continued. "An era in which vampires will no longer hide their existence from humans, but will dominate them. London will be ours and humans will be the ones having to hide. The current Dark Lord and Apostles work together with the Queen of England and the Archbishop of Westminster to ensure that humans and vampires coexist, and that our existence remains in the shadows. They are weak. We are the dominant species, it is our birthright to rule them all!"

As Tim listened to his father's narcissistic ambitions and prejudice against his sister, he had only one desire: to punch him in the face. But even he could sense that Heath was more powerful than him, and would only kill him on the spot.

"You wanted to say something?" Heath asked him, as he noticed the dark flames in his eyes.

"Holly and I are both Thompsons too." Tim simply warned him.

"You *will* be an Apostle." his father told him again.

"Goodnight, Father." he said, rising from his seat.

The next evening, he inquired where he might find Yojinbo and Yurei, and was told they stayed in a humble inn in the East End, near an old church. Tim was surprised that high-ranking Apostles like themselves should pick such a place to stay, but then again, with their foreign features and attire, it was probably a better choice for them. Yurei could never pass as a human child under any circumstance, and Tim did not know yet *what* he was. He naturally frowned at the idea of going so close to a house of God, but after all he had died, hadn't he? And there was no God on the other side, no light, there was absolutely nothing.

He went to the inn and asked the owner to let the two know that Tim was there to see them. The old man went up a creaking stairway then returned and gestured him to go up. Tim went to their room and they let him in. Yojinbo sat around a wooden table with him while Yurei amused himself with toys on the bed, like an ordinary child.

"The Apostles are not ready to render their decision yet." the samurai told him, thinking he had come to find out the results of his request.

"I didn't come for that." Tim said.

"Then what do you want?" Yojinbo asked.

"My father... my father said that I will be an Apostle." he told him in a sad voice. "Where did he get that information?"

"It is being discussed." Yojinbo said.

"Why?" Tim asked. "Why me? I didn't ask for it. I didn't ask for any of this!"

"There are two ways to become an Apostle: one is to be chosen by us, the other is to challenge and kill one of us. That is how your father became one of us." the man said.

"What if I refuse both?" Tim asked.

"As an Apostle, you could pardon your friend." Yojinbo said. To him, it was that simple, but not to Tim. If he did become an Apostle, he would have to work with them, either imposing outdated rules on his kind, or imposing his father's reign of terror on humans. Of course, Cyril could then join him and live with him openly, but he would not be happy at court.

Yurei made what sounded like a soft hissing sound and Yojinbo turned to him, then back to Tim.

"Yurei and I support you." he said.

Supported him in what? In his plea for Cyril? In his opposition to his father? Or in his potential claim to the title of Apostle?

He shook his head.

"I will wait for my hearing." he said.

"Tim, an Apostle is not only a powerful vampire, but also one with a sense of justice. That is why you are being considered for the role." Yojinbo said.

"I don't believe in the rules the vampire society goes by, they are outdated." Tim said. "Master and servant... what nonsense!"

"It is a system based on collaboration." Yojinbo explained. "In my country, I was once a samurai. The word *samurai* means 'to serve', yet it is not the same as the word 'servant' here. Service is an act of devotion and courage. The lord is the decision-maker and offers protection to the samurai, who offers him his sword and loyalty in exchange. I think of the relationship between Naturals and their sired vampires as the relationship between a lord and his samurai."

"Except you are a Natural serving... something else." Tim said, gazing at Yurei.

"I am the bodyguard of an important person." Yojinbo simply answered. "Please, Tim, consider your options."

"Thank you, but I know what I want – and don't want." Tim said abruptly.

He left them and returned to his roaming of the streets – it seemed to have become his favorite pastime, hadn't it? He had come to court only for one thing, one he was not sure to obtain, but one he could obtain if he simply followed his nature and accepted the place they were most likely going to offer him. I was an extremely simple choice, and yet it went against everything he believed in. Could he renounce who he was for Cyril's sake? Could he rule over his kind as an Apostle? Could he work as a mediator between them and humans? Could he accept their system of service? No, he could not. He would never call Cyril his "servant".

He was preparing to return to his father's mansion when he heard footsteps coming from the seemingly abandoned old church, and moved up closer to it.

⁓

Shen sat alone in the dark back room of the White Lotus, staring at the wooden door. He needed to think, and usually did so better alone and in the dark. He had returned briefly to the apartment he shared with his mistress Xiaolian, only to find himself an intruder there, again. Xiaolian, the daughter of a general under the early Qing dynasty, had changed into her Natural form at the age of thirty, and sired her manservant and lover Shen, who then became her eternal servant, bound by the vows of blood they exchanged. At first, they had truly been in love, and their love had lasted for a century or so. But time had eroded their feelings, and now the only thing that held them together was that bond of blood and the obligations that came with it. An intelligent and hard-headed businesswoman, Xiaolian had built an empire of opium dens with his help and was involved in international human trafficking as well. They were filthy rich, but she was the mastermind behind it all and she never failed to remind him. He was only the pawn she moved as she pleased on the great chess board of her financial and political ambitions.

That night, he had found her, as usual, trying on some new jewelry she had purchased with the money he made for her in the dirtiest parts of town. He sat in a corner of the bedroom they had not shared in decades and observed her.

"Where are you going tonight?" he asked her in their language.

"To an important salon... not to some bitch, like you." she said, not even turning away from the mirror in which she admired her own reflection.

She was perfectly aware of his new affair, and did not care. She *did not care*. She could at least pretend to be angry or bothered by the fact that another Natural was stepping into her territory, but she did not. She acted like she was above that. He frowned.

"At least she doesn't ignore me like you do." he said calmly.

"I'm talking to you right now. You're the one who is never around." she remarked.

"And why would I be?" he said in an angry voice. He rose and kicked his chair to the ground. "I'm tired of being just a dog you drag on a leash! I'm a man, a man you once loved!"

Finally, the stone-cold woman turned around, but her words only froze his heart even more.

"Pick up that chair. Now." she said calmly.

"You pick up the damn chair!" he retorted. "If only you were not my mistress..."

"But I am, and you will *obey*." she said firmly.

"In our country, a woman serves her husband, not the other way around." he said.

"In our world, sired vampires serve their Natural master or mistress, not the other way around. Or does that wench get down on her knees and calls you 'Master'?" she asked.

"She does not care about my rank, she sees me as a man." he said. He clenched his fists with rage. He could not suffer to hear his mistress insult Holly like this, yet he was bound to obey her. He physically could not harm her.

"Are you falling in love?" she laughed. "How sweet! I hope this naive little girl knows who she is standing up against."

No. He hoped Xiaolian knew who she was standing up against. For Holly would not be alone in that fight, it would be the both of them against the vicious old woman.

"She is neither naive, nor a little girl, and someday she will become an Apostle." he warned her.

Xiaolian broke into a loud laughter. Again, she did not care. She did not imagine she could have any rivals in her servant's heart or at court.

"Be glad I keep you on a very long leash. I could keep you in a cage instead." she told him. "Now be a good servant and pick up that chair."

Everything inside him wanted to resist her, to defy her, but when the vampire master ordered, their servant was bound to do as they said. They simply could not go against them. Burning with rage inside, he picked up the chair, put it back in place, and left the room. He left the apartment where he was always ignored and humiliated, and took a cab back to Limehouse, to the warm, welcoming opium den where the other woman in his life, the one who had so simply and innocently claimed his heart, would meet him.

Holly was headstrong but also innocent and knew little of their world, and if she had fallen into another man's arms, he thought, that man could easily have taken advantage of her. He could have taken advantage of her too if he wanted. But she had found a way into his heart. She simply loved him for who he was and it deeply moved him, it had melted the ice around his cold heart. As for her, how could any man not love her? Her beauty far surpassed that of any other vampire, and behind that baby face was an intelligent mind as well. She was not cunning and scheming like Xiaolian, but she was quick to understand things and she did not think like every other vampire. Holly was unique, and devoted to him, and he was willing to do anything for her.

And that night, Holly indeed returned to the White Lotus. Tim's words about Shen troubled her a little, but not enough to keep her away from the man she loved. As for scandal, she already had a bad reputation anyway, she might as well own it. She had never really cared about what others thought of her, and was concerned only about how they treated her. She wanted to be respected, but between her father who saw her as an imbecile and her brother as a cheap whore, it seemed like no one would ever look past appearances. A book was judged by its cover and that only, especially at the vampire court. She was more than what they saw in her, but she had no idea how to express it and be respected. But Shen saw it all, or so she thought.

He smiled when she entered, like a captive would smile to his savior, and immediately went to take her cloak. He then led her to the bedroom upstairs where they always met. He had noticed small details about her, like the colors and fragrances she liked, and used them to create for her a romantic atmosphere. He had also noticed how she adopted his colors in her dress, the blue, gold and white of the White Lotus, perhaps in defiance of her father.

Once in the bedroom, he pinned her gently against the door and kissed her. He had truly missed her since their last encounter, and even though they met almost every night recently, he could not get enough of her, or she of him.

"I've missed you." he said in a sweet voice.

"I'm hungry for you." she said, kissing him again.

She let herself fall to her knees and pressed her head against his belly, breathing in his scent. Her hands then reached under his tunic and began to unfasten his pants, and he leaned back against the wall.

"Holly..." he gasped, as she found her favorite toy and began to play with it.

"You're mine." she said in a whisper.

Holly was not shy and she learned quickly. She already had all of his body mapped out and knew exactly what he liked the most. Unlike him, she did not play for hours, she gave him the best first, and then they could play as much as he wanted. Never had any woman been so eager, so devoted to him, and he only adored her even more for it.

When she had awakened his senses enough, she led him to the bed so he could finish what they had started, and he gave in to her demands again with tender devotion, and they lay together afterwards, breathless. She gazed at him with sparkling eyes, and kissed him, and he held her tightly, feeling her heart beat against his.

"What are you thinking?" she asked him when their lips parted.

"I'm losing myself in you..." he whispered.

"Then don't worry, for you are safe in me." she said, kissing his hand.

He had never been conquered by a woman like her before, but he loved how she took initiatives with him. She made him feel like a king, not a servant, not a plaything. A king.

"Have you any new information?" she then asked him.

Pleasure first, business later, such was her style.

"I do, actually." he said, sitting up and inviting her to do the same.

They put on silk robes and went over to the sofa, where he prepared her favorite blend of opium for her.

"I have new information regarding your plans." he then told her.

"What?" she asked, excited.

"First, your brother Tim visited an inn tonight. My informants told me that Yojinbo and Yurei are staying there."

Her undead blood froze. He had just come to court and was already selecting his allies, while she had been making only enemies. He was following their father's plans after all. It only made her even more bitter.

Shen then pulled a piece of paper from a cabinet and set it on the table before her.

"I also have this for you."

Holly couldn't believe what she was looking at. There, right before her, was a list of five names: those of the vampire Apostles.

"How did you get that?" she gasped.

"My humans talk, when given the right blends." he said. "Now we know who the Apostles are, all we have to do is stage a challenge with one of them, and you will take their place."

"But there's no way I can win a challenge against an older and more experienced Natural!" she said.

"I said *stage* a challenge." he said with a wise grin. "Now pick the one you hate the most."

She gazed at the list again: Didier, Thi, Yojinbo, Ashok, Heath, then pointed at Thi's name.

"Alright then, this means we also have to take out Didier." he said.

"Are you trying to discourage me? What's your plan?" she asked him, growing impatient.

He rose and put on a pair of gloves, then carefully opened an ornate box on a side table. He drew two silver stakes from it and placed them on the table before her.

"A double murder." he said. "We will only get one chance and we have to take out the pair. If we miss, they will report us to the Apostles. I will testify that you challenged Thi and that Didier tried to intervene in the duel, and thus had to be eliminated. Your father will support your claim to the title of Apostle if he believes you challenged them."

A vampire could legally challenge another to a duel and no other was allowed to interfere. But she was not so sure her father would support her.

"Father wants Tim to become an Apostle, not me." she said. "There's no way he will ever believe I won a duel."

"Heath Thompson eliminates those who are of no use to him, yet he has not touched you yet." he said. "I think he has plans for you to become an Apostle and he is waiting for you to prove yourself. He will certainly suspect you had help, but he will oversee it because he would rather support a member of his clan than anyone else."

"I wish I was not a Thompson, and I wish becoming an Apostle would displease him. I hate that man!" she said, biting her lip.

"But you are, and you can use it to your advantage. Who cares how you get to power, so long as you get there?" he told her.

"What if our plan fails?" she asked him. "My father will eliminate me then."

"If that's the case, we will be long gone before he hears of it." he assured her. "Every Chinese man in Limehouse and Shadwell is loyal to me. They will help us escape through the Shanghai tunnels. Xiaolian is the only other person who knows of them, and she won't collaborate with any non-Chinese. We keep our business among ourselves."

"Like the Thompson clan doesn't mingle with others?" she wondered.

"In a way, yes." he said.

"Aren't you breaking that law by sharing all of this with me?" she asked him.

"You are part of my clan now, Holly." he said, kissing her hand.

"Not until we exchange blood vows." she said.

She had mentioned it often, and he was liking the idea more and more. But it was still too early for her to challenge Xiaolian, he needed to make her an Apostle first.

The couple left the opium den and headed in the direction of the address where Thi and Didier were attending a salon that night. There, they waited for the pair to leave and followed them, and approached them in a secluded area. They could not murder them in plain sight, even at night, if there was the slightest chance of anyone seeing them. So instead, they invited them back to the White Lotus.

"You want to make friends with us now? And just why should we follow you?" Thi asked, placing her hands on her hips in a dominant stance.

"We know things you might want to know as well." Shen said.

"There is nothing that we don't know." Thi laughed at them.

"You don't know who are your allies and your enemies." Holly said.

Shen found it quite interesting how she could be so innocent with him and such a cold liar with others. They were a perfect match.

"And a spoiled little bitch like you is going to teach me?" Thi retorted. "What does your dear father think about you sleeping with someone else's servant?"

Holly was about to strike her but Shen discreetly placed his hand in front of her, holding her back.

"Tim Thompson has made a move." Shen told them. "He has begun to select his allies, and unless you want to see him become an Apostle very soon, you probably want to hear what we have to say."

Thi and Didier exchanged worried glances. They were not afraid of the explosive and disorganized Holly, but her brother was cold and calculating like their father, and he too was an ultra-dominant, they had sensed it. So they agreed to follow Shen and Holly back to the White Lotus. The four of them seated themselves in the back of the establishment, hidden behind wooden screens, and Shen served two separate brews. He watched quietly as the couple tried his special blend.

"How do you like it?" he asked.

"It's good quality." Thi said. "So, you like Asian men after all?" she asked Holly.

"And you have a problem with it?" the young woman replied.

"Not at all, as long as you only pet him." Thi said.

"What happens in my opium den stays in my opium den." Shen stated. "We have rooms we rent by the night too... if you ever wanted to try an exotic experience with our waitresses."

"I'll think about it." Thi said, and her husband moved closer to her.

"Anything for my queen." he whispered in her ear.

"Well then," she said, "here we are all together as good friends. What information did you want to share with us?"

Good friends? What a joke, Holly thought.

"My brother has made a move already." she said again, gazing at her. And the fierce woman appraised her with her shining eyes.

"Continue." she said.

"He was seen visiting Yojinbo and Yurei tonight."

"And why should this concern us?" Thi said.

"It should concern an Apostle." Shen said.

"I have no idea what you mean." she said.

But the brew was beginning to work its effects on them, and soon they became drowsy and eventually fell asleep. With methodical precision, Holly and Shen drew the silver stakes from a hiding place under the table, rose, and put them through their hearts. Holly watched the two bodies dissolve into ashes before them. So it was that simple after all. As a dominant Natural, all she had to do was put a stake through the hearts of the vampires she didn't like.

"So, how do you feel about your first murder?" Shen asked. Obviously, it was not his first.

"Powerful." she said almost in disbelief. She had liked it much more than she had expected.

"You are powerful, and beautiful." he said. "You are a queen."

"Your queen." she told him with a smile.

It had been an intense, thrilling – and uniquely arousing experience for Holly, and in the heat of the moment she drew her lover back to the bedroom. There, she pinned him against the wall and they kissed slowly and longly. Having his heart was no longer enough, she wanted to bite him and make him hers forever.

"Shen, do you love me?" she asked him, breathless from the way he aroused her.

He leaned over to her ear and whispered: "*Wo ai ni...*"

He kissed her again, and again, and she knew he was losing the battle to her. She was going to win.

"I don't care what happens anymore, I have to make you mine..." she said, as her lips brushed against his neck. The attraction of his scent and the desire for his blood were dizzying, intoxicating, but she needed his permission. He was not her servant, she would never treat him as such. But to her surprise, he pressed her head down against his neck and said: "I'm ready... Take me Holly!"

"Yes, my love." she whispered.

She bit his neck fiercely and drank his blood while her hands made their way underneath his clothes. She was showing her dominant side again, but surrendering to her was the most wonderful thing he had ever done. He leaned back against the wall and let her have her way with him, quivering under her sharp fangs and her playful fingers. The ecstasy of having their blood drank was the greatest experience for a vampire, but she intended to make it even better for him, and she worked her magic so well on him that he could not suppress a few cries when the pain and passion took him over the edge.

And when she was done drinking him, he sank to his knees, still breathless and dizzy, and lifted her skirts. Making his way up her leg, he chose a tender spot on her inner thigh and bit there. He was in a frenzy now, eager to drink her and become one with her forever in body and soul. He was surrendering both his heart and his life to a new mistress, but this time one who loved him and would make him free.

"It's your turn, my love... take me!" she whispered under his delicate touch.

Her knees weakened and she moaned with delight as he drank her blood, feeding on her slowly and amorously while his hands worshipped her legs. And as the waves of pleasure rushed through her body, so did her heart fall deeper and deeper in love with him. She would be his new mistress, but she was the one at his mercy. She felt strong, safe, and whole at last. So they were sinners now, forever. But being together forever was worth it!

When he removed his fangs from her skin, she let herself fall limply into his arms, unable to speak, unable to do anything but press herself against him, and he held her in a tight embrace.

❧

As she left his bed later that night to return home, Holly lay a kiss on her sleeping lover's hand and took the silver stake with her. Like her father said, the Thompsons were meant to rule over all others, and within the clan, she was third in the hierarchy. Tim had already made a move and selected at least one Apostle as his ally. How long until he saw a rival in her and eliminated her? She would not wait to see that happen, she would strike first! She would sneak into his room during the daytime and put a stake through his heart. All she would have to do then was get rid of his ashes and no one would know.

He was solitary and brooding, people would just assume he decided to leave court and not return.

As she swept through the empty streets she eventually noticed that she was being followed by another vampire, which was not in itself unusual. She turned around and faced Astrid. After all, this was her hunting territory, she had expected her to come out. They were in the slums, near an old church. A quiet place to hunt, or talk.

"Who's the stake for?" Astrid asked her roughly.

"It's none of your business." Holly replied.

"You're on my territory, so yes, it's my business."

"Well maybe I can use it on you then, and make this my territory." Holly said, drawing her weapon.

"Are you challenging another Natural? You've become bold all of a sudden." Astrid said. She wondered what was taking Magdalena so long: she had brought the target to her. Perhaps they were still out of range. She moved in a half-circle around her opponent, forcing her closer to the church.

"Halt!" a man's voice said.

It was Yojinbo, followed by Yurei. The man drew his katana sword and placed it between them.

"The life force of two Apostles has just vanished in the vicinity." he said, turning his gaze to Holly, then to Astrid, who was truly as surprised as him.

"I have no idea what's going on! She's the one with a weapon!" she said, pointing at Holly.

"Holly, did you kill them?" Yojinbo asked her.

"They challenged me!" she said.

"Have you any witnesses?"

"Shen... Shen is a witness!"

"She's lying!" Astrid retorted. "I saw the two of them lure Didier and Thi into the opium house! So that's what happened, you little bitch? You took care of them quietly like a coward?"

Needless to say, she was planning to do the exact same thing with her, and then with them.

Yojinbo gazed at them again, then said: "The council will review the incident. But weapons have been drawn here tonight. Holly, are you challenging the vampire Astrid?"

Damned rules! She had no choice now but to go on with the ritual, since it would be witnessed by an Apostle. Astrid, on the other hand, tensed. She had not planned this, and if Magdalena took a shot now they would both be exposed – and go to trial.

"Yes, I am challenging the vampire Astrid." Holly said in a confident voice.

"Very well then. Yurei and I will witness the duel." Yojinbo said. He retreated a little, leaving them enough room to fight.

And then, a shot was fired.

Holly barely had the time to hear the bullet coming at her when she was knocked to the ground by something – or someone. She looked up and saw her brother towering over her, and then she looked to her left and saw little Yurei on the ground. The silver bullet had hit him and he had fallen face first rather than dissolving into ashes like vampires and ghouls did.

"Shit!" Astrid said aloud.

"There's a sniper in the tower! Take shelter!" Tim shouted, pulling his sister away as more shots were fired. He had sensed the burning feeling of the silver bullet as it brushed against his skin and he knew that bullet was meant for vampires.

Yojinbo got into an alley in time, but Astrid didn't. A stray bullet hit her in the back and she fell to the ground in a sparkling rain of ashes. Meanwhile, Yurei's body lay there still. It was not bleeding nor dissolving.

"What the hell is going on?" Holly gasped, crouching with her brother behind the stone wall surrounding the church.

"There's a sniper up there. I heard noise earlier so I came here and watched what would happen." he said, gazing up at the tower.

"A sniper? You mean Astrid's pet, the girl with the pistols?"

"Yes, I think so."

Holly suddenly felt guilty for thinking about murdering him. The stupid fool had saved her life and now she couldn't go through with her plans. In all her youthful arrogance, she had thought herself strong and cruel enough to eliminate all her enemies, but she had misjudged Tim and almost murdered an innocent who wanted her no harm – at least not right now. She let go of the silver stake and it fell to the ground.

"What were you planning to do with that?" he asked her.

"I was going to murder you." she muttered.

"Fantastic." he said with sarcasm. Nothing surprised him anymore in the world they lived in.

"Look!" she suddenly said, pointing in the direction of Yurei's body.

The body was moving again, lifting itself back to an upright position as though it were a wooden plank. The child then turned around and gazed at the tower with a smile that chilled them all to the bone. The air turned cold, so cold, and even time seemed frozen.

"The Dark Lord..." Tim whispered.

"What?" Holly said, terrified.

More shots were fired but this time they went right through Yurei's body, that had become almost transparent like a ghost. The child levitated up to the tower and loud shrieks were heard, and then there was no sound.

⬿

Magdalena had been sitting there, trembling with fear and shock as she watched one of her stray bullets hit her mistress. And then she saw the demonic child rise again from the dead, or the undead or whatever he was, and fly up to her. Terrified, she fired more shots, but he seemed invincible to her bullets. And then he was floating in her face like an apparition from another world, smiling like a child ready to commit some mischief, except his crimson eyes were not those of a child. She screamed as her limbs were pulled apart in every direction, twisted and turned until her bones broke with a crunching sound. And he was still in her face, forcing her to look into his cruel eyes.

Finally, gathering the last of her strength, she grabbed her silver crucifix in her mouth and lunged forward. Only then did the child back away. And then his eyes turned black all the way, from pupil to sclera, and Magdalena felt her skin splitting across her entire body. She was being skinned alive and her lips could not make a sound. She rolled her eyes up to the dark sky and it was light again... the light she thought she had lost! And there were warm, welcoming arms stretched out to her. Mary's? No, these were the arms of the strong Astrid, her friend, her mistress. She was not going to Heaven, no, the gates of that world were closed to her. But if she could be with Astrid at least, in a quiet place, it would be enough. And so she left her body.

Tim and Holly's instincts told them not to move, not to intervene, for the creature they had just seen was no vampire, and they had no idea how to fight it, should it decide that they too were prey. After some time, Yojinbo came and stretched out his hand to them. Both of them tensed and huddled closer together.

"You have witnessed the Dark Lord's true form and powers, and you were wise to stay away. You may come out now. It is safe." he assured them.

"How can you say that *thing* is safe?" Tim said. His entire body was shaking now, thinking of what might have happened to them if they were in the way – or if the Dark Lord turned against them someday.

"Very well then. Yurei and I will leave." Yojinbo said. "Holly, you will present yourself to the Apostles tomorrow evening to explain what happened with Didier and Thi."

It was an order, an order from an Apostle. Holly shook with terror and gazed straight ahead. Yojinbo then left them and went to the tower, where

Yurei, now a seemingly normal vampire child, came out to meet him, and they walked away together in the night.

Tim and Holly relaxed a little. The young man let his head sink, overwhelmed by everything that had just happened and still trying to make sense of it.

"So... you murdered Didier and Thi, and then you were on your way to murder me, but Astrid, who was planning to have her sniper shoot you, caught up with you, and the Dark Lord got hit instead..." he said.

"Yes?" she said, unsure. It was a convoluted story indeed, but it was true.

"You murdered them... in cold blood." he repeated.

"We are dominants, Tim. It's what we do. We eliminate our enemies before they eliminate us." she said in a soft voice, as to convince herself, but it did not work.

"And may I ask why you wanted to kill me?" he asked.

"You secretly met with Yojinbo and Yurei. I thought you were plotting to kill me..." she said in a small voice.

"If I was plotting to kill you, why would I protect you from the sniper?" he said. "What makes you think everyone around you is your enemy?"

"Because they are!" she cried. Tears now streamed down her cheeks. "Tim, isn't what happened tonight proof enough? The moment I found myself alone, Astrid tried to kill me! But she couldn't gain anything from killing me, I think her true target was one of the Apostles. I was probably just an easy practice target for her."

"Am I... a fool for not seeing any of this?" he sighed.

He shook his head in defeat, and Holly burst into tears. He wrapped his arm around her shoulders and drew her closer.

"You're right to hate me... look at me!" she sobbed.

"You did what you thought you had to do in order to survive in our world. And you were right, for the most part." he said. "But I'm not your enemy. I'm your brother, Holly. I will always be your brother."

He rose and helped her up, and wiped away her tears.

"Don't cry, sister. We are Thompsons. Father may be a terrible man but he is right to say we are the dominant clan among all Naturals. We won't be so easily defeated, will we?" he told her with the same confidence as their father. She stared at him for a moment.

"What are we going to do now?" she then asked him.

"Go home, what else?"

"I can't! If they find me and Shen guilty, they will eliminate us!" she said.

"So what's your plan? To become a fugitive like my partner?" he asked.

"I knew it... I knew you were Cyril's master!" she said, pulling away from him. "So you and I are both guilty of the same thing."

"Did you... bite Shen?" he asked her in disbelief. "Holly, what were you thinking?"

"I'm in love!" she retorted. "Just like you are..."

They still resembled each other much more than they had thought.

"It looks like we both turned out to be rebels." he said with a soft smile.

"Let's run away together!" she said, taking his hand. "Shen will help us! We can escape through the Shanghai tunnels!"

"I can't. I came to court to ask the Apostles to pardon Cyril. I'm not leaving until they do."

"Holly!" a man's voice suddenly shouted. It was Shen, he came running to them and she threw herself into his arms.

"Where the hell were you? My sister almost got killed!" Tim told him, angry.

Shen gazed around them, then turned to Holly.

"Astrid exposed us! They know we did it!" she said, gripping his tunic in her trembling hands.

"Astrid had laid out a trap to have her sniper kill Holly, but Yojinbo and Yurei intervened. They were looking for whoever just murdered Didier and Thi." Tim explained. "Things got messy. Astrid and her sniper were killed, and Yurei... he's not one of us."

"Are you going to report us to the Apostles?" Shen asked him, pulling Holly away in a protective gesture.

"No. But it doesn't mean I approve what you did." Tim said. "I want no part in any of this."

"He was the one who was seen with Cyril as a human, and set our house on fire. They've exchanged blood vows, he's a criminal, like us." Holly told Shen.

"Do the Apostles know what you did?" Shen asked Tim.

"I lied to them and asked them to pardon Cyril. They have not granted me an audience yet." Tim said.

"Tim, the Apostles do not pardon sired vampires for their crimes." Shen warned him. "You will only attract your father's wrath and he will have you eliminated, just like his other daughter!"

"What? He killed Esther?" Holly said in shock. She had her suspicions, but no actual proof.

"Come with us, Tim. It's not worth it." Shen advised him.

"I can't." Tim replied. "I want to live free with Cyril."

"You're a Thompson. You can only serve your father or become his enemy. He will never let you live free. Neither you nor Holly." Shen said. His arms tightened around the woman he loved.

"Come with us, Tim." Holly begged him again. "Better to be outlaws than dead!"

"We need to go, now!" Shen urged him.

But Tim only shook his head.

"Shen," he said, "you are my brother now, please protect Holly."

The man nodded, and he pulled his sister away into the shadows.

⁘

Tim returned to Heath's mansion with a heavy heart. No, he did not want to run away, nor did he want to become an Apostle in order to obtain Cyril's pardon. He did not want to challenge other Naturals to assert his dominance or commit murder. The Thompson blood was cursed indeed: it was a lineage of power-hungry vampires competing with one another to rule them all. He would not be a part of that, never.

Cyril... Cyril was waiting for him back in Yvan's castle near Portsmouth. He lay in his bed feeling the emptiness around him. He thought the blond vampire should be there, by his side, where he could hold him again. He had been such a fool to leave what he had and come here. Now he may never get a chance to return to him!

Unable to sleep during the day, he got up and went around the mansion without a purpose. His father had nothing of interest to him and he wondered why the man spent so much time decorating the place to hold salons there. He was trying to make his way up by acquiring allies and keeping them near – something neither himself nor Holly could ever do.

He wandered into Heath's library, hoping to at least find a book to read until he could fall asleep. He noticed a pile of books with loose sheets of paper stuck in them on a corner table and went to examine them. Several of them were in a foreign language, Chinese or Japanese perhaps, and one was a dictionary of that language. He opened one of the books and browsed through its pages, appreciating the illustrations since he could not read the text. One page contained a sheet of paper with several words written on it: *yojinbo*, bodyguard, *yurei*, spirit, and *zashiki-warashi*, which was circled. Tim then opened the dictionary and looked up the word: it meant the ghost of a child. He immediately shut the dictionary, struck with horror. The last book in the pile was a book of exorcisms. Heath was investigating the true nature of the Dark Lord... to eliminate him! What was he thinking? Tim had seen Yurei's true form and it terrified even a dominant vampire like himself. It was so incredibly powerful, and its childlike appearance only added to the fear it inspired him. So Heath truly was intent on challenging forces beyond them in his insatiable quest for power.

And what if he warned Yojinbo and Yurei, he suddenly thought? Did they even need to be warned that an Apostle was planning to challenge and kill the Dark Lord? It was not hard to guess. Why had they not intervened then? Perhaps because they were ready to face him. He did not want his own father to meet the terrifying fate of that sniper whose desperate screams he could still hear. But Heath was looking for that sort of ending, wasn't he? None of this was Tim's business, but now he was involved in a lot of things that were none of his business. So he returned to his room instead, and lay on his bed, and waited. He'd had enough of all the intrigues, the danger, the power struggles. Now he only wanted to sleep. And he fell into a heavy slumber.

7.

Cyril gazed out the open window of his room, searching for the moon and stars, but there was nothing out there that night but the dark sky and clouds. It had only been a few weeks since Tim had gone, but it seemed like eternity had left him hanging on a cliff all this time, and his hero was not coming back to save him. Ever since Tim, the dark and brooding human, had entered his life, he had not been himself anymore. He had longed for him, missed him when he was gone, and lost appetite for all things other than Tim. And he loved him because Tim said out loud the things he thought and felt: the human said the truth about death, loneliness and grief in a world where those things were not discussed. Like all vampires, Cyril too had gone through terrible grief in his immortal life, which he hid under a smile, and Tim understood it. It was comforting to finally find someone who didn't put on a mask when facing the cruel reality. And from then on he had wanted them to work together, to face this reality and make it better. But they couldn't if Tim died at the hands of the Apostles.

There was a knock on the door and Fiona came in, carrying a tray with a bottle of blood and another of wine, and a glass.

"You should feed a little at least." she told him gently.

"I don't want to... I can't. I'm too worried." he said in a weak voice.

"Tim is fighting for you." she reminded him. She didn't say *"He will return."* for she too was not sure of it.

"Do you think they killed him already?" Cyril asked, slipping out of his seat. He came to her and grabbed her arms, and then, too weak to stand, he let himself fall to his knees.

"I don't know." she told him honestly. "But I know that if he returns he will want to find you in good health."

She helped him into a chair and poured him a glass of blood she then mixed with wine, as he liked it, and brought it to his lips. He drank reluctantly.

"You know, right now Tim is probably missing all the delicious food we get here." she told him with a smile and he laughed softly.

"Tim is a reckless fool for going away." he said.

"You knew that before exchanging blood vows with him." she remarked.

"True."

"He is also wary of others. He will be as careful as one can be." she said. She sat in a chair across from him.

"I came to let you know that Hanson, Humphrey and I will be leaving the country shortly. We can make arrangements for you to travel with us." she then told him.

"Where to?" he asked.

"Paris. I was going to reopen my business in England but it has become too dangerous for me and Hanson."

"It wouldn't be if you transformed him."

"Cyril, we're all going to be watched closely by the Apostles now – always." she said.

"But... if I came with you and Tim does return, how will he find us?" he asked.

"I gave Yvan the address. You can trust him."

"But Tim... Tim will be coming back for me. I can't leave him."

"I understand."

She rose and left him, and returned to Hanson who was waiting for her in their room. He sat on the bed and she joined him.

"He's staying." she told him.

"I would too in his place." Hanson said, drawing her into his arms.

She rested her head against his chest and listened to the sound of his young beating heart.

"I'm an old vampire... why did you fall in love with me?" she whispered.

"And you with me?" he said, amused.

"Because it was meant to be."

She had no doubts, no hesitation about the fact that he was meant for her. At first, when he began courting her, thinking she was a human like himself, she had thought him foolish. But he declared his love to her over and over, and with such passion she had finally given in and allowed him a few kisses. And then came the inevitable question: why was her skin so cold? She had tried to break up with him, but found herself helpless before his pleas. He told her he wanted to make her his wife, and that it didn't matter who or what she was. She had been a wife, a long, long time ago, before she awakened as a Natural, but it had been an arranged marriage. She did not know what it was like to be the wife of someone she loved. She decided to tell him she was a vampire, expecting him to change his mind and leave her, but he didn't. That was when she had decided that there could be no other man for her. Hanson was entirely devoted to her, ready to accept her and everything he did not yet know about her. And now she thought she had been foolish to refuse him the one thing he had been begging her for all along.

She moved to gaze into his eyes and he smiled at her gently.

"I don't want a servant, but..." she said.

"Cyril and Tim are not master and servant. They are partners, companions." he reminded her, cupping her delicate face with his hand. "And I am ready to be your *partner* for all eternity."

"Hanson..." she whispered.

He kissed her and drew her to the bed, and lay on her. They were not exactly fast in their relationship: they had been together for several years but had never done more than just kiss, mostly out of fear Fiona would lose control and bite him. And she did not want that.

"Hanson... I'm ready." she told him in a soft voice.

"I've always been ready." he said.

"I want it all, your flesh, your heart, your soul... I want you for all eternity." she whispered.

"I can't wait." he whispered in return.

He kissed her again and again, diving deep into her embrace, and she welcomed him without restraint this time. Removing their clothes, they lay naked together, exchanging more vows of love through their kisses. His hand finally discovered the cool softness of her skin, and explored it eagerly. He had been waiting for her for so long, he was like a lone wolf starved for her. His lips ravaged hers and she responded with even more passion, moaning softly as she reached the heights of a vampire's arousal.

"Hanson!" she begged him now, asking to be taken before she took him in the vampire way.

He obliged, giving himself to her. He held her as tightly as his human arms could, as their bodies rocked together in the quiet of the night. She no longer knew whether it was her heartbeat or his passion that rocked them so beautifully; she was lost, lost in him. He gazed into her eyes, penetrating her with his tender love and the heat of his passion at the same time. She cried softly as he again and again made her reach heights of ecstasy she had never known before. He was an insatiable lover, and she held back as long as she could, wanting to give him a chance to find his release. But soon the arousal was too painful to endure, and she sunk her teeth in his neck while he still made love to her. He moaned with delight, and as she drank him he finally reached his limits, crying out for her love.

She was the insatiable one now, pressing him against her chest as she drank, and drank him. He could feel lukewarm tears rolling down her cheeks and onto his skin now as new emotions overwhelmed her, and he too wanted to cry. He tensed when he felt like he was losing too much blood, and she immediately withdrew her fangs. They gazed at each other for a moment, breathless. She then slashed her wrist with her long nails and offered it to him. He took it and sucked the blood from the wound.

Having finally drank enough of her blood for the transformation to take place, he began to feel dizzy and let his head fall onto her shoulder. She held him in her embrace as his body changed, over the course of an hour or so. He was cold and stiff in her arms. For a moment, she wondered whether she had accidentally killed the one she loved so much. But then his heart started beating again, and his body went from stiff to soft again, and lukewarm like hers. When he opened his eyes again he was like her: a vampire. They were one at last, bound for all eternity by these vows of blood.

"How do you feel?" she asked him in a soft voice.

"It was a little scary but I'm happy now, happier than I've ever been..." he said with moist eyes. "It's like we're married now, isn't it?"

"It's more than that." she smiled.

He wiped away one last solitary tear from her cheek.

"So when does our honeymoon begin, my love?" he asked her with shining eyes.

"Now." she said, ready for more.

Days passed and Tim waited and waited for the hearing that would determine his and Cyril's fate. Holly had disappeared into the shadows with Shen shortly before the Apostles declared them guilty of the double murder of Didier and Thi, and a bounty was placed on their heads. She was right to run away. She had greater survival instincts than Tim, who thirsted for justice above all things. It was his one and only obsession: to obtain Cyril's pardon.

And one night, his father came to him.

"Come." Heath simply said.

He took him outside and they followed the street down to a small stairway leading to a tunnel closed by a heavy gate. To any humans, it might have seemed like an entrance to the city sewers, but it was not. Heath unlocked the gate and they went inside. They walked for a long time in a pitch black tunnel, but that was no problem for their vampire eyes. The paved way under their feet seemed to go down, deeper and deeper into the earth, and the tunnel narrowed to the point their shoulders were brushing on either side as they walked. The place smelled like mildew and gunpowder, and now and then Tim's feet crushed bones and skulls. Probably the leftovers of some vampire's snack, he thought. At the end of the tunnel were three doors, one in front of them and two on either side.

"From here on, you must go alone." Heath said.

He turned sharply and took the left door. Tim opened the door in front of him and continued. It opened onto a stairway going up this time, and as he went up he could see more and more light, until he came out into what he at first thought was broad daylight. He immediately covered his eyes and face with both arms, thinking he had been led into a trap and would burn alive, but he didn't. He was in the great hall of a cathedral and it was lit with this new thing called "electricity". He had heard of how bright and piercing its light could be but he had never actually seen it. Great chandeliers lit by this strange magic hung from the ceiling of the cathedral.

Around him on elevated rows were nine people, all wearing purple hooded robes and masks as to not be identified. He could sense that five of them were mortals and four were vampires. One of them would be his father. It suited him well, he who had been a lawyer as a mortal. Now he was a prosecutor. Ahead of Tim, on a gigantic gold throne that seemed to tower above them all, was an eleventh person, a child, dressed in a crimson robe and also wearing a mask: Yurei. So this was the Dark Lord's court of law...

"Timothy Thompson," a man started, "you have brought to this court new evidence regarding the incidents involving the vampire Cyril Stewart.

You stated that you were the one who set fire to your own house, and that you were alone that night. Is this correct?"

"Yes." Tim said boldly. There was no going back now. He would not escape them, but at least, if they believed his lies, perhaps he could save Cyril.

"The council will now vote to decide whether you will be eliminated or not." the man continued.

Eliminated. Straight to the point. Well at least he would get an answer quickly, he thought.

"Your Highness." another man's voice intervened. Tim recognized Yojinbo.

The child nodded in his direction.

"I would like to bring to your attention the fact that the defendant protected an Apostle from what appeared to be a premeditated murder attempt. He knew of the type of weapon used by the sniper and warned us to take shelter before more of us could get hit."

The child nodded again and gazed at the other council members.

"Council members, now cast your vote. Is the vampire Timothy Thompson a danger to our kind and should he be eliminated? Raise your hand if your answer is yes." the first man asked the others.

Four Apostles raised their hands and five didn't.

"Your Highness, please render your verdict. Life, or death?" the orator then said, turning to the Dark Lord.

The child stretched out his little hand and turned his thumb up, just like an ancient Roman emperor would decide of life or death on a gladiator. Apparently a thumbs up meant "let him live" in this court.

"The court has ruled that the defendant is not dangerous and should not be eliminated." the orator said. "Now the council will vote on whether or not it should pardon the vampire Cyril Stewart. The defendant attests that the rumors stating Cyril was seen regularly with a human were false, as he was the one seen with him and is not human."

"Your Highness," Heath's voice intervened, "the court should be made aware that the defendant has a personal interest in the vampire Cyril Stewart."

He spoke coldly and without any intent to support his son in obtaining the pardon of his beloved, whom he only saw as an obstacle in his ambitions for Tim.

"Objection!" another Apostle said, and Tim was surprised to recognize the voice of Joe the Mad Hatter, the eccentric man who had brought him to court.

"One of the Apostles here has a personal interest in keeping the vampire Cyril Stewart away from the defendant and should not be allowed to vote on this matter." Joe said.

The Dark Lord nodded. They voted again like the last time and the Dark Lord gave a thumbs down. Their answer was "no". Cyril would not be pardoned or live. Tim felt his heart sink. All this... all this for nothing! He was ready to rip all their heads off!

"The council will now vote to decide whether Timothy Thompson is to become an Apostle." the orator then said, to Tim's surprise.

They voted before his befuddled eyes and the final answer was a "yes". They wanted him to fill the empty seat on the side of the vampire Apostles.

"Timothy Thompson, the robe is yours, you may take your place among us." the orator then said, turning to him.

If he just took the robe and became one of them, then he would have some leverage on granting Cyril pardon. But that would also mean bowing to them, becoming involved in their intrigues, and always living with the fear of being challenged, murdered, or even dismembered and skinned alive by an angry Dark Lord.

"No." Tim said in a low voice at first.

"No?" the orator repeated, surprised. Apparently no one had ever refused the offer.

"No!" Tim shouted this time, furious. "What I have seen at court was nothing but greed, lies and manipulation! I can't believe such corrupt vampires deliver justice upon us who merely try to exist in this world! I want no part in it!"

There were whispers exchanged among the Apostles, and then all heard the voice of the Dark Lord for the first time.

"Tim is good. We like him." he simply said in his childlike voice.

Well at least the Dark Lord liked him, and he would not be dismembered today. He left the council without an escort and was not followed back to his father's mansion. Once there, he packed a few items including an extra silver stake, just in case, and headed out. As he passed his father's library though, he went to the foreign language book and took the piece of paper with the words written down by his father, folded it and tucked it into his pocket.

As he was about to cross the threshold of the mansion, Heath appeared behind him. When had he returned? He stood there in the hallway, tall and imposing in his black and red suit, his arms crossed.

"Where are you going?" he asked in a dangerous voice.

"Somewhere... anywhere but here." Tim replied.

"You made quite an impression today. Now the Dark Lord wants you as an Apostle even more." he said.

"My answer is still no."

"You are making a very grave mistake by refusing the place that was offered to you."

"And you have no idea what you're getting yourself into." Tim retorted. "I have seen the Dark Lord's true essence. What are you thinking? That you can destroy him with an exorcism? A talisman? Your ambitions will destroy you!"

"Then stay here. Let us fight that thing together!" Heath said.

"I want no part in any of it, neither do I ever want to see that... *thing* again." Tim said, shaking his head.

"Think about it." his father urged him. "Better to make friends with the right people and accept your place in the hierarchy. You could do anything you want as an Apostle, even obtain Cyril's pardon."

"You've heard their decision: I created much more of a scandal by burning down our house than him being potentially seen with a human, and yet I am the one who gets to live!"

"Cyril is not important to the vampire society. You are."

"That's exactly why I don't want to live among all of you!" Tim said in an angry voice.

"If you cross the threshold of this house, you will become my personal enemy." Heath now warned him. His eyes were darker and angrier than Tim had ever seen them before.

"If you kill the Dark Lord's pick for an Apostle, you'll be the next to die." Tim warned him in return.

"I don't need to do anything. I have minions everywhere working for me, and they have servants." Heath smiled.

"Farewell, Father." Tim said.

And he crossed the threshold and shut the door.

He was in real danger now. There was no official bounty on his head but Heath and his followers would be after him. He had to escape the city quickly before word got out to them – and it always got out very fast in the vampire world. Heath had told him that Cyril was not important because he was of low rank. How could they so naturally classify vampires according to their use and importance in society, and why were Naturals superior? He had only seen Naturals scheming and plotting to kill each other. Was that what made them superior? Did "important" simply mean "dangerous"? And why was he important then since he was not plotting to kill anyone?

He was headed in the direction of the port, to find the old Chinese man near the Dragon Gate, when he heard noise behind him. Already. That was fast, he thought.

He grabbed one of his silver stakes with his gloved hand, spun around and prepared to fight. Behind him were five vampires concealing their identity under black cloaks. One of them was slightly more powerful – a Natural. Without a word exchanged, they threw themselves at him. He rolled on the ground to avoid three of them and put the stake through the fourth and the fifth. Then, back on his feet in a second, he leapt onto the top of a building and the three others gave chase. He led them in the general direction he was going and didn't fail to notice several police blockades in the streets – probably not destined to stop him, rather to catch human smugglers. Dammit! That plan wouldn't work twice.

The three vampires including the Natural caught up to him on the flat roof of a storage building and attacked. He avoided them by leaping high and then staked one in his fall before rolling on the ground under the other. He accidentally put the stake through his private parts rather than his heart, but that disabled him long enough for Tim to strike again and hit the heart. The vampire dissolved into ashes, leaving only him and the Natural.

There was an extremely odd unspoken rule that many vampires – especially Naturals – would not carry weapons and fought with their bare hands. It was all about etiquette. Tim could too, of course, but he found that a stake did the job just fine. The other lunged at him and he threw his stake in the air and landed a punch in his stomach while the vampire swung at his face with his clawed hands. Tim then swiftly avoided another blow and, wrapping an arm around the man in a solid headlock, pulled out the other silver stake he was carrying and stabbed him in the chest.

"Sorry brother, you just have to be prepared in this world." he said as the vampire dissolved in his arms.

The sky was turning blue on the horizon now. Tim needed to find shelter and quickly. He could not afford to spend another day in London though, as more vampires would come after him. He could not even trust humans. Some of them may be future servants of vampires, waiting to be sired. He gazed at the police constables down on the street, standing in front of a makeshift barricade. No one was entering or leaving the port by carriage today. He then remembered Holly's words about the Shanghai tunnels – whatever that meant. Shen was an outlaw and not one of his father's minions, but surely his opium dens would be under surveillance now. He moved quickly, leaping from one rooftop to another, until he got to the area of the docks controlled by the Chinese. There, he let himself down into an alley and slipped into the back door of a building, which had been left unlocked. It was a small pub and it was closed. He hid behind the counter and closed his eyes, just for a moment.

When he awakened, a Chinese man was leaning over him and gazing at him with curious eyes. He was a human.

"I need to find Shen." he immediately said, and the man took a step back, realizing what he was. He rose and the frightened man took another step back, holding on to the counter.

"You're not in any danger." Tim assured him. "I need to get to the Shanghai tunnels."

The man seemed puzzled for a moment, then nodded and stretched out his hand. Money. Yes, of course, Tim had plenty of it with him. He drew a small purse filled with gold coins and threw it to him. The man opened his eyes wide as he counted the money, then smiled. He gestured him to wait there and left the room. He returned after some time and invited him to follow him. He took Tim to what appeared to be an ordinary storage room and closed the door. There was nothing of interest to him in that room, only crates – all of which were full anyway so he couldn't hide in them. And, then, as he was walking around the room, a revolving trap door opened under his feet and he fell onto an old dusty mattress. He had found the tunnels. Around the mattress were ropes and shackles, and he wondered what kind of business these tunnels were used for, but he could think about that later.

He immediately darted off into the dark corridor before him and ran as fast and as long as he could, until he came to a closed door. He opened it cautiously and came out into a large excavated underground cave equipped with railroad tracks, locomotives and freight wagons. It was a complete underground train station, fully equipped to transport illegal goods and probably people as well. A group of men, mostly Chinese, was busy loading goods onto the wagons. Each wagon was filled with crates smelling strongly of opium, which were then covered with coal. They froze as they saw him.

"I need to get to Portsmouth." he immediately told them. He pulled out another purse filled with coins and presented it to them. They took it cautiously and counted the money.

"*Ni qu nali?*" a man then asked him in Chinese.

Tim had no idea what he was asking. He shook his head and just said: "Portsmouth?"

"*Pucimaosi!*" another said, having apparently understood his request. They all nodded and smiled.

Tim promised himself he would learn Chinese after this.

He got into a wagon of coal as they indicated, and hid as best he could. He would need another suit, along with the Chinese language book. The underground train eventually took off and he was able to catch a few hours of sleep.

As he drifted into a heavy slumber, images of what had just happened in the past few days came back to him, mixed with the haunting screams of the unfortunate Sister Magdalena. He was a part of that world now. He had seen it and could never erase it from his memories. And that world wanted him – badly enough to try to prevent him from escaping the city of London. But he was returning to Cyril. He had chosen him over the life of intrigue and power struggles his position as a dominant Natural destined him to. He would be a criminal now too, even if no bounty was issued on his head; his father's hitmen would chase him relentlessly. Heath had made it very clear that no one could stand up against him and live. Had he also taken care of Esther as Shen said? Probably. Would he find Holly? She was smart enough to escape him, at least he hoped so. And he hoped Shen's love would calm her angry heart and turn her away from the path of murder. Not that he really cared about the act of murdering dangerous Naturals, he just thought there were more interesting things to do with one's undead life. Like working for a funeral home. He smiled in his sleep as he remembered the place and people that had made him feel safe.

The underground train eventually came to a halt in a small dark station, where more foreigners, this time mainly West Africans, unloaded the goods. Nobody seemed otherwise surprised to see a vampire jump out of a wagon and politely ask them the way out. They pointed to a small door leading to a staircase, and that staircase led to the back of another pub. Shen had this all figured out, Tim thought. There, he waited for nightfall and bought a horse to get out of town.

Heath had been wary of his son the moment he set foot in his mansion. It was something in his eyes. Once a reclusive and dark youth, wasting his time in books and contemplation rather than going out into the world, his son had turned into a powerful dominant like himself and he trusted no one. He was not displeased with that. But the Dark Lord wanted Tim, and Tim was gone. He needed to at least pretend to be searching for him to please his lord. He needed not tell him what he would do with him once he found him.

"The Dark Lord is very unhappy. As Tim's father, you should have kept him in your house." Yojinbo spoke in a low but dangerous voice.

Heath stood across him in the great cathedral. They were alone, he Yojinbo and Yurei. This was a private audience with the Dark Lord – and no one who valued their life looked forward to that.

"I did everything I could to convince him, but my son is young and stubborn." Heath said calmly.

"The Dark Lord thinks he is likely to gather followers and turn against us." Yojinbo continued.

"Followers? Tim? He is an antisocial." Heath said with a smile.

"That makes him all the more appealing to a certain kind of vampires."

He was talking about eccentrics and vampires with alternative lifestyles, like Joe and Fiona.

"My men are already looking for him." Heath assured them, and they seemed satisfied.

He returned to his mansion and one of his vampire servants, Lizzie, advised him that his guest had arrived. The poor Lizzie was just one of the many humans he had seduced, sired, and put to work for him. He worked her hard and drank her hard too, and as she stood, weak and thin before him, he could see that her days were numbered, unless he allowed her some time to hunt and recover. But that was a waste of his time. He would just have to kill her and replace her.

He went to the parlor and there found someone actually important: a guest from a faraway land.

"Greetings Miss..." he said, having forgotten how to pronounce her name.

"My name is Murasaki, High Priestess of the Shiwa Inari shrine of Iwate." the woman said. She too was a dominant Natural but he was dominant over her. She was a short Japanese woman dressed in the traditional attire of a priestess of her country under a dark cloak. Her smooth black hair fell well under her waist like a dark veil and everything about her appearance inspired respect. They sat together in the parlor and the servant closed the doors.

"Your servant will betray you and reveal your secrets to someone." she immediately said, gazing at the doors.

"My servant will die before she gets that far." Heath said with a smile. "No one knows of your presence here."

She took a sip of the wine that had been poured for her and frowned. She did not like the taste of it. She set it down on the table and he noticed how perfectly smooth and precise her moves were.

"You move with a grace of a feline." he noted.

"Surely, you didn't call a Japanese high priestess to your country to talk about my grace." Murasaki told him.

"Indeed." he said. "I am curious about one thing though. You said you are a high priestess, yet you are a vampire."

She smiled.

"Humans in my country do not live in fear of the underworld. Rather, they accept its existence and simply try to stay away from it. As undead beings with bodies, we vampires act as a liaison between humans and the underworld. We can provide guidance, and spells for them. In return, they turn a blind eye to our hunting practices."

"I see." he said.

"There is a Japanese Apostle in London. You want to know about him." she then said.

"Yes, but not only him." Heath said. "Yojinbo is a Natural like us, but the Dark Lord he serves, Yurei, is not. I've been trying to find out exactly what he is."

"In my country, *yurei* is a spirit or ghost. *Yojinbo* simply means 'body-guard'." Murasaki said.

"So they go by code names, like I thought." Heath said.

"A Natural should not be ashamed of their name, unless they are a criminal – or something else." she said.

"I think Yurei is a *zashiki-warashi*. Can you tell me more about them?" he said.

"*Zashiki-warashi* are ghosts of children that haunt houses." she said. "They are pranksters, but they are usually benevolent. Also, there would be no reason for a ghost to interact with the vampire world, let alone try to govern it."

"What if he was the ghost of a murdered child?"

"Still, he would be tied to the home where he died." she said.

"Do you recall any stories, any local tales where you come from?"

"There are many."

"I see. Is there no way you can find out more?" he asked.

"I would need to see them without being seen." she said. "I can do this through the ritual of fire."

"Perfect." he said with a grin. "And what will you need for this ritual?"

"I need a quiet place and a bonfire."

He took her to the basement of his mansion and cleared out a hole in the floor with a sledgehammer to build a bonfire. Then, after having purified herself with water and put on a clean robe, Murasaki installed herself in front of the flames.

"I shall now call upon Inari, the spirit of the fox. He will be my eyes and ears. You will lead him to the place where I can observe Yojinbo and Yurei." she instructed him.

"They will be at Miss Grey's place tonight." he said.

Murasaki sat on her heels in front of the flames for some time, reciting prayers, and the flames turned a deep purple color and adopted the shape of a fox spirit. Heath observed her from a distance. The purple fox stepped out of the flames and became almost transparent. It gazed at Heath now, ready to follow him.

They went to Miss Grey's mansion, and there positioned themselves in a corner. The fox slipped under a chair, unnoticed.

"Heath Thompson! I thought you wouldn't make it!" an old female vampire with an abundance of powder and rouge on her face said.

"I am a busy man. I shall probably not stay all night, but I wanted to greet you at least. You look divine, as always." he said, kissing her hand.

She was as ugly as they came, but it was his natural tendency to flatter and please everyone he met, until he determined how they could be of use to him. If they were of no use, like Holly, he didn't bother with flattery.

It was not long until Yojinbo and Yurei showed their undead faces. As always, they only stayed among the crowd long enough to greet the court members present, and then retreated to a corner to observe them. Yurei's gaze was fixed on Heath. Could he guess the presence of the fox spirit? Heath waited until the two were distracted to escape with the fox. He returned to the basement of his mansion where the priestess still sat in front of the fire, reciting prayers. The fox spirit returned to its home of flames, and then she finally turned to him.

"So, what did you find out?" he questioned her.

"Yurei is a malicious *zashiki-warashi* with a personal revenge against our kind, and Yojinbo is somehow involved. Only when his vengeance is accomplished will he return to his world." she said.

"That doesn't help me. I'm not going to lick his boots forever, nor help him do whatever he came here to do." Heath said, angered. "Have you nothing more to tell me?"

"Vampires cannot defeat ghosts because ghosts are vaporous in nature. They do not have a real body." she explained. "Unless you plan on becoming a ghost yourself."

"How does one do that?" he asked, interested.

"There is an exorcism..." she said, turning her gaze to the flames. "It is however irreversible."

"I don't care, as long as it makes me more powerful." he said.

"I can turn you into an *onryo*, a vengeful spirit. They are in essence more powerful than *zashiki-warashi*. You will lose your physical body but you will be able to interact with, and fight Yurei. In order to interact with the rest of the world, you will have to use your mind, or a bodyguard like he does."

"Then turn me into an *onryo*." he said without any hesitation.

"If you become an *onryo*, like the *zashiki-warashi*, you will be tied to the object of your revenge. Therefore, if the object of your revenge is Yurei, then you will disappear if he is eliminated." she warned him.

"Yurei is not the object of my anger or revenge." he said. "I just want to take his place."

"And why do you want to be Dark Lord of England? What is your purpose?" she questioned him further.

"To establish my family's dominion over all vampires." he said. "The Thompsons are meant to rule and dominate others. It is in my blood and my children's. Power should not be in the hands of the weak and complacent, it should be held by a firm hand."

"Very well then. And who will be your bodyguard?" she asked.

"I don't need one, I have many servants already."

Murasaki nodded and began to prepare the ritual. She wrote down symbols on a paper talisman and also collected some of Heath's blood in a goblet. She dipped her hand in a bowl of water, took the goblet and placed it in the fire while reciting more payers, and the flames did not hurt her. She then proceeded in the same way with the talisman. The moment it touched the flames, it caught fire and so did Heath's body.

"What are you doing to me, you bitch?" he cried out in pain.

"Shut up!" she ordered in a dangerous voice.

She continued to recite prayers as the vampire fell to the ground, twisted and turned, and howled in agony. His skin burned away and then his bones, until there was nothing left of him but a shapeless green mass. The mass then shaped again into a man's body and solidified, losing its green color for a white one. And Heath rose again, having reached his new form. He gazed at his hands in awe, and then his legs and the rest of his body. He sensed a new and incredible power rise within, as well as the burning desire to kill. And he could not resist the urge to kill right here, right now. He moved closer to Murasaki, who immediately stood and held a wooden amulet with symbols in his face.

"You shall not harm me!" she said in a low snarl. "*Akuryo taisan!*" she then shouted in her language, and he could not move. Of course, as a priestess she knew of exorcisms to protect herself too. He took a step back.

"I will not harm you." he agreed.

"Know your master and the one who made you." she reminded him.

He nodded and left the building. He would deal with her later. Now in the form of a spirit himself, he could move even faster than a vampire, on the ground, in the air, underwater – anywhere! He flew across the night sky to the outskirts of town, then back. He entered the houses of unsuspecting humans, frightening them almost to death. Too bad they didn't die, he thought. He was no longer thirsty for blood: now inside him raged the insatiable hunger for *death*. He wanted to kill, to see piles and piles of bodies rotting before him, and blood running across the pavement on the streets. He wanted to dismember and shred to pieces every living and undead soul out there. He knew this was probably the result of his new shape, and he tried to focus on his original goal. Yes, he was going to defeat Yurei and take his place. He was going to *annihilate* him.

And so, after exploring his new powers at length, he found Yojinbo and Yurei in their small room in a human inn, and entered through the wall, as walls meant nothing to him anymore.

Yojinbo immediately stood and drew his katana, while Yurei stood on the bed, his eyes fully black.

"I came to challenge the Dark Lord and take his place!" Heath said.

"You cannot fight here." Yojinbo said. He knew of Heath's ambitions and was not surprised to see him adopt another form to challenge his master.

"Teleport." Yurei said, and the next moment they were no longer in the inn but in the cathedral where the council met. The electric lights were off, and the large building was dark and empty. The perfect place for a duel.

Yojinbo retreated, as was the custom when witnessing a duel, and took shelter in one of the upper rows. The air turned cold and the room began to spin around the two opponents. It spun and spun, and sparks lit up the darkness on either side of them.

"Your tricks do not impress me, ghost!" Heath warned Yurei.

The child then flew over to him and he felt pressure applied to his limbs, but they were only illusory so it could not hurt him. He lunged forward himself and attacked. They were of equal strength, their mental forces colliding with the sound of thunder in this contained space. This was not a fight Heath could easily win, and he regretted not asking the priestess for more information about his opponent. From the corner of his eye, he noticed Yojinbo drawing an amulet from his clothes – the same Murasaki had used on him. He needed to take him out first.

Moving his arm in his direction, he ripped off the hand holding the amulet. Yojinbo cried out in pain and fell to his knees. He was wounded, but the loss of a limb would not kill him. All he had to do was put the hand back in place and it would attach again to his arm and heal, leaving only a scar. Yurei immediately moved to protect him. Why? Did the ghost's revenge have something to do with the mysterious samurai? Yurei attacked again, this time sending Heath crashing into the golden throne. A mistake. A moment of distraction was all it took. Heath immediately moved to dodge another attack and Murasaki appeared, seemingly out of nowhere, and placed herself between them. Reciting prayers, she moved slowly in the direction of Yurei, whose moves were restrained by her exorcism. With great difficulty, she stuck a paper talisman on the child's forehead and shouted: "He is immobilized. Heath, kill the vampire!"

"The vampire?" Heath asked, surprised.

"The vampire is his slave and the object of his revenge! Kill it and the *zashiki-warashi* will disappear!"

But how did a spirit kill a vampire, since all he had left were his mental powers? And then an idea came to him. Using his mind to detach a gigantic silver cross from the wall, he hurled it at Yojinbo. The cross impaled the vampire, who dissolved into sparkling ashes. Yurei let out a loud piercing shriek and disappeared and the paper talisman fell to the ground. Too bad the fight had been so short, Heath thought.

He went to Murasaki and gazed around them. They were alone now, the duel was over and he was the new Dark Lord of England.

"How did you know Yojinbo was Yurei's slave?" he asked her.

"I remembered a local folktale from Iwate." she said. "A samurai served a very young lord with connections to the Shogun, the ruler of all Japan. His late father had hopes that he would become the next Shogun. But the samurai lost his mind and began to drink his comrades' blood. He eventually attacked and killed his young lord and the child was said to haunt the family mansion. Struck with grief, the samurai committed suicide. The mansion was recently sold to an Englishman. Frightened by the presence of a ghost, he burned it to the ground."

"I see." he said. "So the samurai died and was reborn as a Natural, the *zashiki-warashi* chose a new country to govern and made the samurai serve him forever."

"That is what I believe happened."

"Why did you help me?" he then asked the woman as she picked up the paper talisman.

"I told you... know your master." she said, turning around. She gazed at him with shining eyes and he knew she had some sort of power over him.

"What... what did you do to me?" he asked, startled, as he realized the trap he had fallen into.

"I did exactly what you asked of me." she said, smiling. "I did forget to tell you one thing: the *onryo* is bound to serve the master who created him. If he kills the master, he too disappears."

"You... bitch!" he hissed, balling his fists.

"Let's make a deal." she then proposed. "You will need a bodyguard now, to accomplish your will in the physical world. I will be your bodyguard. You can rule as you please over England, and you will expand your rule to Asia, which I will control."

He relaxed and smiled. She had tricked him but they wanted the same thing, like all Naturals: to dominate all the others. He could learn to work with her, until he found a way to reverse her exorcism.

"You win. You can be my bodyguard." he agreed.

"Another thing..." she said, moving up close to him, her powerful talisman in hand. "In private, you shall call me *Mistress*."

Not even a night passed before the entire court knew the Dark Lord's throne had been taken by an Apostle, and most knew, or could guess, the name of their new ruler. There were now two vacant Apostle seats, two seats all the dominant Naturals would fight for.

235

"Ah! What interesting times we live in!" Joe said, leaning back in his chair.

Joseph Stein, otherwise known as Joe the Mad Hatter, was not exactly a regular of the Hell's Pit, but he went there with friends, sometimes. Born in the year 355 of the Christian calendar to a Jewish family in what the Romans then called Germania Inferior, he had died and awakened as a Natural around the age of twenty-three. He had seen the world change, the maps change; he had witnessed the persecution of his people across the ages, and he had lived through the great plagues. He had seen it all, he thought, until the recent events that unfolded in London.

He did not know Heath Thompson very well, but he knew without a doubt he was the new Dark Lord of England, and the mysterious Japanese woman who now stayed with him would be an Apostle. That still left one empty seat. He wondered who would claim it. The dark and rebellious Tim Thompson would be the perfect candidate, one who would bring change and keep the Dark Lord in check at all times, but he had declined the position, for now at least. Joe had no doubt Tim had exchanged blood vows with the vampire Cyril Stewart, who legally belonged to Sofia, but he had no intention of bringing it up to the council. After all, a little drama made immortal life so much more interesting, and the world would be such a boring place without a few renegades.

"Interesting? I would say *dangerous*." said Hugo, who sat across the table.

A middle-aged Scot, Hugo preferred the safety of a life in the shadows. They were both Naturals without servants, and good friends. They were not exactly socialites, but they enjoyed dining in both high-end and small restaurants like this one, and sometimes even appeared in salons.

"Isn't the daily special just amazing today?" Joe said, swallowing a mouthful of meat and vegetables.

"It's *heart*." Hugo said.

"Amazing..." Joe said. "Now, about the Apostle seats..."

"I'm not claiming one, are you?" Hugo asked. He did not know his friend already was an Apostle. He had been appointed to the role after Didier and Thi's deaths. Joe raised his shoulders.

"Who do you think will?" he asked.

"Why wonder when their identity will never be revealed to us anyway?"

"We could place bets." Joe said.

"And never know the result." Hugo pointed out.

"True." Joe said. Well, he would know at least.

Hugo did not really care who would become an Apostle. He was one of those for whom eternity was boring and though he secretly hoped to form a bond someday with a servant, he had never found that human yet.

"It's a pity Tim Thompson left the court..." Joe said.

"He wouldn't have stayed." Hugo smiled.

"You both need to brighten up." Joe said. "If I had your attitude I would've gone mad over the centuries!"

Hugo raised his shoulders, unconcerned.

"Gentlemen!" another man said cheerfully, who had just entered. He came to their table and seated himself with them. His name was Theodore and he too was an old but young-looking Natural. His servant Marc was not with him that night.

"Long time no see, Ted!" Joe said. "Anything interesting happening in Portsmouth?"

"Maybe." he said with shining eyes.

"Anything of interest to us?" Hugo added, not interested in small gossip.

"Well... one of our own just may have seen a vampire resembling Tim Thompson there." Ted said.

"And?" Hugo asked, already losing interest.

"Well, I don't know." Ted said. "Why would a powerful dominant like him suddenly leave the vampire court and London to go to Portsmouth?"

"Because he doesn't like our court." Hugo said.

"Or perhaps it was not him." Joe said. He knew exactly why Tim was headed there, and who he would meet, but they did not need to know.

"I find it very suspicious." Ted continued. "There are already rumors about him gathering a rebel force to overthrow the Dark Lord."

"I seriously doubt that." Joe said. "I've met him a few times: he is as antisocial as they come."

"Really? That's too bad." Ted sighed, disappointed.

"Do you have any problem with the Dark Lord?" Joe asked him, curious.

"No, not at all." Ted immediately said. "I just wonder about Tim Thompson's intentions, like many of us."

"If anything, I would be more worried about his sister Holly." Hugo said. "She escaped the city with Shen and they're likely to come back with the whole Chinese triad under their thumb."

"Fascinating." Joe said. "Love, intrigue and betrayal in the Orient... I will pen that down in a new book!"

Among other things, he was an author and ironically wrote many vampire stories for unsuspecting humans. Since they were merely works of fiction and his vampires slept in coffins, feared garlic and water, and he never revealed anything of their actual world to the public, this was tolerated by the other Apostles. It was his classy and innocent way of breaking the rules, just a little.

"Young Naturals these days are quite the rebels." Hugo remarked. "Hopefully the new Dark Lord will bring back order and tradition to our society."

"I do hope he doesn't, what a tragedy that would be!" Joe said.

"It's a wonder you two get along at all. You have nothing in common." Ted laughed.

"We do." Hugo said. "We're old."

Ted laughed even more.

"Well, gentlemen, I shall excuse myself now." Joe said, standing up. He dropped some coins on the table.

"Where are you going? The night is not over yet." Ted asked.

"I want to catch the night train." Joe said.

"*Where* are you going?" Hugo asked again.

It was not unusual for him to suddenly take off to some close or far away destination, and they only wanted to know whether he was traveling to another city, or to the Americas or Russia and when they could expect to see him again.

"To the coast. I might get some ideas there for my new book."

"You spend too much time playing, you should claim your place at court and among the Apostles." Ted advised him.

Joe laughed. If only they knew...

Holly sensed something, and she knew that Tim could sense it too, wherever he was. She turned to Shen who was browsing through a scroll in his language. They had escaped through the Shanghai tunnels and found passage to Asia on a boat, in the safety of large crates. They came out only at night, and sometimes took a little bite from an unsuspecting sailor in the shadows. Humans, unaware of their presence, thought they had contracted a fever and went about their business as usual. Their voyage would be a long one, but at least they were safe – for now, and they were together.

"Shen..." she whispered.

"What is it?" he asked, turning to her.

"Something happened... to my father." she said. "I don't know what it is but I can sense it."

Naturals like herself could feel the life force of their peers emerge, grow, or disappear – especially that of their blood relatives, but it was the first time she experienced it so strongly.

"You think he is dead?" Shen asked, frowning.

"Not dead, no. It's like... his power has increased tenfold!" she said.

"Perhaps he defeated the Dark Lord. He's been coveting the throne for a long time." he said.

"Yes, perhaps that's all it is. I hope so." she said with concern.

"You think it could be something else?"

"I'm not sure... but it frightens me. Just like that *thing*, Yurei."

"Either way, it's all behind us now." he said, practical. "We will find another place and make it our home."

"Until Xiaolian finds us." she remarked. He still belonged to her for all eternity – or at least until they murdered her. Too bad they didn't have a chance to do so before leaving England.

"If she does, I will kill her." he said coldly.

"What happens to a servant when their master dies?" she asked.

"It's like dying inside... or so I've heard." he said.

She did not want him to go through such suffering, yet it would ultimately be the only way to regain his freedom.

"You've changed." she said. "You, the man who worked in the shadows behind closed curtains and doors, have openly become an outlaw, both by murdering your kind and exchanging blood vows with me."

"I have no regrets." he said.

"Neither do I." she smiled.

He smiled and kissed her. And she kissed him again and again, hungrier for him than ever. Who cared about being an outlaw? The more dangerous their life, the more exciting it was! She knew she would never have found such excitement in the life at court she was eyeing. At most, she would have become an Apostle and bowed her head to people she hated all day, and eventually sired some uninteresting mortal to keep her company in the great loneliness of eternity. She understood now why vampires like Cyril and Tim broke the rules. There was nothing better than breaking them!

She unbuttoned the collar of his tunic and kissed his neck, breathing in his scent.

"Holly... soon I will have no more blood left." he gently protested.

"Then try to stop me." she said, taking a little bite.

He dropped his scroll and wrapped his arms around her as she drank his blood slowly, pouring into him the ecstasy of her love. And as she drank his hands found their way under her dress and up to her inner thighs. He played there, brushing his fingers against the scar he had made. He would drink her there again, and in other places too.

"You're the one who wants to be devoured." he reminded her.

"Whose fault is that?" she asked playfully.

After having thoroughly expressed their love for each other that night, they crept out onto the upper deck, where only one drunken sailor kept watch, and he was asleep. Together, they gazed at the endless black waves around them.

"What will we do in Hong Kong?" she wondered.

"Start a new life, open a new business." he said. He had done it before many times, but never with someone he cared for like her.

"Like the sort of business you conducted in England?"

"I'm ready to try something new – and less dangerous." he said.

"I could be your business partner." she said.

"You needn't worry about work or money." he told her with a smile. "I don't want another Xiaolian, I want Holly. Just Holly."

And they gazed longly at the waves together, as the ship took them quietly across the ocean to a new life.

8.

The bumpy road to Yvan's castle seemed the longest Tim had traveled in his life, but he was on his way home to the one who had been waiting for him, at last. A great sense of relief swept through him the moment he left the city of Portsmouth. He had not been followed. He could relax a little now, away from the court and its dangers. Away from his father. He could return to being just Tim, the undertaker, or whatever job he would find next. So long as Cyril and him were together, it didn't matter. But the road before him was long, so long!

Finally, after what seemed like the entire night, he reached the old gates of Yvan's castle. They were closed, of course. He abandoned his horse and climbed over the gates, and dashed across the property. He knocked loudly on the heavy wooden doors, but no answer came. Perhaps there was no one home, or perhaps something had happened. After all he had witnessed, he would not have been surprised if something had also happened to Cyril. It was possible, there was a bounty on his head after all. He began pounding on the doors frantically, until finally the old servant opened them.

"There is no need to knock so loudly..." the old man said.

"I... I'm sorry. I was worried something happened." Tim said.

"Nothing ever happens here." the man said before letting him in.

Relieved, Tim did not even bother to find Yvan, he ran up the stairs straight to Cyril's room and all but broke down the door. Cyril jumped out of the chair he had been seated in and stared at him in disbelief for some time.

"I'm back." Tim said, smiling.

Cyril ran to him and threw himself in his arms, crying and repeating his name over and over.

"It feels like an eternity since I could hold you like this." Tim whispered, overwhelmed with emotion.

"I never thought you would return, I thought they would kill you!" Cyril said in tears.

"My father did try... but I escaped." Tim said. "I'm sorry Cyril, I couldn't obtain your pardon after all." he then said, lowering his gaze.

"It doesn't matter. Having you here with me is much more important!" Cyril said. He kissed him, and they sat together around the table where Cyril had been having his dinner, or not so much of a dinner since he had little appetite. And gazing into each other's eyes and holding hands, Tim told him everything that had happened to him in London, and the choices he had made. It was different now, telling the story away from the heat of the intrigues and the dangers of court. It seemed like something that should belong in a novel rather than reality – especially the part about the Dark Lord of London being the ghost of a Japanese child lord with a revenge.

"If someone had told me what awaited me in London, I never would have believed them, not in a million years." Tim joked when his story was over.

"I would believe it. I have seen such things in our world." Cyril said.

"I should have listened to you and stayed away from it all. Now they want me as an Apostle." Tim said.

"Why did you refuse? You could do anything you want as an Apostle." Cyril asked, curious.

"No, I could not do the one thing I want most: to live a simple life with you." he smiled, and kissed his hand.

"And what are we going to do now?" Cyril asked.

"I don't know. Perhaps find Fiona, Hanson and Humphrey. Do you know where they moved to?"

"Paris."

"Then let's go there!"

After resting during the day, they went to Yvan in the evening and dined with him. He was intrigued by Tim's story, although he did not reveal to him the names of any of the people he had met, nor which of them were the Apostles, for his own safety.

"Well, all the more reason to stay away from London. I'm too old for all of that." the old vampire said.

"This is so good!" Tim said as he stuffed himself with the old servant's vampire-friendly human food. It had been a long time since he had eaten so well, and more importantly, in pleasant company.

"Seriously, Yvan, if anyone ever puts together a vampire cookbook, your cook's recipes should be in it." Cyril agreed, and Yvan laughed.

"A vampire cookbook?" Tim said, also laughing.

"I will try to talk him into writing them down, but he doesn't like to share his secrets." Yvan said.

Tim gazed at Yvan and what he saw was no longer an isolated, solitary vampire, living in the loneliness of his castle with only a servant, but a man living the life he wanted, with a human servant not bound to him by anything other than trust, and they both were happy in this mutual agreement. Undead life could truly be the continuation of one's normal life, only living by night and feeding on blood – sometimes. It did not have to be a separate society, run by a dark lord.

As much as Tim liked the old castle and the countryside though, he thought Cyril would prefer to be in a city with a lot of people and distractions, a city like Paris. It probably had its own dark lord, but nobody would know them, or bother them there.

"So I hear Fiona has moved her business to Paris." he said.

"Indeed. She left the address with me in case you wanted to join her." Yvan said.

"Will you come to visit?" Cyril asked.

"I don't really travel anymore, but you're welcome to come back here anytime." Yvan smiled.

And so the next evening, Tim and Cyril headed out to Portsmouth on horseback, this time enjoying the pleasant ride together. Once in the city, they abandoned their horses and went on foot to the port in search of a ship they could board easily and without being seen. It was there they were approached by Joe. He stepped out of the shadows where he had been waiting and approached them casually. Tim's hand immediately moved to his stake while Cyril hid his face under the hood of his cloak.

"There is no need for that, my friend." Joe said, waving his hand in a friendly gesture.

He was dressed elegantly as usual, and carried a small travel bag.

"What do you want?" Tim asked him, suspicious.

"I just want to talk. Let's go to one of the pubs, it will be more comfortable. There are no boats leaving until morning anyway."

"I have nothing to say to an Apostle." Tim said firmly.

"Ah, well that's good because I am no longer one. Your father should be receiving my letter of resignation tonight." Joe said.

"My father? What do you mean?" Tim asked, surprised.

"Come with me and I will tell you all about the new Dark Lord." Joe said with a smile. "I carry no weapons." he added.

Tim and Cyril reluctantly followed him into a pub, where he ordered them all some food and drinks, as any human customers would. The little pub was packed, and many of the late-night diners were passengers from the last ship grabbing a bite before heading to their hotels for the night.

"A lot has happened at court since you left." Joe told Tim. "Your father brought in some Japanese priestess, and they defeated both Yojinbo and Yurei. Your father is now the Dark Lord, and she his favorite Apostle."

"He defeated that thing?" Tim asked in shock. He had indeed sensed a change in his father's life force but he did not know how to read into such feelings.

"Thing? Explain." Joe said, curious.

"You mean you don't know?" Tim said.

"I only know the part I told you. Only you know exactly what happened between the murders of Didier, Thi and Astrid, the sniper in the tower whose body was found in shreds the next day, and the disappearance of Holly and Shen."

"I saw... something terrifying, even for a dominant vampire like myself." Tim said.

"Yurei was not a vampire, right? What was he?" Joe asked.

"I'm not sure." Tim said. He remembered the piece of paper he stole from his father's library. He drew it from his pocket and placed it on the table.

"Bodyguard... spirit... *zashiki-warashi*." Joe read, fascinated. "I wouldn't be surprised if Heath recruited that Japanese priestess to exorcise the damned thing."

"So now he is the Dark Lord..." Tim said.

"What are his next plans?" Cyril asked.

"He wants the Thompsons to dominate all vampires, and vampires to dominate humans." Tim said.

"Glad I left then. I don't think I would enjoy that." Joe said, stretching out on his chair. "I'm going to be in trouble soon anyway."

"Why?" Tim asked.

"Everything you have told me is so exciting, I plan to write a book about it." he said with a grin.

"Doing that would expose all of us!" Tim said, raising his voice.

"Calm down." Joe urged him softly. "No real names will be used. But I think someone needs to tell the story of Tim, the vampire who said 'no' to the Apostles and the rules, and Holly and Shen's forbidden romance laced with murder. And they need to know that the Dark Lord was not even a vampire.

Tim, we are all being duped and you brought things to light! The vampires need to know!" he insisted.

"And then there will be a bounty on all three of our heads." Tim said.

"We'll be in other countries by then, and your sister is probably headed to China, or even India now." Joe said. "Vampires need a new hero to free them from this stupid caste system of masters and servants, a hero like you, Tim. We need to stop enslaving and murdering each other for power, and begin to live at last!"

"You're playing with fire." Tim said.

"Well I've been around for over a thousand years and never got burned yet." Joe said with a grin. "Besides, once I become the number one public enemy by sharing the Apostle's secrets, you and Cyril will quickly be forgotten."

"I think he should write that book." Cyril said. "We're all outlaws anyway at this point, how much worse does it get?"

"You said you were leaving England, where do you plan to go? We're headed to Paris." Tim told Joe.

"Paris? Fantastic! What a wonderful place to write a book! I can't wait to see Montmartre again. I haven't been there in ages!" Joe said.

"Oh, right. You've probably traveled a lot." Tim said. "Is there a dark lord down there too?"

"There used to be, but I don't know anymore... the French don't like monarchs very much."

"Well then, you'd better come with us." Tim said. "Just for resigning from your position, you'll be on my father's blacklist by tomorrow night."

"Very true!" Joe laughed. "Well then, shall we go board a ship to France?"

The trio headed back to the docks and found a ship going to Le Havre, from which they would be able to travel to Paris either by boat on the Seine river, or by train. The ship left mid-morning and it was only a journey of a few hours on a ferry boat, so they hid inside it until sundown, then went out into the city.

Le Havre was one of those charming French coastal cities, with stone buildings and their stone tile roofs lined up along the port, and cobblestone streets. Seagulls flew around the port, calling out to each other, and fishermen prepared their boats to go out fishing during the night. Spring had only just arrived and the townspeople were preparing to celebrate Carnival. There would be parades and costumes, and the whole city was getting ready for the festivities. Restaurants and hotels were packed with travelers, so the trio went to the town square as they waited for a place to open up so they could eat and perhaps rent a room. The small square too was pretty crowded, and people enjoyed the music played by a band here, while a man entertained a crowd with stories there. A small circus had also settled in town, and Tim saw lions and elephants for the first time. Cyril laughed when he asked him which one would taste better, and replied he had never tried either. They lost Joe the Mad Hatter, but only for a moment, for he was soon found entertaining a small crowd with magic tricks.

"I never imagined life could be so pleasant." Tim told Cyril, slipping his arm around his shoulder.

"It can be, when you decide to live it." Cyril said with a smile.

They rented a room for the night, and hid there out of sight during the day. It was not so easy in the small room they found for it had large windows, so they hung up blankets and their cloaks to block out the light. In the evening, they boarded an overnight train to Paris.

The ride was long and monotonous, but Tim and Cyril were happy, and so was Joe, jotting down notes in a notebook for his scandalous novel about the vampire court of England.

"How is your book going?" Tim eventually asked him.

"Fantastic!" Joe said with shining eyes before returning to his writing. "Should my passionate heroine fall immediately for the handsome Indian prince or should she put up a fight against her responsible but controlling brother first, then run back to her lover in despair?"

Tim laughed.

"She should try to murder her brother." he said.

"Great idea! I love it!" Joe said, excited.

"And I think the prince should be Egyptian." Tim said.

"And give her a good whipping." Cyril added.

"Oh, I see you are a reader of my other books too!" Joe said, exchanging an accomplice smile with him.

"You seem quite experienced with women, for a man I've only ever seen around other men." Tim said, intrigued.

"Me? Oh no! I've never been with a woman, not even once." Joe laughed, slightly embarrassed.

"Then why do you write about it? You could just... do it." Tim said, now truly confused.

"I'm terribly shy with women actually." Joe confessed. "Perhaps my stories are a way to do things I would never do in real life. Yes... I like to think of all my female readers hiding my books under their pillows and secretly reading them at night, after their husbands have fallen asleep. I'd rather give them beautiful dreams with my words than touch their bodies."

"You give men beautiful dreams too." Cyril said with a grin.

"All the better." Joe said, smiling.

"You're a strange man." Tim said.

A sudden jolt was felt and the train came to a halt. All passengers exchanged curious glances, wondering what happened.

"Are we being attacked?" Tim whispered, frowning. He reached for the silver stake he now always carried strapped around his body, in a protective leather case.

Joe gestured him to sit still while he poked his head out a side door to find out more. He returned a few moments later and sat in his seat, looking annoyed but not angry or worried.

"Well, what happened? Did they find us?" Cyril asked, anxious.

"No." Joe said. "The train hit a cow."

"A cow?" Tim said, puzzled.

"This is France, not the East End of London." he said. "We're in the middle of nowhere. There's nothing around us except farms and cows."

"Will the train be able to continue?" Cyril asked.

"I heard them say there's damage to a wheel, they will need to bring a new locomotive from the next town on the line. I doubt that will happen before dawn. We could try to make it to Rouen on foot and get a hotel, or find a barn around here where we could sleep tomorrow."

He gazed out the window, evaluating their options.

"What would you rather do?" Tim asked Cyril.

"I don't really like barns..." Cyril said.

"Neither do I." Joe said. "Well, my friends, how about a little night stroll in the countryside?"

So they left the train and continued on foot. The city of Rouen was only an hour away, and they were able to check in to a hotel there, where they hid from the sun the next day.

After the sun set, Joe told them he wanted to visit the city that night. He hadn't been there since the Middle Ages, when his people were driven out of the city, and he wanted to see how much it had changed since. They had no objection: after all, they had all eternity to enjoy themselves and make it to Paris and their friends.

∽

The city of Rouen, on the banks of the Seine river, had been one of the largest and most prosperous continental cities in the Middle Ages, and had retained an antique, fairytale-like charm with its half-timbered houses and cobblestone streets. Notre-Dame of Rouen Cathedral, a beautiful gothic cathedral with its great arches and ornate facade, stood solemnly in the downtown area, surrounded by theaters and small restaurants. Rouen Castle was the place where Joan of Arc had been imprisoned before being burned at the stake – a favorite story among vampires, who loved dramatic tales with a sad ending. The most interesting sight for Tim though was the *Gros Horloge*, Rouen's Great Clock installed in a Renaissance arch crossing the street. It had a painted sun dial and also pictured the moon phases and – more impressive – it still worked after five centuries. While Cyril appreciated its aesthetic qualities, Tim wondered how long humans had been observing the sky, the sun, the moon, calculating and mapping time. Joe then took them to the botanical gardens and the opera, and they very much enjoyed it. Vampires traveling for leisure and sightseeing. Tim had never thought it possible. It was in fact just like humans traveling, except they had to be cautious of the sun. In the crowded streets, they had not heard the footsteps following them, and were very surprised to hear someone calling out to them.

"Joseph? Incroyable!" a man said in French.

They turned around and found themselves face-to-face with another Natural. Tim immediately tensed, fearing another Apostle or some French equivalent. But Joe went to him and embraced him.

"Philippe!" he said, overjoyed.

The man named Philippe kissed his cheeks and Joe did the same with him.

"Where have you been all these centuries?" Philippe asked him.

"Where have *you* been?" Joe asked in return.

"Are these people your friends?"

"Yes, this is Tim and Cyril."

"Enchanté!" Philippe said. He went up to them and kissed both their cheeks.

Tim stared at the man with wide eyes and Joe laughed.

"It's just how people greet each other here." he explained.

"Good to know." Tim said. He would never get used to that custom.

"Oh, sorry, sorry." Philippe said. "Are your friends British?"

"Yes, they are." Joe said. "We're here sightseeing."

"Out here, with all the *sweepers*?" Philippe said, frowning.

"You mean vampire hunters?" Tim asked.

"Yes... they hunt us. Especially near the cathedrals and churches."

"We haven't met any. Our greatest excitement along the way has been our train hitting a cow." Tim said with what sounded to the Frenchman like typical British humor, and he laughed.

"Oh, *mon ami*, your friends are amazing! Please, do come to my house so we can talk more." he said.

"Are there any other vampires there?" Tim asked, always cautious.

"Oh no, not tonight. Why?" Philippe asked.

"Tim is a solitary." Joe explained.

They followed him to the large mansion he owned in the downtown area, and he offered them expensive wine and cigars. Philippe was a fashionable French vampire with long blond hair and a friendly face. He had changed in his early thirties and had the tastes of many a gentleman his age. He liked music, theater, and also photography. He begged them to agree to be immortalized – as though they were not already immortal – in a photograph, which he gave them after developing it.

"I hope you'll forgive my innocent pastimes." he said. "I just love all things new and modern!"

Tim liked his comfort and was wary of anything new. He didn't understand Philippe, nor did he understand why a black and white image of them showing all their scars and imperfections was better than an embellished painting in color, but Cyril liked it, so they kept it.

"Nowadays everyone wants a photograph, especially at weddings. Are you married?" he asked him and Cyril. They had never thought about it. Vampires didn't *marry*. Or did they here? Was there a possibility for a master and servant to marry in the French vampire society? And could they still marry if they were both men?

"Don't you have masters and servants here?" Tim asked him.

"Of course we do, but it's not practiced so strictly. France is famous for its libertines. I too was one, back in the day." he laughed.

So he had sired several servants, and they did not live with him.

"I take it you aren't anymore?" Joe asked him playfully.

"Oh, there are only so many different types of people in this world. One gets tired after a while." he said.

"Where are your servants then?" Tim wondered.

"Let's see..." Philippe said. "Hortense lives in the South of France – she's a lovely girl who runs a hat shop open only at night. Olivier and Francine became a couple and they live not too far from here. We have dinner together sometimes. Marianne, Chloe and Gabrielle I have lost track of."

"So these vampires were all your lovers at some point, and now they don't live with you but are still bound to obey you?" Tim asked, confused.

"Obey me? No, my dear. I don't want or need anyone to obey me. Why can we not all live peacefully, enjoying love when it comes and friendship when love fades away?" Philippe said.

Tim did not think he would tolerate any outsiders in his relationship with Cyril.

"And what about rulers?" Tim asked. "Do you have a dark lord?"

"Not anymore. We beheaded him during the Revolution." Philippe said.

That was one way of dealing with the problem. The French were very straightforward apparently.

"Then who rules over the vampires?" Tim asked.

"Well we have the Freemasons, I guess." Philippe said. "They are a secret society of humans and vampires that protects us. But they are not our kings or lords, they are more like the police."

Tim was relieved to find that there may not be such a thing a the vampire court with Apostles here. He might actually like this country after all. He would have to learn French, along with Chinese.

"Freemasons? Interesting." Joe said. "Do they help with the *sweeper* problem?"

"The upper clergy is on our side and tolerates us as long as we remain out of sight. It is the lower clergy that preaches to passionate young humans that they should hunt us down and kill us. They don't realize most of those they recruit will meet an early end. We don't want to kill these ignorant humans, but they attack us..."

"Why not hire them instead, and turn them against the clergy?" Tim suggested, remembering Astrid and her human pet.

"That's an interesting idea. I will definitely pass it along." Philippe said.

"And what do you do about criminals within the vampire society?" Cyril asked him. He was not aware of bounties being issued internationally, but things could always change.

"Depending on the crime, they can be banished or put to death, though most of us are in favor of banishment."

Cyril relaxed a little.

"Now tell me all about you." Philippe said. "You seem very interested in politics, Tim, were you thinking of joining our Freemasons?"

"No, I have no interest." Tim shook his head. He'd had enough of that world.

"And what about you Cyril?"

"I just want to live my life in peace." Cyril said.

"I see. You two must be an old couple!" Philippe laughed, and they laughed along with him.

He refilled their glasses and brought more cigars.

"And you Joe, surely you're involved in some new and interesting business, or perhaps in the arts?"

"I'm writing a new scandalous book actually." Joe said.

"Oh, we love scandal here! What is it about?" Philippe said, excited.

"I don't think you should..." Tim began to say, but it was too late. Joe was already telling his friend all about it.

"It's about the dreadful vampire society of England, bound by archaic laws oppressing us." Joe said. "The hero is a bold and rebellious young vampire who goes to court to save his love from a certain death. There, he stands up for his fellow vampires of all ranks and status, defying the Apostles, and refuses to take part in their schemes. He reveals to all vampires they are being duped, and their Dark Lord is actually a ghost. Deceived by the court, his sister, a passionate, sensuous youth in full bloom, tries to murder him. But her attempt fails and he forgives her, and instead helps her escape with her lover, a handsome Egyptian vampire sired by another woman. Free at last, the hero and his sister decide to follow their hearts and never return."

"That sounds absolutely fabulous!" Philippe said, clapping his hands. "I do hope the hero's sister and the handsome Egyptian make passionate love in the end on the ship taking them away from England!"

"Hey!" Tim said, angered at the way his friend had portrayed his sister.

"Oh... that's a great idea!" Joe said. He took out his notebook and jotted down a few words.

"You should read the Marquis De Sade for some sultry ideas." Philippe suggested.

"I most certainly will." Joe said, who was always in search of new and preferably salacious or scandalous reads.

Cyril laughed at the mortified expression on Tim's face, and he eventually laughed too.

Life was not that bad after all, not as dark and gloomy as it had seemed back in England. They went to bed in the early hours of morning, feeling free and happy at last. But Joe and Philippe's world was not Tim's. As he lay with his companion that night, he asked him: "What do you think of Philippe?"

"I think he is pleasant company." Cyril said.

"How do you feel about the things he said? Is it true that love inevitably fades away and turns into friendship?"

"It can... Are you worried about us?"

"I don't know."

"Tim." Cyril said, bringing his hands to his face that still bore the scar from that fateful night. "We are not Philippe, and Philippe is not Joe. Everyone is different."

"I don't want to share you with anyone else – ever." Tim said, drawing him closer.

"I'm all yours." Cyril assured him.

"I do miss our friends though." Tim then said.

"We'll be heading to Paris soon." Cyril told him. "I know they are safe. Fiona has been around longer than me. She knows what to do."

"I just want a normal life with you and our friends. I want us to live in a normal house and work an honest job. In fact, I'd like to continue working as an undertaker for Fiona."

"It doesn't pay that much. We may have to share a small room somewhere, unless you plan on robbing a lot of humans." Cyril remarked.

"A room is enough for me." Tim said.

"We'll need a little library at least." Cyril said.

"Of course." Tim smiled.

The next evening, it was decided that Tim and Cyril would continue on to Paris, while Joe would spend more time with his friend and gather ideas for his novel before joining them. So, after a quick feed near the station, Tim and Cyril boarded the night train, and this time enjoyed an uninterrupted ride to Paris.

Paris was, like London, a very large city with a bustling nightlife. They arrived at the Saint-Lazare station near the Paris opera and not so far from the Louvre palace – two places they would have to see sometime, but they were headed to the Quartier du Marais on the other side of town. They easily found a carriage outside the station that would take them to their friends.

"Shall I make haste or would you like to take a more romantic route?" the coachman asked them with a wink.

"The romantic route." Cyril immediately said.

Tim was not enthusiastic about it at first, as he really wanted to see their friends, but the Marais neighborhood was not that far, the coachman assured them, and he did find the ride quite pleasant after all. He had never paid much attention to monuments and landmarks in his life as a human, but Cyril's excitement as he recognized places he had been a century ago was worth it. They followed the Seine river, of which the banks were crowded with colorful stalls and merchants late into the night. They passed the Tuileries palace, where Cyril told him the first Constituent Assembly of humans and vampires had been held, and they had decided to behead the Dark Lord. They saw the Louvre palace and Notre-Dame Cathedral in the distance as well, before turning into the Marais.

"I never realized there were so many beautiful things to see." Tim told Cyril as he gazed out the window of the carriage.

"That's because you were never truly alive until you became undead." Cyril said. "From now on, we will truly *live*."

His hand tightened around Tim's, who smiled. He was right: Tim had lived his mortal life as a dead man, buried in grief. Now as an undead vampire, and having found that his family were also alive as vampires, he no longer had a reason to grieve. It was time for him to learn to enjoy life again, and he was ready to enjoy it with Cyril.

⌒∽⌒

It had been nearly a month since Fiona, Hanson and Humphrey had opened their new business in Paris, in the Quartier du Marais, not far from the Bastille prison. Vampires loved to congregate around old prisons and monuments with a tragic history – except churches. Perhaps it was some innate taste for everything dark and historical, or perhaps it was just where they were less likely to stand out. Their new dwellings were not dark and dusty, but as colorful as Fiona's bourgeois taste permitted. Fiona had decorated her and Hanson's apartment with simple but tasteful paintings and brought home fresh roses every time she could. As she was arranging flowers in a vase that night, she gazed at the gold ring on her finger. Hanson and her had married, like the French vampires did, and they did not call themselves master and servant, but wife and husband now. The passionate young man had since also adopted a more sober style, appropriate for a man married to a much older woman, and loved to dote on her. Granted, she was the one giving out the paycheck, which he then turned around and spent on her, but it gave them the satisfaction of living a somewhat normal life.

Humphrey was still the man he had always been. After much negotiating, he had agreed to receive a new suit. He spent his free time reading newspapers and articles, and had a newfound interest in railroads and trains. Even he, the stoic middle-aged man, would get passionate about the new project for the construction of the *Métropolitain*, a series of underground trains for public transportation in Paris, and could not wait to see it with his own eyes. Fiona did not like trains, their noise or their smell very much, and she hoped people would continue to go in carriages forever. Hanson told her it was simply not possible, that progress could not be stopped, and Humphrey would then proceed to remind her of all the benefits an underground train would offer.

Days and nights went by peacefully, and yet Fiona worried about Tim. She had received word from London that an Apostle had challenged the Dark Lord and taken his place. She did not know who it might be but it was always possible that Tim had become entangled with the court and seduced by the lure of power. She wondered about Cyril too. She had written to Yvan but had not received a response yet. Hanson came to her. It was four-thirty in the morning, and he always served her her favorite blend of rose tea and blood, except now they could enjoy it together. He sat with her and they smiled at each other.

"Are you worried about them?" he asked. "I'm sure they're safe. Tim is smart."

"Tim went to meet his father." she sighed. "He is a strong dominant like him. I'm worried he may have decided to stay at court."

"I don't think so."

"There is a new Dark Lord of England."

"You think Tim became the Dark Lord?" he said, doubtful.

"I don't know." she said.

"Well, he is dark, but not power-hungry." he said.

"That is true. But by becoming the Dark Lord or an Apostle he could easily pardon Cyril and live with him in peace."

"Tim is not like them." he simply said. "I know him, and I trust him. Don't you?"

"I trust that people's hearts can be swayed by such things as power, or love." she said, lowering her gaze.

He took her hands in his.

"Like Tim's sister." he said.

Next to the new Dark Lord, the hottest gossip in the vampire world lately had been the story of Holly Thompson, a Natural of the highest rank, who, after a brief and unsuccessful struggle for power, had chosen instead the love of a dashing sired vampire and escaped with him to a faraway land.

"I'm a little envious of her. She is bold. I wish I had been more like her when I was young." Fiona said.

"You are Fiona, and Fiona is the woman I chose." he said, laying a kiss on her hand.

"I made you wait a long time." she said. "I was scared, so scared of life and love."

"It was worth it."

She finally broke into a smile again.

"Well, let us finish our tea and go to bed." he said. "I have to be up by nightfall for my shift."

"And I must be there to answer this *telephone* thing..." she sighed.

She did not like progress, technology, nor having all this electricity in her business, but this was the way things would be done in the future, or so Humphrey said.

Since Hanson had been sired, they'd had to make a few changes to their schedule. Humphrey had the day shift, and sometimes hired some human help, and Hanson had the evening and night shifts. They finished their tea by five o'clock, and then went to bed before the first sun rays and the first calls.

Humphrey was up and ready at six that morning, as usual. With modern equipment like the new telephone they had installed, business was booming, and he had a lot of work. He picked up and brought back the *clients* during the daytime, and Hanson and Fiona kept watch at night for the occasional ghoul they missed and that would awaken.

The French died a lot more than the British, or so it seemed. They had the curious habit of still engaging in duels, mostly over women, to the point the government had to outlaw the practice. Nevertheless, enamored young men still shot each other every day over a lost lover and provided a fresh supply of clean blood for the mistress – and Hanson. Today, he was picking up a few of them from the local morgue, and a few old folks from the neighborhood. Nothing he couldn't handle. He took out their brand new hearse and made his rounds as usual. When he returned at dusk with the last *client*, he parked the carriage in front of the heavy wooden doors, beside which now hung an elegant sign: "*Pompes Funèbres Inc.*". He smiled, satisfied. Yes, business was going well. And then he heard footsteps behind him, footsteps that were not human. He turned around, prepared to fight, and then smiled again. Tim and Cyril stood before him.

"I'd like to apply for the night shift." Tim said, smiling.

"I don't know about that, it's getting a little crowded with vampires here." Hanson's familiar voice said from the doorstep.

They were pleasantly surprised to see his transformation. But Humphrey simply stretched out his hand to Tim, who shook it, now with undead strength.

"Welcome back... to Undertakers Incorporated." he said with a grin.